Murder by the Seaside

Jackie Baldwin

This is a work of fiction. Names, characters, business, events and incidents are the products of the author's imagination. Any resemblance to actual persons, living or dead, or actual events is purely coincidental.

Ebook ISBN: 978-1-80508-053-4
Paperback ISBN: 978-1-80508-055-8

Cover design: Eileen Carey
Cover images: Trevillion, Shutterstock

Published by Storm Publishing.
For further information, visit:
www.stormpublishing.co

Also by Jackie Baldwin

Dead Man's Prayer

Perfect Dead

Avenge the Dead

To Rhanna Baldwin

Prologue

The woman blended into the shadows as she hugged the wall, her eyes intent on following her quarry. Where could he be going at this time of night? She'd thought she was the only one here. Was he brazen enough to meet his lover in the college? Rage flared inside her, causing a shiver of hatred and longing. She'd make him pay for this insult. He had cast her aside like dirt on his shoe. Ever since, she'd been biding her time.

It was pitch dark up here on the top floor and all she had to guide her was the flicker of his torch ahead. Where on earth was he going? He was nearing the end of the corridor now. Her breath caught in her throat as she realised that he might double back on himself and by now she'd crept closer than she'd intended. If he caught her trailing him, she'd be humiliated. Turning to flee, she felt a draught of cold air prickle her neck. A door clicked shut and she realised he'd gone up onto the roof, taking the pinprick of light with him. The dark closed in with suffocating finality. All she could hear was the whisper of her own breathing. *I should turn back while I have the chance*. But she had to see with her own eyes. To douse herself in the petrol of his betrayal and set fire to any residual feelings she had for him.

With renewed determination, she felt along the wall until she came to the door. Bracing herself, she opened it and slipped through. Hurrying up the last flight of stairs as quickly as she could in the dark, she slid through the door at the top and ran across to a chimney stack. She could hear voices raised in anger but, confusingly, both of them were male. This was no love tryst. It didn't take long to realise the identity of the second man. She almost groaned aloud. What had she been thinking? She leaned back against the far side of the chimney stack, turning her flushed cheeks up to the stars. Her feet were numb with the cold. Could she make it back off the roof without being seen?

Suddenly, the voices went quiet. A set of footsteps rushed past her, and she caught a glimpse of a receding back. The stars twinkled overhead, their beauty emboldening her.

Her heart beating like a drum, she stepped out of the shadows...

Chapter One

Grace McKenna shrugged off her towelling robe and stood, braced against the wind on a chilly February morning. The waves danced towards her, spraying her face and sending icy shivers up and down her spine. She charged through the heaving water until it was deep enough to dive under the waves. As the numbness worked its way up her body, her arms scythed through the sea with mechanical efficiency. After a few minutes the acrid burn of salt water up her nose caused her to stop and splutter, her rhythm interrupted. Treading water, she glanced behind her, her body undulating with the waves. When she was lifted up, she could see the shoreline she had left behind, people walking their dogs like figures in a Lowry painting. Her teeth were now chattering relentlessly. She turned her back on the shore and looked at the horizon, feeling the pull of the tide. After a last lingering look at the swollen slate-grey clouds ahead, she turned again, put her head down, and fought her way back the way she had come, her powerful shoulders thrusting against the ebb of the tide until her feet hit the grainy sand of Portobello Beach.

She always left her robe in line of sight with The Espy pub. Swooping down, Grace grabbed it and thrust her feet into her waiting sports sandals. Although it was on the fringes of the Scottish city of Edinburgh, Portobello still felt more like a town. The long expanse of golden sand running parallel to the paved Esplanade offered a range of chic eateries, bars and other businesses all fronting towards the sea, most with flats above them. It was particularly popular with dog walkers and, when it was warmer, Grace loved nothing more than to sit outside facing the sea, enjoying the antics of the assorted dogs with their owners walking by.

Now, as she hurried up the beach at a diagonal, she felt a quiet satisfaction when she took in the newest sign hanging over the Esplanade. Fashioned from a piece of driftwood she had found herself, it was painted blue with silver lettering that spelled out *The Portobello Detective Agency*. Although she had only been open since the beginning of the year, business was already starting to pick up.

Despite the cold of the February morning, Grace's body was already on fire as circulation returned to her frozen limbs. As she opened the door to her comfortable flat above the office, an indignant woof greeted her. She sank down and buried her nose in the fur of her golden retriever, Harvey.

'Don't you go getting uppity, you cheeky boy. You've already had a walk this morning!'

He thumped his tail and stared at her, unabashed. He'd given her a reason to live during some very dark times, for which she would always be grateful.

Once she had fed Harvey, Grace jumped into the shower. Afterwards, she sat nursing a cup of coffee, her short blonde hair already drying, as she flicked through the news headlines on her iPad. Her no-nonsense blue suit was the same one she had worn when she worked for the police. Glancing out of the deep bay window at the roiling sea, she blew out the candle in the storm lantern on the windowsill. The scent of beeswax filled the air. Although it had been two years now since her son, Connor, had been presumed drowned, she couldn't yet bear to relinquish this guiding light in case any essence of him remained out there, floating in the sea in the dead of night. It was the closest she had come to a prayer.

'Come on, boy,' she said, fondling her dog behind his ears. 'Time to go and earn a crust.'

Five minutes later, Grace and Harvey were entering the cramped reception area of the Portobello Detective Agency. She was pleased to see that her assistant, Jean, a plump motherly woman in her early fifties, was already installed and opening the mail.

She greeted the other woman and picked up a thick bundle.

'There's some cheques in there,' said Jean.

'Music to my ears.'

Putting the envelopes aside, Grace glanced at her watch and frowned but, before she could comment, the door was flung wide open and young Hannah blew in along with some sand, slamming the door behind her.

Harvey rushed over to greet her with his customary enthusiasm.

'Sorry I'm late,' Hannah muttered, her eyes downcast as she patted his head. 'The bus...' She tailed off as though she didn't have the energy for a lie.

The two women glanced at each other, but Jean shook

her head slightly when Grace opened her mouth. Biting back a retort, Grace looked at the girl more closely. She was ghostly white apart from the dark circles beneath her eyes.

'It's fine,' Grace said with a smile. 'Grab a coffee. I've emailed a few background reports to you to type up. Pretty straightforward stuff.'

'The work's certainly starting to come in,' said Jean, then made a face.

'But...?'

'It's just not how I imagined it would be. All the credit reports, employee vetting and erring husbands. It's not very... *exciting*, is it?'

Grace had thought the exact same thing herself of late but was damned if she'd admit it. To have gone from being a detective inspector on a major enquiry team to a glorified administrator was not what she'd had in mind when she started the business.

'It may not be exciting, Jean, but it keeps the wolf from the door.' Feeling tense and with the beginnings of a headache, she retreated to her office and bent her head to her work.

An hour later there was a light tap on the door and Jean popped her head round.

'I've a woman in reception. She won't give me her name or say what it's about, but says she needs a discreet investigator on an urgent matter.'

Grace sighed. It sounded as though this was going to be another cheating husband job, but beggars couldn't be choosers.

'Send her in,' she said, pinning a smile to her face that failed to reach her eyes.

Chapter Two

The woman who swept into her inner sanctum was probably in her early forties but could have passed for younger. She was muffled against the cold in a long, black woollen coat, a purple velvet beret nestled on top of dark curls. Her face was immaculately made up.

'Grace McKenna,' Grace said, standing up and offering her hand. The woman removed a hand from her glove reluctantly to meet hers and Grace immediately understood why. Her nails were bitten down to the quick. This was a woman who clearly liked to always put her best foot forward.

'Sylvia Gordon,' she replied, her voice low and husky. 'You might have heard of what happened to my husband, Paul Gordon, a few months ago? It was plastered all over the papers.'

'What can I do for you?' asked Grace sympathetically. She recalled reading in the press three months ago that Sylvia's husband, Paul Gordon, a well-known celebrity psychic, had jumped off the roof at his place of work. Perhaps she wished her to trace a missing beneficiary?

'I need you to find out who murdered my husband.'

Grace sat back in her chair and regarded the woman opposite.

'But didn't he...?'

'Commit suicide? No, he did not. Paul would never have done such a thing. I need you to prove that he was murdered. Someone pushed him off that roof.'

'I'm sorry for your loss,' Grace said. 'But I remember reading about the case. The fatal accident inquiry ruled that it was suicide. There was never any real doubt.'

'That's as may be, but I *know* he was murdered.'

'Have you any idea who might have wanted him dead?'

The woman gave a mirthless laugh. 'There was no shortage of candidates.'

'Including you?'

Sylvia gave a twisted grimace. 'Yes, including me, though I can assure you that I wasn't involved.'

That's all right then, sniped Grace in her head. She had to admit that her curiosity was piqued. Her intuition, however, was telling her that this case was going to be a whole heap of trouble. But it could also put her fledgling agency on the map. That is, if she managed to solve the case. She buzzed through to reception for a tray of coffee.

'I'll listen to what you have to say,' she told her prospective client. 'If I decide to take the case, I'll email you my terms and conditions, and my charges. If I decide not to take the case, then today's meeting will be free.'

'Agreed,' Sylvia said, with a small tense smile.

Grace noticed Sylvia's eyes boring into the back of the framed photograph on her desk and stifled the impulse to grab it and lock it in a drawer. She pushed aside her growing unease in this woman's company. If she wanted the agency to survive and safeguard the jobs of her staff, she damn well couldn't afford to be picky.

There was a light tap on the door and Hannah walked in with a tray. The teacups were rattling as she set it down on the side table behind them. What was with the girl today?

Grace thanked her and flashed a smile, but Hannah didn't meet her eyes and quickly scurried away. Grace walked over and poured out the coffee, handing a cup to Sylvia. Settling back behind her desk, she grabbed a large notebook and leaned forward.

'What makes you so sure your husband was murdered?'

'He told me.'

'Excuse me?' said Grace, startled.

'You know, from beyond the grave? Look, I know how it sounds.' Sylvia sighed. 'Let's call it a hunch or intuition if that makes you feel more comfortable. Does it matter?'

'Um... well, if he told you that he was murdered then surely he told you who did it?" Grace tried her best not to sound sarcastic.

'He can't remember.'

'You're grieving. The mind can play tricks on us sometimes.'

'That's not it. Paul wasn't the only one with psychic ability.'

'Okay...' Grace's heart had started to hammer in her chest. The woman was staring at the back of the photograph again. Grace wanted to yell at her to stop.

'Why is it so important to you to find out who killed your husband?' asked Grace.

'Six months before he died, he took out a massive life insurance policy. They won't pay out because it was ruled to be a suicide.'

'But that—'

'Makes me suspect number one? Yes, I'm aware,' said Sylvia.

'Why come to me?' Grace's voice hardened. Did this woman choose Grace because of her past? Did Sylvia think she would be easy to manipulate?

The woman looked away, biting her lip. There was an awkward silence.

Grace stood up. 'I don't think this is going to work if you can't be honest with me.'

Still nothing. Grace walked to the door and reached for the handle.

'Wait! I'll tell you. I came to you because of your son.'

Grace froze.

Slowly she turned back around.

'What...?'

Sylvia advanced towards her. 'I didn't mean to blurt it out like that. I knew that you'd investigated murders in the police force. It was in the papers about your son. I thought it might make you more receptive. That's all I meant. I swear!'

Grace felt the surge of adrenaline dissipate and a wave of fatigue swept in instead. Maybe Sylvia was on the level. And this case could make her name. She owed it to herself to take a look.

Grace returned to her seat and sat down, taking up her pen. 'Start at the beginning,' she said.

Chapter Three

'I married Paul Gordon before he was well known. Back then he was a care worker and would do anything for anybody. He'd do readings on the side. Only dabbled, really. He barely charged anything, did it mainly to bring comfort to others.'

'So what changed?'

'Ten years ago, he had a breakdown and, well...'

'Was he sectioned?'

She bit her lip. 'Yes, I had to do it. I had no option. Deep down, I think he never forgave me. He lost his job. Things were tough for a while, then he reinvented himself as a full-time psychic. Overnight, his whole personality seemed to change. I wasn't sure I believed any of it... I thought he was delusional. It felt like I was living with a stranger. But then he started to get celebrity endorsements and it snowballed from there. Finally, things settled down and he was really happy until the road accident.'

'What happened?'

'He was driving home on his motorbike when a car ran a

red light and smashed into him. It was touch and go for a while. Apparently, he died on the table, but they were able to bring him back. He was never the same after that – he was moody and irritable, refused to even talk about it.'

'How long was this before he died?'

'Less than a year.'

'Who do you think might have wanted to kill him?'

'Five years ago, he opened a new Psychic Development College in Edinburgh with his business partner Regan Bradley and another psychic, Xander Croft. In the last few weeks before he died, they'd all been fighting about something. I kept asking Paul what was going on, but he kept it from me. I don't know if they were arguing about money or something else, but the atmosphere at work was terrible.'

'You worked there, too?'

'Yes, but not as a psychic. I didn't ever share my growing abilities with Paul. It was a part of myself I chose to repress. After everything that had happened to him, it frightened me. But I was around the college often – I did all the routine admin for them.'

'Were they having financial problems?'

'Yes, but I didn't know at the time.'

'Is the college still going?'

'Yes. They fired me, though. They said my being there was making it more difficult for everyone to move on after Paul's death.'

'Harsh.'

'I think there was more to it. I think they're trying to cover their tracks. Before Paul died there was an investigative reporter sniffing around.'

'Can you remember his name?'

'Tobias Sloan. He was freelance. I have his card.' She rummaged around in her bag and produced it. 'And the new

Psychic Director, Xander Croft? I don't trust him. He has a massive ego and courts celebrity. I could never work out whether he even has the gift or if he's simply a sophisticated mentalist. Either way, he was jealous of Paul. They were rivals for all the lucrative TV gigs and celebrity endorsements.'

Grace bit her tongue.

'Look, I can tell that you're not a believer. I'm not here to convert you. The police didn't want to know when I went to them. They were bloody patronising and dismissive, in fact. All I need from you is an open mind and your investigative skills. Your personal beliefs don't matter to me as long as they don't get in the way.'

'Does anyone else bear looking into?' asked Grace.

'There's a group of protestors led by a woman called Beverley Thomson. They're outside the college every day waving their placards. They're out there come rain or shine. They think we're doing the Devil's work.'

'Anyone else?' asked Grace. This investigation was going to be tough to pull off with her limited resources and no concrete leads.

'No one else I know about,' said Sylvia. 'Look, I've taken up enough of your time. Here are all the papers I've managed to get my hands on. Let me know if you're able to take things further.'

She stood up abruptly, wobbling a little on her heels, and put a shaking hand on the back of the chair to steady herself.

Grace softened as she realised how much strain the woman was under, beneath the strong image she was presenting to the world.

Maybe they weren't so different after all.

Chapter Four

Grace looked up from the papers scattered over her desk as she heard the sound of laughter from next door. She went and stuck her head round the door and then wished that she hadn't. Her ex-husband, Brodie McKenna, was holding court in reception to a delighted audience. She scowled. Every time she saw him, she was torn between hurtling into his arms and hitting him over the head with an iron poker.

'What brings you here?' she asked, striving for a neutral tone.

He turned to face her, his brown eyes amused. 'Your face will stay like that if you're not careful,' he said, by way of a greeting.

She rolled her eyes at him.

'Jean here tells me you may have landed a big case?'

'Did she now?'

Jean started typing busily, her cheeks pinking up. A stifled giggle escaped from Hannah.

'I suppose you'd better come through before you manage to charm any more secrets out of my staff.'

Grace held the door open and he moved past her. Inhaling the scent of him made her feel weak with loss.

Inviting him to sit, she moved behind her desk, grateful for the barrier between them.

Brodie's expression was serious now as he regarded her. 'How have you been?' he asked. 'The new venture, is it helping?'

She gave a brittle smile. 'It's a distraction, I suppose. How's your new distraction?'

'She has a name,' he snapped. 'Don't do this, Grace. You sent *me* packing, remember? I refuse to feel guilty for being in a new relationship.'

He was right. Grace knew she had no reason to be bent out of shape. It just hurt. It hurt a lot.

She held up her hands in surrender. 'Sorry, my mouth ran away with me. How's Julie?'

'She's good. It's easier somehow being around someone who doesn't also carry the weight of losing him. It helps... a little.'

'We couldn't have you finding the death of your son *difficult*.'

He looked as though she had slapped him. 'Do you have to be so goddamn prickly? I'm trying to have a real conversation here. It's exhausting having to edit every single thing that comes out of my mouth.'

'I know,' she whispered, feeling a lump at the back of her throat.

Brodie shook his head, but reached over and patted her hand. He picked up the framed photo on her desk, his touch gentle as he took it in.

Their son smiled out from the frame with no hint of the tragedy yet to unfold at that time.

'So,' he said, putting it back on the desk, his voice husky as he strove to regain control. 'Are you going to tell me about your new case?'

Grace appreciated him steering the conversation into safer waters. 'Do you remember anything about the death of that psychic, Paul Gordon?'

'Vaguely. Didn't he jump off a roof?'

'According to his widow he was murdered.'

'Why would she think that?'

'She... has a strong... er, intuitive feeling about such things.'

'Tell me this isn't going where I think it's going?'

Grace sighed. 'Look, I don't believe in that stuff any more than you do. But I can't turn down work. I've a living to make, remember?' she said, an edge coming into her voice.

Brodie's face tightened. 'Look, I don't want to fight. That's not why I came here.'

'I know,' she said. 'Don't worry. I'll just do a bit of digging and report back to her. I'm not going to bleed her dry if I think there's nothing to investigate.'

'I'll find the file,' he said. 'See if we missed anything.'

'That would be great,' she said, surprised and a little touched. It was good to see Brodie coming in to his own now that she had left the police. He had joined straight out of sixth form to support them when she fell pregnant while they were still at school. They'd married in a simple ceremony and, thanks to her parents' help with babysitting, she'd been able to go to university to do a degree in psychology. As a fast-track graduate entrant, she had quickly surpassed him in rank and bagged a position in the Murder Squad while he had languished in CID. His recent promotion to sergeant had seen him finally join the team he had always set his sights on.

He stood up to leave. 'I'd best head off. I've left Julie in the car.'

'You should have brought her in,' she said, tongue in cheek.

Brodie laughed. 'Maybe another time. Watch your back out there, Grace.'

'You too, Brodie.'

The room seemed lonelier when he had left. She stroked the face of her son with a wistful finger and then buried herself in the files once more.

Chapter Five

Grace pushed back her chair from the desk and stood up to stretch her knotted muscles. She wasn't designed for being trapped behind a desk. Glancing through the window she noticed it was already getting dark out. She was fed up with winter and craved the feel of sun on her face. A sun that would never again shine on her son. Grace forced her mind away from him. Something she had to do many times each day.

Opening the door into the reception area, she could see the sea from the large picture window. The wind was clearly whipping up; frothy, white sea horses danced into the sand on Portobello Beach beyond the low wall that separated it from the promenade. Harvey thumped his tail hopefully.

'I won't be long, boy,' she said, ruffling the fur at the back of his neck.

Hannah brought her some contracts to sign and she settled down at the table to do it. Her staff thought she was mad to have chosen the room at the back for her office, thus depriving herself of the wonderful views. But the downside to being at the front was that people could see in and Grace valued her privacy.

'So, are you going to take the case?' asked Jean, her eyes alight with curiosity.

'Yes. It'll mean a lot of work for us but such a high-profile case could bring in a lot more high-quality business. I've had a quick look through the papers left by Sylvia. The police did investigate but decided fairly quickly that it was suicide, so it won't hurt to look into it again. I'll digest it overnight then come up with a plan and allocate tasks. Hannah, if you want to pop through there's a matter I need to discuss with you.'

As Grace walked her over to the comfy seating area, she reflected on how little she knew about her youngest employee. Hannah had come to her as a school leaver from sixth year, expressing a keenness to learn. In many ways she had seemed ideal; she loved acting and had a natural aptitude for figures. These skills would serve her well when interviewing suspects or dealing with fraudulent accounting. However, those weren't the reasons that Grace had hired her. It had been the look of blank desperation in the young girl's eyes. She had an air about her of a kid in trouble and in need of saving. Having failed to recognize it in her own son, Grace wasn't about to make that mistake again. A hungry little voice inside her had also latched on to the fact that she had attended the same high school as Connor. In all probability Hannah had known him. It was a conversation they were yet to have.

'I wanted to check in with you, Hannah. How are you finding things here at the agency?'

'I love it here. Really, I do!' She paused. 'Have I done something wrong?'

'No, not at all,' Grace reassured her. 'I simply wanted

you to know that you can come to me with anything. We're a new agency and there are bound to be teething problems.'

'Well... there *was* something I wanted to talk to you about.'

'Go on.'

'So, while I'm enjoying learning how to do all the office stuff – credit checks, employee background checks and that kind of thing – I wondered if you might be able to make use of me in other ways as well.'

'Such as?'

'Well, you know how drama is kind of my thing?'

'Yes,' said Grace, not quite sure where this was going.

'I thought I could maybe do honey traps for those suspected of cheating.'

'Absolutely not!' Grace responded immediately. 'You're only eighteen. It's far too dangerous.'

Hannah reddened and dropped her eyes. 'I can handle myself,' she said, her voice quiet but determined.

'Hannah... at your age you only think you can.'

'We need someone to do this kind of work. Clients will expect it.'

'Maybe so, but I can do it, if need be.'

'*You*?' said Hannah, the surprise in her voice genuine. 'But...'

'But what? I'm too old?' said Grace. 'Too dowdy?'

'Of course not,' said Hannah, unconvincingly.

'Look, I'll think about it,' said Grace, smiling to show there were no hard feelings. 'This new case might need some light undercover work. We could start you on that.'

Hannah's face lit up. 'That's brilliant! I won't let you down.'

. . .

At the flat later that night she recalled the baffled look on Hannah's face at the thought that a man – or woman, for that matter – could possibly find Grace attractive. It had hurt. She was still only thirty-five. Although she had never been the kind of woman who traded on her looks, Grace had always thought she could scrub up reasonably well when the situation demanded. She walked into her bathroom and turned on the lights. Scrutinising her reflection in the mirror, she could see the ravages that grief had wrought on her face. The dark circles under her eyes gave her a bruised look. Her skin was pulled taut over her cheekbones from two years of scarcely bothering to eat. *No wonder Brodie didn't put up more of a fight for you*, her treacherous mind whispered.

'Stop it!' she said aloud. Brodie hadn't left her. In every meaningful way, she had left him. She had wallowed in her grief, picking away at the scab of every negative interaction she had ever had with their teenage son. Brodie had tried to gather up the pieces of their shattered family and move on, yet how could she entertain such a thought when it was her fault that Connor had seen no other option but to walk into the sea that night? It had to be. She was his mother and she had failed him miserably.

This was what happened when she allowed herself too much time to think. She would go for a walk. That would clear her head. She turned around and saw Harvey lying down in the doorway, looking worried at her outburst.

'Relax, boy,' she said, stroking his broad head. 'I was talking to myself, not you.'

He thumped his tail hopefully. 'Come on, time to blow away the cobwebs.'

Clipping on his lead she headed out into the dark, wondering what tomorrow would bring.

Chapter Six

Grace paused outside the modern glass frontage of the Merchiston College of Psychic Studies. Despite what it was going to cost her she had realised that the only way she could succeed in inserting herself into the heart of the college was to turn up at one of their events as herself. She would have liked nothing more than to hide behind a false identity but given the publicity surrounding the death of her son and her subsequent case against the police for unfair dismissal, she felt it was likely that someone would identify her from the extensive media coverage.

To the right of the entrance was a straggly group of middle-aged protestors brandishing homemade placards. *Everyone needs a hobby*, she thought. This must be the group her client had mentioned.

Minutes later, she was standing in a vibrant café watching members of the college work the room. She tried to keep the cynicism out of her expression as she surmised that the eager helpers were probably trawling amongst the recently bereaved for information they could use later. Seconds later it was her turn as an earnest middle-aged woman with washed-out blue eyes arrived in front of her.

'Hello, Matilda Swain, pleased to meet you.' She beamed.

'Grace McKenna, likewise.'

'What brings you here today, my dear?' she asked.

'I'm curious, I suppose. A friend in my bereavement support group spoke highly of your psychic director, Xander Croft.'

'He's a wonderful man. We're so lucky to have him. You mentioned you were bereaved? I'm so sorry. May I ask who you lost?'

'My son.' Grace smiled through gritted teeth.

The woman took her hand and held it between her own dry papery ones for longer than Grace was comfortable with. 'I'm sorry for your loss, my dear, but be assured he's in a happier place, in spirit.'

Bugger that, hissed Grace in her head. *He'd be happier here with me.*

As the woman moved on with a farewell squeeze, Grace sipped her tea and looked around her. She could easily spot the hollowed-out appearance of the bereaved. The wild hope flaring in the eyes of some as they yearned beyond reason for contact from a loved one. Others were withdrawn, driven here despite themselves and clearly not expecting much. She, too, wore her grief in the contours of her face. The whole thing was making her queasy. What the hell had she been thinking, taking on this case? She had a strong urge to walk – no, run – out of the door and never come back.

After a few minutes she felt the hairs on the back of her neck prickle a warning.

She whipped around and found herself staring up into a

pair of assessing green eyes. He immediately looked away, but Grace knew she hadn't imagined him watching her. Annoyed, she gave him a bit of a glare and turned away. She had a feeling from his demeanour that he wasn't one of the bereaved. Maybe he worked here? Unlikely: none of the other staff seemed to be interacting with him.

A bell tinkled discreetly. *Showtime,* she thought, trying to curb her grumpiness. She followed the others into a beautifully proportioned room. Rather than sit at the front, she drifted to the middle. To her annoyance, the man sat down beside her. What kind of a creep came to a gig like this to pick up women?

There was a hum of excitement in the room. A stage stood at one end with magnificent velvet drapes.

'I know who you are,' the man beside her whispered in her ear.

'Is that a fact? Because I have no idea who the hell *you* are or what you want with me.'

'I'm Tobias Sloan, investigative reporter,' he said, sliding a card into her hand. 'I suggest we meet up afterwards.'

Grace paused. 'Okay. The Espy pub at Portobello, noon,' she murmured before turning her attention back to the stage.

Xander Croft suddenly appeared from the wings. She recognised him from his profile on the college website. He was a striking man, probably in his early forties, clean shaven and wearing a well-cut navy suit. He moved to the front of the stage and held up his hands for silence. An expectant hush fell on the room.

'Welcome.' He had the most melodic voice.

Grace felt the power of his magnetism. It seemed as though he was looking directly at her, addressing her personally, and she guessed that everyone else there felt the same. True charisma was a rare thing, but this man possessed it in spades. She found herself drawn to what he was saying. A resolute non-believer in the afterlife, she felt the first tug of such a belief. How wonderful it would be if she could be reunited with Connor one day... *Back in your box*, she said in her head. *You're here on the job and for no other reason.*

Glancing around, she could see that the audience were hanging on his every word. The sun was shining through the stained-glass window, its warmth and beauty throwing the suffering of those left behind into sharp relief. She braced herself against their collective misery.

Xander Croft slumped forwards at the pulpit. His face went slack as though his soul had exited his body. A ripple of excitement raced through the crowd. Behind her there was a mass inhalation as Croft's head went up, his piercing blue eyes staring into the middle distance.

'Lady in the purple coat.' He pointed into the audience. 'I have a beautiful little girl stepping forward. She says her name is Molly. Does this mean anything to you, my dear?'

The middle-aged woman nodded frantically, her face contorted with joyful tears.

'Answer me loud and strong,' he commanded. 'I need your sound waves to maintain the link.'

'Yes!' the poor woman almost shouted. 'She was my daughter. Molly died when she was five. Please, tell her I love her.'

Croft paused, head tilted as though listening.

'She knows that already. Molly sees you kiss her photo every night. She thanks you for burying Blue Ted with her... This might be difficult to hear, but she has found her sister in spirit. I'm seeing her with a child in her arms she tells me you called Katie?'

The woman is sobbing openly now, and Grace narrows her eyes as she looks from Croft to the woman and back again. This was a step too far. Her logical mind snapped back to the fore.

'A few years after Molly died, I had a miscarriage. I gave her the name Katie. I thought she deserved to have her own name...'

'You can rest now in the knowledge that they are both safe and happy in spirit.'

'Thank you,' she whispered, her emotions writ large on her face.

Grace frowned. She couldn't help it. The woman had either told her story to one of Croft's little helpers beforehand or was a plant and faking the whole thing. It was far too specific to be credible. Was she the only one in the room who could see it? Grace felt Croft's eyes on her and quickly schooled her face into a more neutral expression.

The rest of the session was fairly bland and predictable, but Xander Croft's audience lapped it up.

If I was coming through from the afterlife, I'd dish out more inspiring stuff than vague references to anniversaries and dull platitudes, Grace thought. She supposed the one super concrete example had been such a convincer he could get away with less after it. Everyone came back every week hoping that *this* was the day they would obtain such a message from *their* loved one.

The whole thing made her feel queasy. Her focus drifted away from the room. It was stiflingly hot, and she felt a wave of fatigue sweep over her.

Suddenly, her attention snapped back.

'I have a fine young man here taken too soon. Does this mean anything to anybody?' Croft said, his face screwed up in concentration.

Grace froze in her seat.

'He wants you to know it wasn't your fault. There was nothing you could have done.'

Grace felt a wave of nausea grip her and swallowed hard.

He doesn't know, she told herself fiercely. *Nobody knows*.

She had a job to do here and couldn't let her personal feelings get in the way. He was probing, trying to find her sweet spot.

As everyone filed out afterwards, Grace kept her eye on the woman in the purple coat. She suspected she was an actress hired for the occasion. Hanging behind in the throng she saw people pressing her hand or arm and shyly making supportive comments. The woman received them all stoically and Grace started to wonder if she had been wrong after all. Slowly, she followed the woman out and round into the small car park. Grace opened her car and got in, angling one of the mirrors so she could continue to watch the woman whilst appearing to be scrolling through her phone.

At the back of the building, a wooden door opened onto the car park and a hand holding a brown envelope snaked out. The woman in purple took it quickly then, with a furtive glance around her, got into her small car and drove away.

Grace noted down the details of the car then headed off herself, seething with anger at what she had just witnessed.

Chapter Seven

Grace watched Tobias Sloan pick his way across to her through the lunchtime crowd at The Espy. The lines around his mouth gave him a stern appearance, as if he didn't often smile. He nodded as he sat in the chair opposite her, his green eyes flicking around until he was satisfied they wouldn't be overheard.

'Okay, Mr Sloan, spill. What are you doing sniffing around the college?'

'You don't have a monopoly on grief, you know,' he snapped back.

Grace sat back in her seat, shocked. 'Who did you...?' she asked.

'My wife,' Tobias said, 'three years ago. Before that... our child. Sorry, I didn't mean to bite your head off just now.'

'Apology accepted. How about we share as much as we can about our objectives and see if we can't help each other?'

'You want to be my sidekick?' he said, raising an eyebrow.

Grace laughed. 'How about you be mine?' she replied, earning a wintery smile.

'My interest is in Xander Croft. He's a fraud and a charlatan. I want to expose him and those like him who prey on the vulnerable and feast on their grief. I first came across him in London a few years ago. We had lost our daughter and my poor wife got sucked into his web. Eventually, she committed suicide.' He looked away from her and cleared his throat.

Grace considered the situation. If Tobias had an axe to grind, that could perhaps get in the way of her investigation, but hopefully it wouldn't come to that. He would need careful handling, but if he had been looking into Xander for some time, he could perhaps be an asset.

'And you?' he said, his expression shuttered once more. 'This can't be a one-way street.'

He was right. But what could she share without compromising client confidentiality?

'I'm looking into the death of one of the founder members of the college, Paul Gordon.'

Tobias sat back in his chair and stared at her in his direct and intense manner.

'The suicide?'

'Yes. Simply checking that nothing was missed from the original investigation, that's all.'

'I see,' he said, looking thoughtful.

'Do you hate all psychics or only Xander Croft?'

'I don't hate all of them. Some are well-meaning but deluded.'

'So you don't even leave room for the tiniest bit of doubt?' she asked.

'None whatsoever,' Tobias said with a twisted grimace. 'Sorry if that's not what you wanted to hear.'

'Listen, no one's more sceptical than me.'

'And yet?'

Grace surprised herself in a sudden yearning. What

wouldn't she give to be able to hear once more from her son? 'I'm too old for fairy tales,' she said, slamming the door on the topic once and for all. 'So, tell me, how close are you to exposing Xander Croft?'

'I've been investigating him for a while. I understand he's on the verge of signing a deal for a prime-time TV series.'

'Like a sort of psychic televangelist?' Grace shook her head, appalled.

'Exactly.'

'And what did you make of Paul Gordon? Did you ever meet him?'

'A few times. He seemed more genuine, somehow. I would put him in the "deluded" rather than "cynical fraudster" category. Like Croft, he had a compelling personality, but I felt genuine warmth from him, too.'

'When did you last see him?'

'A couple of weeks before he died.'

'How was his demeanour? Did he seem at all depressed?'

'Depressed? No. He did seem a bit stressed, though. He hinted that he might be terminating his connection with the college.'

'He didn't say why?'

'He talked about wanting to strip things back to basics. He seemed to feel the college had become an unstoppable juggernaut that was heading in the wrong direction.'

'Did you tell him you were out to get Croft?'

'Of course not! I told him I was investigating the growth of interest in psychic phenomena. I presented myself as having an open mind and mentioned about losing my wife and daughter,' he said, his mouth twisting in distaste. 'It made me feel dirty, but I told myself to focus on the bigger picture.'

'It makes you feel like you're trading on your grief,' Grace replied with a grimace of her own.

She looked across at Sloan. His abrasive personality wasn't the sort she would normally seek out for assistance with a case. Nonetheless, she had an inexperienced team and limited resources. She'd be wise to take whatever extra help she could get. 'Look, how about we work together? I have a team of two behind me who are still learning the ropes. If I help you get the evidence you need to expose Croft and bring him down, then you can credit my agency as part of the investigative team.'

'And what do you want in return?'

'I want to see your research and findings. I also want your help determining exactly what happened to Paul Gordon.'

'You do realise that if he was murdered, his killer may stop at nothing to prevent the truth coming out?'

Grace shrugged. 'I can take care of myself. Can you?'

'Time will tell,' Tobias said.

'Right. We need to make a plan,' Grace said, feeling a welcome surge of energy. 'Although my team is small, our resources are at your disposal for the duration.'

'I can share my research and I have some ideas on how we can quickly be accepted into the college community. I can start tomorrow, if that suits?'

'Perfect.' Grace smiled, gathering up her things. She fished out one of her business cards and handed it to him. 'I'll see you then.'

As Grace walked the short distance back to the office, she felt a niggle of disquiet. Had she done the right thing, letting Tobias Sloan into this investigation? He had come across as somewhat arrogant and opinionated, not to mention a bit of a crusader. On the plus side, he had the investigative background that her two new employees lacked. Hopefully, it would all work out, and if not... well, she could simply show him the door.

Chapter Eight

Early the next morning, Grace walked Harvey along the Esplanade then turned onto the beach. She threw a frisbee for him and watched with amusement as he cavorted wildly around the beach like a dog half his age. She wished briefly that Connor could be there to watch him, too, but slammed the door on that dangerous thought before it could do any more damage.

The sand was cold beneath her feet. There had been a fierce frost last night. She looked at the blue sea and shivered. The sun was poking above the horizon, brushing the sky with red and gold. She walked to the water's edge and called Harvey to her. He knew the drill and settled down with his frisbee between his paws.

'Stay, boy,' she said, as she discarded her clothes down to her swimming suit, throwing them in a heap on the sand. The tide was on the turn now. Harvey wouldn't be tempted to follow her unless she called out to him. He'd fallen in the garden pond as a pup and ever since he'd had an aversion to going out of his depth.

Shivering uncontrollably now, she plunged into the icy waters and pulled away strongly from the shore, gasping with the shock of it. Once her body was numb, she allowed her mind to drift. She felt closer to Connor out here, like she was accompanying him on his last journey, as if a tracing of him remained and was matching her stroke for stroke.

Not lingering today, she turned round once she tired and raced back to the beach, her mind filling instead with the investigation and how to tackle it.

Harvey jumped up on seeing her and started barking. He knew that the next item on the agenda was his breakfast. Nothing in his world was more important than that.

* * *

A few hours later, the door tinkled a warning as Tobias Sloan ushered in a blast of freezing air. He stood uncertainly on the threshold as if he was in two minds about coming in.

Grace turned to face him with a welcoming smile.

'Jean, Hannah, meet Tobias Sloan. He's the investigative reporter I told you about. He's come in today to give us his insights into Xander Croft and Merchiston College. We're going to help further his work and he's going to assist with our latest case.'

'Morning, ladies,' he said.

'Is that your real name?' piped up Hannah.

'Hannah!' said Jean.

'Actually, Hannah, you're spot on,' Tobias said with a smile. 'I assume a fake identity for every undercover investigation. It's safer that way. I'm a bit of a chameleon after all these years. But I assume you had already worked that out,' he added, turning to stare at Grace.

He was assessing her competence. After her first meeting

with Sylvia, she had researched Sloan to see if he was likely to help or hinder her investigation. He had written some really hard-hitting articles in the broadsheets over the years and seemed to be largely based down south. She had to give him credit. It had taken quite some time to find the man behind his current persona, and even then he remained something of an enigma, though his story about losing his wife and child appeared to be true. She'd discovered death certificates for both of them. It was very sad.

'Naturally,' she said with a grin. 'You've covered your tracks well, Robert Black. We'll continue to use your current identity, however, to avoid confusion.'

She turned the sign on the door to Closed and invited them all through to her room, seating them in front of her desk.

Harvey gave Tobias a thorough sniff. Tobias stiffened.

'Sorry, I'm not really a dog person,' he said apologetically.

'I'm sure you'll grow on each other,' said Grace.

Jean, being proficient at shorthand, a dying art these days, got her pad out ready to take notes.

Tobias Sloan stretched out his long lean legs and at Grace's indication began to speak.

'Lots of us believe in life after death. We're the only species on Earth cursed with the ability to comprehend our own mortality.'

Harvey sighed and buried his head between his paws, looking glum. Grace stroked his ears.

'But all mediums are fakes,' Tobias pronounced. 'A significant number are a bit nuts but have good intentions. I have no particular beef with them. However, others prey on the vulnerable for their own gratification. They are psychic vampires.'

'Are you saying that there are no such things as psychics? Not under *any* circumstances?' said Hannah.

'That's exactly what I'm saying,' he replied.

Jean looked unconvinced. 'A friend of mine has visited one for years. She swears by her! Says she couldn't possibly know the stuff she knows if she was a fraud.'

'Which brings me neatly on to how they do it,' said Sloan, with a weary smile. 'Your average psychic who does it to make a bit of money on the side will use a mixture of hot and cold reading techniques. They use their personal knowledge of you combined with analysing your responses to what they are saying.'

'I still think there are some genuine ones out there,' muttered Jean, crossing her arms.

Sloan's eyes flicked as though he had been tempted to roll them but thought better of it.

'Are you talking about, like, those mind readers you see on TV?' asked Hannah.

'They're similar, except mentalists use their skills to entertain whereas mediums use them to exploit the grieving for their own personal gain.'

'What kind of person would do that?' said Hannah, starting to look angry. 'Definitely not cool.'

'Let me give you a demonstration to prove my point,' said Sloan. 'First of all, I need a willing volunteer?'

'I'm not doing it,' said Jean.

'Please, don't make me,' begged Hannah.

'Fine,' sighed Grace. 'I'll do it. I thought you two wanted more excitement?' She perched on her desk as Sloan came closer. Uncomfortably close.

He fixed his eyes on hers. She found herself unable to look away.

'You've suffered a loss, a great loss. One that ripped the heart from you?'

'Yes,' she snapped, then grimaced apologetically.

'You've been in a dark place and felt totally alone. Is this making sense to you?'

'Yes.'

'You felt abandoned and turned away from your husband. You've turned your back on love.'

Grace reddened. She felt exposed.

'Your son wants you to know he's at peace. He wants you to forgive yourself and let go of the past. I'm sensing a secret, something you've never told anyone because you have carried the burden of shame. Is this making sense to you?'

Grace didn't reply, but wrenched her eyes from his.

'I'm seeing waves crashing on the shore and a feeling of despair. Now, why might that be?'

'Stop!' Grace held up her hand to halt the relentless flood of words. 'You've made your point.'

'How does he know you've turned your back on love?' asked Jean.

'No nail polish, minimal make up, and her body language,' replied Sloan.

'Maybe she's just not that into you,' said Hannah, with a shrug.

Grace held up her hand once more and sent a warning glance to her youngest member of staff. 'Thank you, Tobias, an... interesting demonstration.'

'I'd researched you before coming here, so I knew that your son drowned hence the issue with water. I knew you'd been married but you're not wearing a ring now. Nearly everyone has a guilty secret big or small. So, they were fairly safe bets and your discomfort showed me I was on the right track. It's all about psychological manipulation.'

'I think we can all agree that our eyes have been opened to these techniques,' said Grace. 'It's analogous to some of the interrogation techniques that I learned in the police force. Body language also plays a big part as we can't always control it,' she added with a rueful smile, remembering her own discomfort.

'I need you all to be aware that if you go into that environment as part of this investigation these people will mess with your head. If any of you feel at all vulnerable by reason of your mental health I can't in all good conscience ask you to do this,' said Sloan.

'Count me in,' said Jean.

'And me,' said Hannah but with a worried line between her eyes.

'Great,' said Grace, who suspected that she was the most vulnerable of all, but would rather die than admit it to Sloan.

When it came down to it, she had a bad feeling in her gut about this case that she couldn't shift.

Chapter Nine

It had been a long day. Grace was sitting on the concourse at Edinburgh Waverley Station with a scalding hot cup of coffee. Annoyingly, the Tweedsmuir train had been delayed. Her satchel contained paperwork she'd obtained from the Registrar of Companies on the limited company operating the college. As expected, both Croft and Bradley were company directors. The company secretary was Matilda Swain and her role was most likely restricted to taking minutes of meetings and circulating them. She'd spent the morning in the college library managing to chat over the coffee machine to some of the other students who ranged in age from late teens to proper crinkly. Some of them were studying to be mediums, others were interested in healing in various forms. There was also a parapsychology pathway including modules on quantum mechanics and neuroscience which seemed of interest to both sceptics and believers alike. None of them had a bad word to say about the deceased psychic, Paul Gordon, though word had got round that his wife had been fired, which had made a few of them unhappy. They felt the college should have been more supportive to his widow in the circumstances.

Glancing around at the hustle and bustle of the train station she suddenly froze, her breath stilled in her chest. Sitting opposite was a young lad with dark hair flopping into his eyes as he hunched over his phone. A cry fluttered in her throat like a trapped moth as she half rose from her seat. Hope sprung wildly within her. How could Connor be here, in this place? She willed him to look up, but his head remained stubbornly lowered. She knew it couldn't be him, of course she knew, with most of her brain. But the small, almost extinguished part, where hope resided, suddenly burst into glorious life. After all, they hadn't found a body. Maybe he'd had amnesia and forgotten all about his life with her.

Suddenly, he glanced at the noticeboard and jumped up, walking quickly towards the ticket barrier. The view from the side did nothing to dispel her yearning. It could still be him, however unlikely that was. She rose also, and moved towards the barrier, her gaze never wavering from his back as she followed him along the platform and on to the train.

Grace watched him surreptitiously from a seat behind. His fingers were long and tapered as Connor's had been. A pianist's fingers. Hungrily, her eyes probed him, her blood rushing through her veins like an express train.

She glimpsed the ticket inspector coming in the distance. What train was this? She hadn't even thought to look. Glancing up at the display she saw it was heading for North Berwick, thirty minutes away. She could get off at the first stop of Musselburgh, then hop on a bus to Portobello, though she'd originally been going for the Tweedsmuir train as she'd parked her car at Brunstane Station, only minutes from the office. The boy's phone buzzed and he answered it. Grace listened to the sound of his voice. It was low and deep, just like her son's. She leaned into her pain as she realised it was his mum on the other end of the phone. It shocked her out of her reverie, and she felt her cheeks flush. What the hell had she been thinking? She'd thought she was finally coming to terms with things.

'Ticket, please?'

'A return to North Berwick, please.' She tapped her card on his machine. She would keep her options open. It's not as though she was in any particular rush. It would be nice to have a potter round the shops in the pretty seaside town.

He printed out her ticket and moved on.

If he gets off early, I won't follow him. This has gone far enough.

He didn't. She found herself standing behind him as the train pulled into North Berwick. A waft of Lynx deodorant drifted up to her and Grace almost smiled. Her son and most of his friends had always used it. From behind she could see he was at the stage of adolescence just before filling out. She longed to stretch her arms round his bony shoulders and hold him tight. His back was bowed from the backpack weighted most likely with books.

She stood on the platform, shielding her eyes against the glare of the winter sun. The seagulls squawked overhead as she drifted after him. She wasn't really following him. It was nice to stretch her legs, maybe wander along by the sea, grab a coffee, do a spot of shopping in one of the artsy gift shops. Who was she kidding? She was definitely following him. She knew in her head he wasn't Connor, but her heart sought out the similarities and basked in the warmth of them. Dropping further back, she trailed him to an established residential area where generously proportioned sandstone houses sat back from the road. The boy mooched along, oblivious, concentrating on his phone in the manner of teenagers everywhere. Abruptly, he turned left into a driveway. A few moments later she walked by, casually glancing at the house. She felt a sudden release now that she knew where he lived and hurriedly returned to the train station to catch the next train back to Musselburgh.

It was six o'clock by the time she got home so it was already pitch black. She let herself into the flat above the office and Harvey gave her a rapturous welcome. He took her wrist in his mouth and held on tighter than usual with an air of reproach in his eyes.

'Sorry, Harvey, I'm late with your supper. You're right to tell me off.'

She got down on the floor and hugged him. The unconditional love in his brown eyes made her tear up.

'Come on, boy, quick walk along the beach before your supper,' she said.

Harvey grabbed his lead from the kitchen and presented it to her with a flourish.

Laughing at his goofy expression, she slipped it on, and they headed down onto the deserted coastline. The moon had already risen, a silver path stretching out over the calm sea to the horizon. Inhaling the salty tang, and the smell of damp sand and seaweed, she felt the tension of the day ebb out like the receding tide. It had been a momentary madness. It wouldn't happen again. She had to focus on the case. The cold was numbing her, and she welcomed the distraction. Calmer now, she turned back the way she had come. She would feed Harvey, then chill out with him on the couch watching a film and try to get an early night. Tomorrow was another day.

Chapter Ten

Tobias Sloan and Grace sat at an antique pine table in Sylvia Gordon's spacious kitchen. The Aga radiated a comforting warmth against the chill of the February morning. Sylvia had asked for the meeting to see what progress had been made so far.

'Not much yet,' admitted Grace. 'This is a complex investigation and it's taken a while to set everything in motion. I've brought Tobias onboard to assist me as he has a particular interest in Xander Croft, so we can cross-pollinate the cases. It's his intention to write an expose of Xander Croft and unmask him as a fraud.'

Sylvia gave him an intense look and then nodded. 'I don't want to be named in any articles, I'm a private person.'

'You have my word,' said Tobias. 'I've promised Grace that I won't break the story until she has taken your case as far as she can.'

Grace went on, 'I'm meeting a source within the police later who has access to the original police file and forensics.'

'Good,' said Sylvia, with a tight smile.

'Did your husband have a study or an area of the house that was uniquely his?' asked Grace.

'Yes, he had a study. I should've been in and sorted it out by now, but I haven't been able to face it. It was a bit of a no-go zone when he was alive but suddenly, the other day, the door swung open as I was passing as though inviting me to enter.'

Sloan's face stiffened.

'Sylvia believes she is, er, psychic,' Grace said, beseeching him with her eyes not to go off on one. This was her client, after all.

'Thank you for that ringing endorsement, Grace.'

'I only meant—'

'I know what you meant. Like I said before, it's not something I advertise or even wished for. It's a curse rather than a blessing as far as I'm concerned.'

The more she spoke to Sylvia, the more persuasive Grace found her. But the possibility she might be genuine terrified her.

As if Sylvia had read her mind she smiled and leaned forward.

'Don't worry, I don't intrude where I'm not wanted,' she said. 'Paul was a good man, you know. Latterly, he let all the fame go to his head and went a bit off the rails, but he wasn't a fraud. He actually had the gift, unlike Xander Croft.'

Tobias started to say something but turned it into a cough. Grace shot him a warning look.

'Do you mind if we look through the study now? We need to see if we can find anything to establish his state of mind. It might be that he had received threats that could give us a motive for murder.'

'Help yourselves. I won't join you, if you don't mind. I'm still not ready.'

'Did the police take much away?' asked Grace. 'What about his phone and laptop?'

'They did but I don't think they gave them more than a cursory once-over,' she replied. 'They're back on his desk now. Right from the outset they seemed to be satisfied he had killed himself.'

'I take it you were adamant in your communication with them that it was murder from the start of the investigation?' said Sloan.

Sylvia looked a little uncomfortable. 'No, I wasn't. At first, I assumed he had killed himself like everyone else.'

'Until you realised the life insurance wouldn't pay out,' said Sloan.

Grace shot him a sharp look. The thought had occurred to her, too, but he had no business trying to alienate her client.

'No. Until I realised he wasn't going to leave me alone unless I got justice for him,' she said, staring at him defiantly.

To her amusement Sloan blushed a little and looked away first.

Not quite as hardcore as he'd like me to think, she noted.

'There was no love lost between Paul and Xander Croft,' Sylvia said. 'I mentioned my suspicions to the police, but they did nothing. He's very well connected.'

'I hear that the wife of Police Superintendent Blair is a fan,' said Sloan.

'Yes, Xander helped her when she lost her mother to cancer a few years ago,' Sylvia replied. 'He can, without a doubt, be very charming. The study is through here.' Sylvia walked over and opened a door leading off the lounge. Grace and Tobias followed her over.

'Thank you, we'll try not to be too long.' Grace gently closed the door behind her, then glanced around.

Despite the rest of the house being spick and span, there was a film of dust shrouding everything in the room. It didn't look as though anyone had been in here since the original police search. Even the air felt still.

The room gave off a quietly masculine vibe with muted greens and a lack of fuss and ornamentation. She moved across to the desk where Sloan was already shuffling carefully through papers. He glanced up and froze, looking past her shoulder. Grace felt her skin crawl.

'What? What is it?' she asked, spinning round on her heel.

Then she saw it. The winking red eye of a camera tucked in below the cornicing, beside the wall-mounted oak bookcase.

'Interesting,' she murmured, then turned back to the desk. The desk drawers were unlocked. Quickly, she secured the dead man's phone and laptop. On top of the desk was a framed photograph of the deceased and his wife taken in happier times. Sylvia looked considerably younger and less polished but more joyful. The man in the photograph was handsome. Tall and rangy, with warm laughing eyes and a generous smile. She also located a leather-bound diary and matching address book.

'Anything in his correspondence?' she asked Sloan, who had replaced the sheaf of papers on the desk.

'Nothing that would shed any light on things.' He continued to rummage in the desk, pulling out a half-empty bottle of malt whisky.

'He seems to have liked a tipple.'

'Don't we all?' she said.

A picture fell behind them with a crash and Grace nearly jumped out of her skin.

'There are no such things as ghosts,' she muttered as the

door to the study opened and she saw Sylvia framed there with an expression of fear and anger on her face.

Behind the picture – a framed portrait of the deceased – sat a metal safe set into the wall.

Grace turned back to Sylvia. 'Have you been in the safe recently?'

'Not since he died. I had to get his will and personal papers from there for the solicitor.'

'Has anyone else had access to this room since Paul's death?' she asked.

'Look, Paul died months ago. I've had plenty of visitors since then. I can't recall anyone coming in here, but I can't guarantee they didn't.'

'Perhaps the security camera might help. Can we have access to the footage?' asked Sloan.

'I don't think there is any,' said Sylvia.

'What do you mean?'

'Well, he told me it was just for effect, not real, a decoy type of thing.'

Grace pulled a chair over to just under the camera and hopped on to it. 'It's real, alright,' she pronounced after a couple of seconds. 'Did he tell you why he wanted it?' she asked, as she jumped down and returned the chair to its original position.

Sylvia had gone very white and started to sway. Grace swiftly moved to her side and helped her through to the living room, sitting her down on the sofa.

'I'm sorry,' she murmured. 'I'm starting to think I didn't know him as well as I thought.'

'Maybe a nice cup of tea?' Sloan looked over at Grace.

'Excellent idea,' she said. 'Mine's black. Sylvia?'

'Milk and one sugar,' she murmured, settling back on the cushions, the colour gradually returning to her cheeks.

Sloan stood still for a moment then moved towards the kitchen. 'Right... back in a minute,' he said.

'Do you mind if I take a look inside the safe?' Grace asked her client.

Sylvia bit her lip as though she wanted to say no, but finally nodded. 'The key is under the rug by the chair.'

'I'm sorry,' said Grace. 'I know that this is difficult. All this poking and prying can feel like a violation. However, it's important we get access to everything. It's not always the obvious things that lead us to answers in this line of work.'

She left Sylvia for a moment to locate the key and return to the study. The safe door swung open easily. A musty smell of old paper wafted out towards her. As she rifled through the contents, she pulled out a large ledger with double entry bookkeeping. As she opened it, an A4 envelope fell to the ground and some photos spilled out. They were graphic shots of Paul Gordon and a dark-haired woman in the throes of passion.

Grace scooped them up and walked through to the lounge where Sloan was pouring tea into cups.

'Sylvia, when did you find out that your husband was having an affair?'

Sylvia flushed. 'Not until after he died,' she sighed. 'I discovered those images when I went into the safe to get out his will.'

'Do you know the identity of the woman?' asked Sloan.

'No, I've no idea.'

'How come these photos ended up in Paul's safe?' Grace chimed in.

'Again, I have no idea. He doesn't seem aware of the camera in them.'

'Have you any idea where the photos were taken?' asked Grace.

'None whatsoever. I assume in some hotel somewhere?'

'Was he being blackmailed?'

'Possibly. He never told me if he was. But I imagine he'd have gone to any length to keep those from me.'

'I'm going to need access to all his bank statements and finances in general,' said Grace, rising to her feet. 'I'll also need to look into the feed on that camera in the study. It appears to be hooked up to a small microphone, so hopefully we'll have audio as well. I've some boxes in the car so if it's all right with you I'll pack up all the papers and take them away with me?'

'All of them?' said Sylvia, looking anxiously from one to the other. 'Is that really necessary?'

'I know it feels like a massive invasion of privacy,' said Grace, 'but unless you want me to move in and do it here there's really no other way.'

Sylvia gave a small smile and nodded. 'Take whatever you need. I'm being silly...'

'It's only natural to want to hold on to things,' Grace replied. 'I'll take good care of everything until I bring it all back to you.'

After the paperwork had been loaded into Grace's car, they left Sylvia to head back to the office in Portobello.

'Are you sure you don't want me to take a few boxes away with me to share the load?' asked Sloan.

'That's kind of you to offer, but she entrusted them into my care,' said Grace, her stomach sinking as she realised just how long going through everything was going to take her.

'You do realise that she could be lying about discovering the affair after his death?' he said.

'I'm aware,' she replied. 'If she found out beforehand

then she might well have pushed him off that rooftop herself. She would have had both means and opportunity. Collecting the insurance pay out would be the icing on the cake.'

'And then calling you in to investigate? That would be a very dangerous double-bluff,' said Sloan. 'The woman would have to have nerves of steel.'

'Time will tell,' sighed Grace.

What on earth had she gotten herself into?

Chapter Eleven

It had been a miserable day. Even Harvey hadn't had much appetite for their evening walk. Afterwards, he lay on the rug in front of the wood burning stove, the smell of wet dog heavy in the air, and a gentle snore reverberating. Grace had shed her own wet clothes and jumped into her PJs after a steaming hot shower to counteract the winter chill. The wind was really whipping up now. She wandered over to the bay window, inhaling the comforting smell of melting beeswax from the storm lantern. She could see the waves crashing ferociously against the shore on the empty beach, the water black and threatening. Shivering, she drew the heavy curtains, turning her attention to the boxes of paperwork beside her comfortable couch.

'Netflix is going to have to wait.' Harvey stirred briefly as she poured herself a large glass of red wine to make the job in front of her slightly more palatable.

Grace had lost all sense of time when the doorbell rang, startling her from her work. She didn't encourage visitors, especially not at this time of night. Padding over to the door she peered through the spyhole then flushed in annoyance as she recognized Brodie.

'It's me, Grace, let me in,' he said, sounding impatient.

Harvey's tail thumped treacherously on the floor, and he padded over to the door, whining in excitement.

Trying not to look as grumpy as she felt at being caught at a disadvantage, she opened the door and Brodie waltzed in, dropping to his knees to make a fuss of Harvey who was overjoyed to see him. Her gaze softened as she watched him with the dog.

'What are you doing here?' she asked.

'I did a bit of digging into that suicide you're working on. One of the investigating team owes me a favour. I thought you'd want to know as soon as possible.'

'Here's me thinking you were just after an excuse to nose around my new flat.'

'I figured you might have invited me up before now,' Brodie said, his voice tinged with reproach. 'We're still friends, aren't we?'

'Of course.' Grace forced a smile, her heart thumping. Having him here made her feel twitchy for all kinds of reasons.

Brodie walked over to the large bay windows and drew back the curtains. He didn't say anything about the lit storm lantern but gave her a penetrating look that was tinged with sadness.

'Some view you've got from here,' he said. 'It doesn't bother you, looking down over where he—'

'No, I find it comforting... in a way. Anyway,' she said, firmly steering them away from their past. 'What did you have to share with me? Now that you're here you might as well join me in a glass of wine.'

Brodie took the proffered glass and sank down on to the

settee like he belonged there. Harvey immediately jumped up beside him and shot her a glance as if daring her to make him get down. Brodie stroked him and the dog relaxed.

'He should really live with you,' she said, with a wry smile. 'You always were his favourite.'

'Nonsense! He loves us both the same. Anyway, as you're your own boss you can take him to work with you. He loves being around people. And, er... Julie's not keen on dogs.'

'Oh? That's a shame,' she said. *So, Miss Perky isn't perfect after all!*

'Anyway, about your case. The police investigation was fairly cursory at the time. There was no suspicion of murder. He'd been placed on antidepressants some months earlier by his doctor. Friends said that he'd seemed stressed and withdrawn in the weeks leading up to his death.'

'And yet there was no note?'

'No, but not all suicides leave a note.'

'What about CCTV?'

'The college has some CCTV, but none covering the roof or the trajectory of the drop. It's thought that he died immediately upon impact.'

'No eye witnesses?'

'None. The cleaner discovered the body the next morning when she drove into the car park at the rear of the building. The police and the Procurator Fiscal's office were happy to sign it off as a suicide. The post-mortem raised no red flags.'

Grace sighed. 'I suspected as much. If Sylvia is right and this was a murder, the only way I'm going to be able to prove it is to get a confession from the murderer.'

'Anyone in the frame yet?'

'Too early to say. He was, however, playing away. I found

these in his safe.' She passed across the photos. Brodie's eyebrows climbed into his hairline.

'Blimey, I feel rather unadventurous now.'

'Quite. What I don't yet know is whether he had these taken for his private delectation or whether they were sent to him as part of an extortion plot.'

'Any dodgy payments in his financial records?'

'Nothing that jumps out at me, but I've not been through everything yet,' she said, pointing at the boxes.

'Well, if anyone can get to the bottom of it, you can. Did I ever tell you what your nickname was on the force? Not sure I had the courage back then.'

'No, you didn't. But I knew it was 'The Terrier'. I rather liked it,' she said with a quick grin. She held his gaze for just a fraction of a second too long before she looked away.

It felt both horribly wrong and horribly right having him sitting here. Part of Grace still loved him. It hadn't even crossed her mind to date again. However, their son's passing had ripped them both apart and now there were too many rocks beneath the surface. She dare not go there. She didn't have the strength to go through another breakup. It would finish her.

'I can give you a hand going through these if you like?' he offered. 'If the police did get it wrong and fail to nail a murderer, I'd prefer it was uncovered.'

'Thanks, Brodie, I'll take all the help I can get.'

They worked through the boxes together in companionable silence.

'That's weird.' Grace showed a handful of statements to Brodie where she had underlined the entries in pencil. 'He seems to have been making monthly cash withdrawals to the tune of five thousand pounds from his personal bank account. I haven't been able to find corresponding deposits in any of his other accounts.'

'That's far too much for incidental expenses,' Brodie commented.

'The payments started a few months before he died and ceased after his death.'

'Maybe his wife will know,' Brodie ventured.

'I'll ask her.' Grace added to her notes.

After a couple of hours, Grace's eyes were scratchy with fatigue, and she couldn't help yawning.

Brodie rubbed his neck and glanced at his watch. It had been an anniversary gift from her and she was surprised but pleased to see that he was still wearing it.

He stood up and stretched.

'Mind if I use your bathroom before I head off?' he asked.

'Sure,' Grace answered reflexively. 'Second on the right down the hall.'

As soon as she spoke, she wanted to stuff the words right back in her mouth. This was what happened when you let your guard down. *Had she left the door open or closed? Damn!*

As he left the room, she ran her hands through her hair and paced up and down, straining her ears for any sound, her nerves at screaming point. She heard the flush of the toilet. Maybe she'd gotten away with it? Maybe the door was closed, and he hadn't seen.

She heard his measured tread along the hall. The feet paused on the other side of the living room. *He knew.*

He came in and his expression was difficult to read.

'Grace, this really isn't healthy.'

'You had no right to go snooping around! It's my business how I choose to have my flat.'

'But you've recreated his entire bedroom here. How can you possibly start to move on...? It's bad enough that you've decided to set up shop on the beach where our son drowned, but this is taking things to a whole new level.'

'Just get back to Miss Perky and forget about it,' she snapped. 'After all, that's what you do, isn't it?'

'Don't you dare make this about me!' he shouted. And he was a man who almost never shouted. She flinched, despite herself. 'Connor wouldn't want this. He wouldn't want his bedroom moved into your flat and made into a permanent bloody shrine. He'd want you to live!'

'You're making too much of it,' she said, trying to placate him now. 'It's only my spare room. Anyone can sleep there.'

Harvey started barking and circling them, clearly agitated that his two favourite humans were fighting.

'You need help,' Brodie said, his tone gentler now. 'You need to come to terms with it. Connor drowned. He's not coming back.'

Grace lifted her chin. 'There was no body.'

'You know as well as I do that in all likelihood the currents swept him out to sea.'

'I thought I saw him the other day,' she said, the fight draining out of her. 'At Waverley Station. I was so sure it was him.'

'It's happened to me, too,' he said. 'A glimpse out the corner of an eye, a tilt of the head, the set of the shoulders.'

Grace didn't dare tell him what she had done.

'Look, I have to get going. Focus on the case. You were always a great detective. And if you can't let his room go all at once, then try to do it piece by piece.'

She nodded. His kindness pierced her more than harsh

words ever could. It reminded her of what they had had together and what she had lost.

After he left, she walked into Connor's room. Every morning she sprayed Lynx into the door on her way out to work so that it smelled of him. In here he was forever sixteen, still angular and adolescent with gangly limbs and that painful self-consciousness, starting to push her away with a ferocity that had wounded her even while she understood it.

Brodie was right. She had to find a way to accept what had happened.

Her heart pounding, Grace picked up a guitar from its stand and rushed through to the lounge with it. She laid it down by the door. Tomorrow she would take it to a charity shop. She collapsed onto the couch and tried to concentrate on the financial statements she'd been going through, but her attention kept coming back to the guitar. She could hear snatches of the music it had once played in happier times. Eventually, she couldn't bear the feelings of discomfort any longer and put it back in its rightful place in Connor's room. Feeling calmer, she returned to her position and Harvey settled on her feet.

Chapter Twelve

Grace traipsed up the driveway to her mother's new house. It was architect-designed, yet slightly soulless, unlike the rambling sandstone semi she had grown up in with clematis climbing over the walls. That house had never been enough for her mother, Morag – a relentless social climber who had committed the enormous folly of marrying a gentle man with the soul of a poet. A man she had nonetheless loved deeply, conceded Grace. Or as deeply as she was able to love anyone.

She winced as she rang the doorbell and heard its strident echo throughout the house. Then the door was thrown open and she was engulfed by Brian, her mother's new husband, exuding bonhomie and expensive aftershave.

'Great to see you, my dear,' he boomed. 'Come along. Your mother's in the kitchen putting the finishing touches to lunch. What's your poison?'

'Gin and tonic, please.'

Grace managed a smile, though she felt an unreasonable

antipathy to this brash self-made man who had acquired her mother with barely decent haste after the death of her father.

She made her way to the state-of-the-art kitchen where she found her mother whirling around in a typically energetic fashion. Tall and elegant, her mother was still a good-looking woman and could wield a considerable amount of charm. She tended not to waste it on Grace.

'Grace, how lovely to see you,' she said, gripping her by the shoulders and giving her air kisses on both cheeks. *This must be de rigour these days at the golf club*, thought Grace, trying not to stiffen in her embrace.

Her mother then dropped to her heels to make a more natural fuss of Harvey, prompting big brown SOS eyes from the dog.

'Have you been forgetting to eat again?' her mother said, casting a critical eye over her daughter's lean frame.

'Auntie Grace!' squealed Grace's seven-year-old niece, who grabbed her from behind in a bear hug.

'Emily! Put Grace down,' laughed Grace's sister, wandering into the kitchen with a glass of wine in hand.

'Cally, how are you? It's been a while,' said Grace with a warm smile.

'Whose fault is that?' Cally replied, prising Grace from Emily's grip. 'We're always inviting you for dinner. Tom's starting to get the feeling you don't like his cooking!'

'Have you tasted mine?'

'Er... now you mention it, not for some time. Is that an invitation?' asked Cally.

Not exactly. Before Connor died, Grace and her sister had seen each other all the time but since then, seeing Cally with her kids, and Hamish in particular, was just too hard. He was the same age as Connor and the cousins bore a strong resemblance to each other. It was a constant reminder of what she had lost.

Cally stood eyeballing her, eyebrows raised. She wasn't letting her off the hook this time.

'Yes,' Grace said with a forced smile. 'Why don't you all come round for dinner next Friday?'

'We'd love to!' said Cally, giving her a hug and looking so happy that Grace felt bad for not offering before. They hadn't even seen her new place at Portobello yet.

Grace took her drink from Brian and wandered through to the sitting room with her sister.

It always grated on her that there wasn't even one picture of her father amidst all the family photos. Come to think of it, there was only one of her and Connor, too, compared to the myriad photos of her sister's brood. Her mother had never spoken of Connor since his death. Grace suspected she blamed her for failing to realise he'd been struggling. Grace's father had suffered a heart attack just two months later. Grace suspected it had been the shock of losing his beloved grandson that had killed him. Morag thought so as well, and that knowledge had sat uneasily between them ever since.

'Earth to Grace?' her sister said, giving her a gentle nudge.

Forcing her mind back to the present, Grace gave an apologetic grimace. They sat down together on the couch.

'Any exciting new cases?' asked Cally.

'Yes, I've a big one that's been taking up all of my time. A possible murder. I've been working with an investigative journalist to share the load.'

Hamish lumbered in with Emily on his back and Bruce, the toddler, attached to his leg. Her elder sister had Hamish the same year Grace had Connor, but then her first marriage had broken down and it had been quite a few years before she had met Tom and started a second family.

'He's so good with them,' said Grace.

'I know. He still misses Connor, you know. We were talking about him only the other day. They used to have some laughs together.'

Grace squeezed her hand. Her sister was the only person she could really talk to about her son these days. In the police force, life had been too busy for anything other than work friends and she'd managed to push all of those away in the aftermath of what happened. She returned to work only to start spinning out – driving herself harder and harder until eventually one morning she'd got up and got dressed and then found herself unable to open the front door. She'd been off for six months after that, which hadn't gone down well with her boss, Detective Superintendent Blair. She'd come back to work a somewhat humbled version of her former self, only to find he had no place for her within a Major Investigation Team. When she'd protested, things had got ugly. He'd accepted her back reluctantly, then done everything in his power to diminish and undermine her until, eventually, she'd quit and taken them to an employment tribunal for constructive dismissal. She'd been awarded a massive pay-out. Blair hadn't come out of it well.

'It's time you gave some thought to dating again, Grace,' said her sister suddenly. 'You're far too young to give up on love. I know someone who would be perfect for—'

'Dinner is served!' shouted her mother triumphantly.

'Saved by the bell.' Grace grinned.

As they all trooped through to the dining room, Grace landed beside Brian and groaned inwardly. He wasn't a bad bloke, but he really was so insufferably smug. She intercepted an anxious look across the table from her mother and felt a twinge of guilt. They were right. She really should make more of an effort. Her mother was still young enough to make another life. Her father would have wanted her to be happy. Brian might be a bit brash and materialistic, but in some ways this suited her mother better, much as it pained Grace to admit it. Her mother certainly seemed to be blossoming now and had a social life that put Grace's own to shame. The least she could do was try and be happy for her.

'So, Brian, are you still a member of Granville Golf Club?'

'Yes, I was recently elected to the committee,' he said, beaming with pride. 'It's like the Who's Who of Edinburgh in that clubhouse. Great for business networking, though you have to be subtle.'

Grace had to hide a smile at the thought of Brian trying to be subtle.

A thought suddenly occurred to her. 'I don't suppose that Xander Croft is a member?' she asked. Merchiston, where the college was located, was close to the club.

'Why, yes, he is. A marvellous chap! Very popular with the ladies, I believe.'

Grace sat up straighter in her chair.

'How about Regan Bradley, Xander's business partner?'

'Yes, she's a fabulous golfer. Puts some of our more competitive ladies out of sorts.'

'Does the name Paul Gordon mean anything to you?'

'The psychic chap? Yes, he was a member, too, along with his wife. A terrible tragedy. We were all incredibly shocked when we heard. His poor wife hasn't been back to the club since.'

'Understandable,' she said, an idea germinating.

'Why? Do you know them?'

'Not terribly well,' she hedged. Grace exhaled slowly.

This was it. If she could get into the club, she could gain access to Regan and Xander. She would have to tread carefully. She didn't want to tip her hand. Glancing across the table, Grace noticed her mother's beady eyes taking in the fact that she was chatting with Brian for once. Then her mother got to her feet and motioned to Cally to help her with dessert. Grace seized her chance.

'Is there any possibility you could get me passes for myself and a friend?' she asked, turning her attention back to Brian. 'I'd like to try golf first before I take up such an expensive hobby.'

Brian narrowed his eyes as he thought about it. He was first and foremost a businessman and liked to drive a hard bargain even when it came to family.

'How about we make a deal? Kill two birds with one stone?' he said, sounding pleased with himself.

'Go on,' said Grace.

'We've had some money and jewellery go missing at the club. It looks like there's a thief working there. We're reluctant to get the police involved. Ideally, we want the person identified and sacked privately.'

'You're assuming the culprit is a member of staff?' she asked.

'Who else could it be?' Brian looked surprised.

'Let's just keep an open mind for the time being.'

'Be careful. We can't be seen to be throwing rash accusations around.'

'You've got yourself a deal,' she said, accidentally on purpose dropping a piece of meat from her fork to be scooped up by Harvey who was doing some under-table reconnaissance work.

'Oh, and can we keep this little arrangement strictly between ourselves?' she added. 'I don't even want Mum to know I've... er... taken up golfing until I decide if I'm sticking with it. And I don't suppose you want the golf club matter getting into the public domain either?'

'Agreed,' he said after a moment's pause. 'I'll sort out a temporary membership with the club secretary for you and...?'

'Tobias Sloan,' she said, hoping he knew how to play golf. 'Email me the rest of the information,' she added, passing him her card.

Her mother came back at that moment and the conversation switched to lighter things. Grace, who wasn't used to eating so much these days, could feel her skirt waistband trying to saw her in half. Although glad she had caught up with her family, she was craving the space to be alone with her thoughts. She caught hold of her mother in the kitchen as she was preparing coffee.

'Mum, thanks for today, it's been great. Brian seems like a really nice guy. I'm happy for you, really. I'm heading off now.'

Her mother's sharp expression softened.

'Thank you, Grace. It doesn't mean I didn't love your father. I did. More than you will ever know.' She turned away, busying herself clattering cups onto saucers.

Grace hugged her quickly from behind and made her escape.

Chapter Thirteen

The following day, Grace pushed open the door to the agency and found Jean already immersed in work. The smell of coffee filled the air and the winter sun shone through the windows.

Jean paused and rubbed her neck. 'Coffee's made and there's some traybake in the tin.'

'I don't know what I'd do without you,' said Grace, helping herself to a piece of shortbread and dispensing a post-walk titbit from his treat tin to Harvey.

'I like to be busy. Makes me feel useful again.'

Grace felt for her. Jean had been through a messy divorce from her husband Derek a few years back. Her children had flown the nest and weren't very good at keeping in touch with her.

'Young Hannah's really stepped up, too, since we've taken on this new case. The lass has been running herself ragged.'

The door opened once more, blowing in a chilly draught

of salty air. Tobias and Hannah shrugged off their coats as Grace poured them each a coffee.

Grace ushered everyone through to her office.

'Tobias, have you managed to find the camera feed for Paul Gordon's study?'

'Yes, it was on the laptop and secured by an unfathomable password, but I sent it to a tech guy I've used before and he managed to gain access to Gordon's cloud storage. The camera feed has months of data on it so it will be quite a job to go through it all. It seems to start a couple of months before he died and it's still running now.'

'I noticed a small monthly fee for cloud storage on his bank statements,' Grace mentioned.

'Such a weird thing for Paul Gordon to do,' mused Hannah, her brow furrowed. 'Most people have security footage of the outside of their homes. Why his study? Who wants to record themselves? It doesn't make sense.'

'Sylvia went white when she realised it was a real camera, not a dummy. I can't help worrying that she's not being totally straight with us,' said Grace.

She took the photographs from her drawer and hesitated before passing them around. She had to stop herself seeing Hannah as a child. She was part of this team.

Hannah's eyebrows shot up, but she made no comment.

'The photos show Paul Gordon and an unidentified woman. We discovered them in the safe in his study.'

'Did the wife know?' asked Jean.

'She says no, but she might be lying. After all, she now has her two reasons to have murdered her husband: for revenge and for the money.' Grace sighed.

'What would you do if the murderer turned out to be our client?' asked Hannah.

'I'd turn her over to the police,' Grace said without hesitation.

'That would be really bad publicity for the agency.' Sloan folded his arms.

'We'll cross that bridge if we come to it.' Grace shut down the speculation. 'In the meantime, we give her the benefit of the doubt.'

'Jean, could you phone Sylvia today and see if she can account for these monthly withdrawals of cash by Paul Gordon? I've itemised the amounts and dates here.' She passed across a sheet of paper.

'No problem,' said Jean, taking it from her.

She looked across at Tobias. 'Tell me you play golf.'

He looked startled. 'Yes, I do. I've stalked many a quarry over the golf course in past years. Dare I ask why?'

'I've discovered that the deceased was a member of Granville Golf Club along with Xander Croft and Regan Bradley. I've scored us temporary membership in exchange for a little side investigation. Hannah, there's also a vacancy for a bar person in the club house. I vaguely recall you worked as a waitress in a hotel once?'

'Yes, that's right. Do I have to apply online? Does this mean I'm going undercover?' Her voice rose in excitement.

'Yes, fire off an application and mark it for the attention of Brian Rogers. He'll hire you straight away. I think it's easiest if you keep your own name and personal details. You've had relevant experience so just miss this place off your CV. If you see Tobias or I there just act like you've never met us before.'

'This is so cool!' Hannah grinned. 'I promise I won't let you down, Grace.'

'Jean, this is going to leave you holding the fort,' said

Grace. A flicker of disappointment flitted across the older woman's face, but she managed to smile.

'No worries, I can handle everything here for now.'

At interview Jean's face had lit up when Grace had discussed the possibility of undercover work. Grace felt bad for her, but right now she really needed her here.

'Hannah, the case you're going to be working on relates to some valuables and money going missing from the golf club changing rooms. Obviously, they can't install cameras there. Granville Golf Club is one of the most prestigious in Edinburgh with a very high-end clientele. They're renowned for their discretion, so any breach of trust or petty pilfering harms their brand.'

'Do we have any suspects?' asked Hannah.

'No. Brian's theory is that it must be someone on the staff, as to afford a membership there you have to be quite well-off.' Grace winced as she remembered Brian's smug face as he imparted this information.

'That might not mean anything,' said Jean. 'Maybe someone does it for the thrill?'

'Good point,' said Tobias.

Grace leant back in her chair. 'Hannah, I want you to investigate discreetly and feed all intel back to me. But not at the club, unless it's a dire emergency, or you'll blow our cover. And do *not* put yourself in harm's way. Is that clear?'

Hannah nodded, her eyes lit with enthusiasm.

'Do *we* know each other?' asked Tobias.

'Best not. We can cover more ground there going about independently.'

'In relation to the college, I've made some headway with Beverley Thomson, that protester,' said Jean. 'I've been accepted into their private Facebook group and I'm going to one of their rallies tomorrow.'

'That's brilliant!' said Grace warmly. 'Really fast work.'

'I feel a bit conflicted to be honest,' said Jean, colouring slightly. 'I mean, I go to church myself and here I am going after another Christian. It feels a bit... wrong.'

'It might help to think of it more as crossing this Beverley off our list of suspects,' said Tobias. 'And if she is guilty of bringing about Paul Gordon's death? That's not exactly someone worthy of your protection, is it?'

'No, you're right, of course, I was being silly. All of this...' she said, sweeping her arm around the office, 'is very new to me.'

'It's new to all of us,' said Grace.

Chapter Fourteen

Jean approached the small group of protesters outside the college with some trepidation. She'd wanted more excitement in her life but wasn't sure she was up to the task. Her mouth was dry, her heart was pounding, and she felt sure they would see through her in no time. As she drew closer, she could see the words on the home-made placards. It was fire and brimstone stuff and she shivered, in fear or excitement she couldn't say. The group had a fairly even division of the sexes. Some of the women looked like her, as if they had stopped by on the way to Marks and Spencer. However, there was a handful at the front that were sporting more of an activist vibe in duffel coats and skinny jeans. She guessed that she would find her target within them. Drifting towards them, she tapped one of them on the shoulder.

'Er, I'm looking for Beverley?'

The woman looked her up and down with cold eyes.

'We've been messaging on Facebook. What's going on in

there...' she said, nodding towards the college. 'I couldn't let it continue.'

The woman stuck out a hand in a grubby fingerless glove.

'Welcome. Grab a placard and join us. Beverley!' she shouted. 'New recruit.'

Beverley Thomson strolled over and stared deep into Jean's eyes. Dressed in a warm jacket and dark jeans tucked into hiking boots, with her ash blonde hair tied up in a casually chic bun, she was a handsome woman in her sixties. Jean felt a bit afraid of her and resisted the urge to flee.

'Don't worry... Jean, is it?'

She nodded, not trusting herself to speak.

'Glad to have you join the good fight. We're going to be here for another two hours then head to The King's Arms just a couple of streets away. Ready?'

'Er... yes. Sometimes you just have to stand up and be counted,' said Jean. She grabbed a placard which read 'Mediums do the Devil's work' and held it aloft. *If my kids could only see me now*, she thought.

The rally began. Without being obvious, Jean tried to position herself so that she was behind Beverley to ascertain her closest associates and overhear the odd scrap of information.

After a while, she noticed the protestors had thinned out a bit. Suddenly, a bell sounded, and people started putting their placards in a pile. Jean brightened. Her feet and back were killing her from all the standing about. Were they preparing to knock off early?

The placards were put away in the van and a large cardboard box was brought out. Everyone huddled around it and what looked like rubber masks were passed around for people to put on. They were all images of the devil and incredibly creepy. Jean reluctantly put hers on, not wanting to stand out. It smelled of rubber and old sweat and felt claustrophobic. She felt sick to her stomach. Something else was being passed round. She could hardly see through the mask and was struggling to breathe. Something slimy was pushed into her hand. It looked like a water balloon, but it was heavier. A class must have ended because college students were streaming out in front of them. An angry chant sprang up from around her.

Don't do the Devil's work!

Don't do the Devil's work!

Jean joined in, but felt things were getting out of control. Those she was with seemed to feel freer in their masks and she could sense the aggression. The first balloon was thrown, and a woman's scream rent the air. She turned her face towards them, and it looked like she was covered in blood. People rushed to help her then everyone else threw their balloons, too. Jean took care to miss with hers.

'Police!' someone behind her yelled. 'Run!'

Jean looked around and saw the police car advancing on them, blue lights flashing. Panicking, she threw down her mask in the box and followed the others who were running round the corner.

Jean ordered a large red wine from the bar to warm herself up and casually followed Beverley over to a table in front of a log fire.

The group extended to around twenty members and were middle-aged to elderly. Snatches of conversation drifted over to her, ranging from quotations from the Bible to the best way to make a Pavlova.

'You picked a helluva day to join us.' Beverley smiled, leaning over to talk to her.

'Do you do that kind of thing often?' asked Jean.

'Not often enough that they expect it, but often enough to keep the college on the back foot.'

'I take it what we were chucking wasn't blood?' ventured Jean.

'You don't need to worry. Water soluble paint is all.' Beverley laughed. 'So, which church do you go to?' she asked.

'St George's in Portobello,' Jean said, praying this wouldn't get back to her minister.

'A very conservative parish,' Beverley said, nodding in approval. 'As is mine.'

'Conservative or not, what that lot are getting up to in there is utterly beyond the pale!' Jean declared, earning a 'hear, hear' from across the table. 'It's diabolical, that's what it is,' she added, screwing her face up in an expression of disgust. Her companions had fallen silent, listening. 'I can't stand by and watch them do the Devil's work in broad daylight.'

Beverley clapped her on the shoulder and one of the gentlemen brought her another glass of wine.

Jean stayed on as the group gradually thinned out until it was just her and Beverley left. The wine had done its job and she was feeling more relaxed. She needed to get Beverley to open up, but how?

'How long have you been an activist?' she asked.

'Since my teens,' Beverley replied, laughing at Jean's surprise. 'I've always followed my conscience. I stopped eating meat at the age of seven, dairy products at thirteen and it went from there, really. How about you?'

Jean remembered Grace's advice to stick as closely as possible to the truth.

'My marriage is over, and my kids have flown the nest, so I've only recently had the luxury of thinking much about anything at all. Before that I was all about working enough hours to provide for us all.'

'Why now? Why this issue?' asked Beverley, giving her an intense stare.

'Sometimes you just have to say, "This far and no further",' said Jean. 'I never approved of psychics or anyone dabbling in the spirit world, but most of them do it in such a small way that it was easy to look the other way. The opening of the psychic college? Well, that took things to a whole new level. They're exploiting the spirit world and all those vulnerable people for monetary gain. It's evil, that's what it is. Someone needs to stop them.' Jean hoped she had been convincing enough.

Beverley high-fived her, which was another new experience for Jean.

'Amen to that, sister,' she said. 'Have you ever met anyone who worked there?'

'No, but I've heard plenty about what goes on. A few people from my church got sucked in. They mostly saw that guy who committed suicide, Paul Gordon? Proper messed with their heads, he did. The poor souls didn't know which end was up by the time he finished with them. One of them was even sectioned,' said Jean, who was starting to get in the swing of things now.

'Oh, him. He got what was coming to him,' sneered Beverley, swigging from her glass.

'Did you know him?' asked Jean.

'I know what he was. An emissary of the Devil.'

'Do you think he jumped off that roof or someone decided to take him out for what he was doing?' asked Jean, taking a nervous gulp of wine.

Beverley narrowed her eyes. 'What are you implying?'

'Me?' stuttered Jean. 'Nothing at all! I was only speculating and wondered what you thought, that's all.'

Beverley gave a quick snort of laughter.

'Relax! I'm only kidding around. I've no idea what happened. All I know is that the Lord works in mysterious ways. One way or another, Paul Gordon got his comeuppance.'

Jean nodded and took another sip of wine. Her heart was hammering so loudly in her chest that she feared Beverley could hear it.

The brief exchange had completely unnerved her, and Beverley's assurances hadn't convinced her. It was now clear to Jean that this woman could potentially be a very dangerous adversary.

Chapter Fifteen

Grace drove into Edinburgh via Leith where she was dropping Harvey off to stay with Brodie who was off for the day.

Driving up to his small, terraced house on a new estate, she thought back longingly to their old house in Duddingston Village. They'd both had to severely downsize after the split. Fortunately, Grace also had her pay-out from the employment tribunal, or she wouldn't have been able to afford to buy the flat and office at Portobello. Harvey was paying keen attention to where they were going and when she pulled up on the drive he barked with impatience, his tail wagging furiously. She let him out and rang the doorbell.

Julie answered the door and Grace schooled her face into a smile.

'Grace! How lovely to see you,' said Julie. 'You look nice. Hello, boy!' She bent down in a rather twitchy way to try and make a fuss of Harvey but his response, to his credit, was somewhat lukewarm.

'I'll be back for him this evening. Thanks for taking him.'

'It's our pleasure,' Julie cooed, producing a titbit which Harvey wolfed down, shooting her a guilty look.

Grace walked back to her car, then turned as Brodie hailed her from behind.

'Hey Grace, you look great,' he said. 'Going somewhere nice?'

She could feel her skin flush. *God, what if he thinks I've done it for him?*

'I'm working. Off to the golf club on a charm offensive. I need to try and get in with the main players at the college who all seem to be members.'

Brodie looked worried. 'Well, be careful! I know what you're like, chasing down a suspect.'

'Thanks for having Harvey.'

'No problem. Take it easy out there.'

She got in the car and drove away. Her eyes prickled with unshed tears, and she strove to get a grip on herself. So what if they lived together? She wanted Brodie to be happy, didn't she?

By the time Grace was walking into the golf club she'd regained control. The interior was opulent and more like a world-class spa than any sports club she had been to. The women she encountered all looked rather high maintenance with their designer clothes, artfully coloured hair and fancy painted nails. Grace was pleased she had forked out for some discounted designer gear at the retail park. With her newly lightened hair, carefully applied makeup and naturally lean physique she fitted right in. She was also wearing some very convincing costume jewellery and a fake designer watch that she hoped would convince a would-be thief to scope her out as a potential victim. She'd even had her nails done for the occasion, though she couldn't normally stand nail polish. It made her feel as though her hands were useless. As she was signing in, she noticed that Regan Bradley was already there. She'd likely be coming into lunch soon. The sign-up sheet on the club noticeboard showed that she was out on the course with an instructor, so hopefully she might be lunching alone. Her lesson should be over in five minutes and then no doubt she'd want to shower and change before lunch. Grace had about twenty minutes to kill, she guessed. There was no sign of Xander Croft.

Heading into the bar area she noticed Hannah serving there, with another two staff members. Moving to one end, she motioned to her to come over and was pleased to notice she looked as cool as a cucumber.

'A sparkling water, please. How's it going?'

'I've only been working for a couple of hours. Your stepdad briefed me when I got in. It turns out there have been about a dozen cases of stuff going missing now. If we don't solve the case quickly, he's going to call in the police.'

'No pressure, then,' said Grace.

Another customer came looking for service and Hannah rushed off. The members started wandering in for an early lunch and a queue built up. Grace waited until one of Hannah's co-workers was near then wandered off, leaving her purse on the bar. At that moment Regan Bradley strode in looking immaculate, her glossy dark hair and expensive yet understated linen dress oozing money and class. She recognised the woman from a photograph supplied by Sylvia. Grace waited until she had seated herself at a small table then approached the bar once more. Her purse had vanished.

A staff member appeared, holding it aloft.

'Are you looking for this? You left it behind,' she said.

'I'd forget my own head if it wasn't tied on!' Grace exclaimed. 'It's good to know that everyone here is so honest.'

Grace turned round and approached Regan Bradley.

'May I join you? They seem to be rather short on space.'

Bradley gave Grace an assessing look, then motioned for her to sit down with a small nod.

Grace noticed Tobias Sloan wander into the bar area, looking very 'country gentleman' in a tweed jacket. More than one of the women assessed him out of the corner of their eye. He caught Grace looking over and blanked her. Irrationally, she felt snubbed.

'You want to be careful with your belongings in here,' Bradley said suddenly, not bothering to lower her voice.

'Really?' Grace replied, sounding shocked. 'I didn't have it down for that sort of place.'

'I've lost stuff in the changing room myself,' said Regan, looking angry. 'A gold necklace was removed from inside my locker.'

'How do you know it didn't just fall off?'

'All my valuable pieces have safety chains,' Regan snapped. 'I don't wear cheap rubbish.'

'No, I can see that,' soothed Grace.

'I haven't seen you before. New member?' asked Regan, her eyes weighing her up.

'Yes, I've just joined.' Grace smiled. 'I'm a bit rusty. Is the golf pro any good here? I'm thinking of having lessons.'

'He's perfectly... adequate,' Regan replied with a faint smirk.

They both ordered lunch, then talked about the club and its facilities for another few minutes.

Hannah soon arrived with their food, looking stressed. As she was putting Bradley's salad down, the plate slipped from her grasp, banging onto the table.

'I'm so sorry!' she gasped.

Regan glared at her. 'Careful, you idiot!' she exclaimed. 'This isn't a truck stop, you know.'

Hannah backed away, her face beetroot, and Grace felt for her but had to hide it. She needed to get this hideous woman to trust her. She grimaced across the table. 'You simply can't get good staff these days,' Grace said with a shake of her head.

'What do *you* do?' asked Regan, her eyes shrewd and assessing.

'I run my own private investigation business,' said Grace.

'Interesting,' Regan murmured, her tone cold.

'How about you?' asked Grace.

'I'm a business partner in a psychic development college.'

'Really? That must present some unique challenges.'

'You have no idea,' Regan said drily.

'I'm quite open to that sort of thing. I lost someone a couple of years ago. I saw a medium at the time. He was very understanding. It really helped me to move on.'

'Mind if I ask who?'

'It was Paul Gordon, a friend recommended him. He really opened my eyes.'

Regan went white and Grace noticed that her eyes had moistened.

'Oh, perhaps you haven't heard?'

'Heard what?'

'I'm afraid he died a few months ago,' Regan's voice wavered, and she looked stricken. Not the response that Grace had been expecting.

'I'm sorry to hear that,' Grace said. 'He looked so well the last time I saw him.'

'He wasn't ill, well, not physically anyway.'

'If you'd rather not say...'

'No, it's fine. He... well... took his own life. He jumped off the roof of the college.'

'But that's awful! He couldn't have been in his right mind.'

'It left us all with so many unanswered questions.'

'A sudden death is like someone walking off in the middle of a conversation,' said Grace.

'Yes, well, anyway,' said Regan, sitting up straighter. 'There's no point in dwelling on things. Life goes on. You should consider joining the college. We do spiritual readings and all sorts of classes. You can even get your teeth into subjects like neuroscience and quantum mechanics. You may have heard of Xander Croft? He's developed quite a following.'

'I'll definitely look into it,' said Grace. 'Are you a psychic yourself?'

'Heavens no!' Regan laughed. 'I'm afraid my gifts lie in other areas and usually involve a spreadsheet or six.'

Grace finished her lunch and excused herself. She felt pleased with what she had accomplished. She looked round for Hannah on her way out, but she was still rushing around serving and she didn't want to disturb her. She walked into the ladies' and saw a member of staff in there wearing a burgundy tunic over black trousers, rifling through a small worn make-up bag. Their eyes met briefly in the mirror and the woman, who looked to be around the same age as Grace, quickly averted her eyes. She had clearly been crying and was trying to repair the damage.

Grace hovered for a moment, washing her hands, but by the way the woman angled away from her she thought it best to leave her in peace to regain her dignity.

Chapter Sixteen

Hannah hunched in her duffle coat as the wind whistled about her ears. It was freezing cold on the Esplanade and the water over the wall to her left was gun-metal grey, but she needed to pause and collect her scattered thoughts before the team meeting at the agency. She clutched her cardboard cup of hot chocolate with both hands to encourage some warmth back into her fingers. The odd walker whizzed by in a winter coat, dog on a lead, their fur standing on end.

She was rattled by her first shift undercover. It wasn't nearly as much fun as she had thought it would be. Some of the staff had been so nice to her that Hannah had felt really guilty that she was there to spy on them. She'd planted the fake money in a couple of members' jackets and also in a locker that she'd left unlocked, but no one had nibbled at the bait so far. Hannah brightened and her lips lifted in a small smile. Maybe that meant that no one she had been on with today was the thief. Or maybe she'd given herself away somehow and they'd rumbled her.

Grace made it all look so easy. She had looked so natural chatting away to Regan Bradley in the club today. Mind you, she used to be a hot-shot detective, so probably had nerves of steel. Hannah wished Connor was still here. He would have got such a kick out of what Hannah was doing now. Grace had never asked her if they had known each other, and Hannah didn't know what she would tell her if she ever did. It was complicated. She sighed then drained the last of her hot chocolate and walked on until she hit the boardwalk. The spray from the sea wet her face and stung her lips as the water writhed under the onslaught of the wind. She glanced in at The Espy on the way and it was full to bursting with people taking shelter, a happy clamour floating towards her as someone came out laughing. It would be nice to have some mates to have a drink with. Everyone had turned on her in her final year at school. After what had happened.

Hannah pushed the morose thoughts firmly away. Lifting her head, she pasted on a happy expression and pushed open the door of the agency.

Jean welcomed her with a warm smile.

'Just go through. Everyone's there already. I'm getting the coffee.'

'Are you sure you don't want me to do that?'

'No, you go in and take the weight off. You've been on your feet all day.'

'Hannah! How did it go?' asked Grace.

'It was hectic, but I still managed to set the traps. Annoyingly, no one went for them.'

Grace's face fell. 'No worries, it's early days yet. I'm afraid you'll have to do the same tomorrow but mix it up a bit. Maybe leave something in a corner by the hairdryers, leave a handbag under the seat, that sort of thing.' They had acquired a convincing stash of bait items such as jewellery, bags and purses from judicious charity shop hopping in Portobello High Street. 'How many suspects are we looking at, potentially?'

'There are eight staff members with access to the changing rooms. They all seem really nice,' she added, with a worried frown.

'Appearances can be deceptive in this game,' said Grace. 'Stay on your guard.'

Jean came through with the rest of the coffees and sat down.

Hannah settled back in her chair, feeling a wave of fatigue hit her as the adrenaline drained away. It was exhausting leading a double life. She'd thought it would come easier to her than it had done.

Harvey crept up alongside her and nudged her hand. She stroked his silky ears, finding comfort in his presence.

'We've made some progress at the golf club,' Grace told Jean. 'Hannah has been working all day behind the bar and has identified eight suspects and laid traps for them with treated banknotes and various trinkets. So far no one has taken the bait.'

'I saw you talking to Regan Bradley,' Hannah put in. 'She treats the staff like dirt. They can't stand her!'

Grace nodded. 'I think I made some headway with her. She's encouraged me to check out the college, so that's given me an in there. I'm also having a lesson with her golf professional tomorrow to see if I can persuade him to reveal anything that might help us. Tobias, anything to report?'

'No sign of Xander Croft, so I left after lunch. I did mention Paul Gordon to a few of the members, however, and no one had a bad word to say about him.'

Jean cleared her throat. 'Er, I joined the protest group and managed to get invited for drinks with them afterwards.

The ringleader, Beverley Thomson, styles herself as a lifelong activist and really seems to have loathed Paul Gordon. It's as if she considers him the embodiment of everything she is ideologically against.'

'Well done, Jean,' said Grace. 'You've made a great start. Keep digging!'

'As well as this investigation, we also need to make some headway with Tobias's investigation into Xander Croft's fraudulent practices.'

'I think it's important to get to the bottom of Paul Gordon's death first: to expose Croft properly, we will need to reveal who we really are and that will compromise your original case. However, you will also appreciate that I can't wait forever to move in on him,' said Tobias.

'Noted,' said Grace. 'You guys get off home and I'll close up here. Before you go, Jean, can I go through one of the reports with you? I'll need it typed first thing in the morning.'

They all moved through into the next room as Hannah slowly got to her feet. She walked to the desk and picked up Connor's photo, staring at it – wishing him back to life as her finger traced the remembered contours of his face.

Gently, she replaced the photo and turned to leave, giving a start as she saw Grace standing in the doorway staring at her intensely.

She rushed past, her cheeks scarlet.

'Good night, see you tomorrow.'

'Good night,' replied Grace quietly, the intensity of her scrutiny still burning into Hannah's back as she walked quickly along the darkened esplanade.

Chapter Seventeen

Grace opened the oven door and gasped at the hot blast of air that greeted her along with billowing smoke. Turning the oven down, she slammed the door shut and opened the kitchen window as the smoke alarm started beeping insistently. Grabbing a brush, she jumped up on one of the kitchen chairs and poked the alarm viciously until it subsided. Why on earth hadn't she just ordered in, messed it about a bit, then passed it off as her own? It didn't help that her sister Cally was a domestic goddess. When she was first married, she had hated going to Cally's for dinner in case Brodie began to realise what he was missing.

'Sorry, Harvey,' she murmured, dropping a soothing hand on his head after that affront to his hearing. 'At least there will be lots of titbits later.' She grinned at him which earned her a thump of the tail. Titbits was his second favourite word after walkies.

The pots were bubbling away, and the roast was well cooked, to put it mildly. She flung open a drawer and rummaged about for the steak knives, hoping they would cut through the charred meat. Thankfully, there was a rich sauce to smother it all which could hide a multitude of sins.

The doorbell rang. Dammit, could her perfect sister not be late for once? She hadn't even had a chance to change. Glancing at her sweaty red face in the mirror as she flew down the hall she cringed with embarrassment. *There's a reason why I don't entertain*, she thought grimly as she flung the door wide and forced a welcoming smile onto her face.

'Oh, it's you,' she said as her face fell.

'Not quite the reaction I was hoping for,' said Tobias with a wry smile. 'Am I interrupting something?' He took in her dishevelled appearance.

'No, er, yes!' she spluttered, her brain working overtime. Her sister was always nagging her to date again and probably had at least two horrendous suitors waiting in the wings. If she paraded Tobias Sloan in front of Cally, she might just get off Grace's back.

'Which is it?' he said, looking amused.

'Quick! Come in.' Grace pulled him in by the arm. 'Have you eaten?'

'Not yet. Grace, what's going on?'

'My sister, her husband and their kids are coming for dinner. Fancy posing as my date in exchange for a free meal and lots of wine?'

He sniffed the air and frowned.

'Do I really have to?'

'No, but you'd be doing me a solid if you agree. I'd owe you one. Plus, we can talk about whatever you came here about once they're gone.'

The buzzer sounded.

'I need a decision,' said Grace, beseeching him with her eyes.

He shook his head and gave her a crooked grin. 'Fine, I'm in.'

'Wonderful!' She exhaled in relief. 'Now can you let them in and introduce yourself while I quickly get myself ready?'

Tobias opened his mouth to protest but she'd already sped off to her bedroom. She jumped into the shower for five minutes then threw on a fifties style dress with a nipped in waist that her sister had bought her for her last birthday, pulling off the price tag as she did so. Cally didn't need to know that this was the first time she'd worn it. A slick of lipstick, a dash of mascara and she swept her hair up into a pretty clip Connor had got her. She wrestled her mind back from Connor and rushed to join her guests.

'You look stunning,' said Sloan, presenting her with a large glass of red wine on her return.

She flashed him a grin of thanks. He was really getting into the whole date thing, which was just as well as her sister would be paying close attention. In her absence, he'd supplied everyone with drinks.

Tobias leaned close to her ear.

'I saw what you're serving for dinner,' he whispered. 'I figured it would need copious amounts of alcohol to flush it down.'

Startled, she looked at him. Grace hadn't realised he had a sense of humour. Of course, perhaps he wasn't joking?

'Cally!' she said, striding over to her sister and enveloping her in a warm hug. She greeted Tom, Cally's husband, and hugged the kids, holding on to Hamish just a fraction of a second too long. As always, he let her, as if he realised a bit of the hug was for someone else.

'Right, you,' said Cally, 'I want a tour of your new pad.

I'm sure Tobias will manage to hold the fort for a few minutes?'

'No problem, I'll just check on the dinner,' he said.

Grace showed her sister round the flat, eliciting enthusiastic comments. She was reaching out her hand to the door of the lounge when her sister stopped her.

'Hang on, what's in here?' she said, opening the door to the spare bedroom. She reached for the switch and froze, tears coming to her eyes.

'Oh, Grace, I thought things were getting better? That this was going to be a fresh start?'

Grace squirmed under her sister's compassionate regard.

'I'm working on it!' she exclaimed. 'Honestly!'

'This is why you haven't invited any of us round, isn't it?'

Grace nodded, unable to find the words.

'Anyway,' her sister said with a faux-cheerful smile. 'We're here now so let's enjoy ourselves, eh? Tobias Sloan? You're a dark horse. He's very good looking. There's a brooding intensity about him.'

Grace didn't have the heart to reveal they weren't really dating.

She headed back to the kitchen to find Sloan had miraculously transformed her cremated roast into something approaching edible. As she walked in, it felt strange but not altogether unpleasant to see him at the cooker looking perfectly at home. It opened her eyes to the possibility that there might still be someone out there for her. Moving close to him, Grace started to serve the food onto warmed plates.

'Thanks so much for this. I really appreciate it,' she murmured.

To her surprise, he put an arm around her and pulled her close. Reflexively, she stiffened.

'Relax,' he whispered in her ear, 'all part of the boyfriend service.'

Grace felt her cheeks redden in embarrassment and smiled at him as she grabbed another plate.

Sitting in the midst of her family, who were all in fine fettle, Grace felt her flat come alive for the first time, instead of being her usual furtive mausoleum. She'd almost forgotten the sound of her own laughter, she realised, as she got caught up in the hilarity between the kids and their parents. She may have lost her son, but she still had all these wonderful people who wanted to be in her life, even after she'd done her best to push them away.

After they'd all left, Grace turned to Tobias, who was sitting on the comfortable couch with his long lean legs stretched out in front of him.

'Wow!' She grinned, sitting beside him with a fresh glass of wine. 'That was impressive. You're hired.'

He threw his head back and laughed before turning towards her. 'It wasn't a hardship, Grace. Any man would be proud to have you by his side.'

There was an awkward pause. Grace's heart hammered against her ribs. She wasn't ready for this or the intense way that he was looking at her. Time to get things back on an even keel. She sat up straighter and put her wine glass down on the coffee table.

'You came to see me about something earlier, before I dragged you into my family dinner. What was it?'

'It's about the camera feed file from Paul Gordon's study. I spent days going through it and have copied anything of interest onto this,' he said, passing her a memory stick.

'That's great, thanks for doing that,' she said warmly. 'However, I'd also like the whole file, too, just in case.'

'Don't you trust me?' he said with a raised eyebrow.

'No, it's not that.' She laughed. 'Call it a hang up from my days in the police. I also know how tedious it can be watching camera footage for hours with nothing happening. You may have nodded off at some point and not even realised.'

'Good point. I'll get a full copy across to you.'

It was late and Grace desperately wanted to be on her own. It had been a long day.

As though sensing the sudden change in mood, Sloan uncoiled his long body and rose to his feet.

'Time to head off, I think.'

'Thanks so much for tonight. You've saved me from my sister's matchmaking for at least a few more months.'

'Happy to be of service.'

He leaned in to kiss her on the cheek as he left.

Chapter Eighteen

Grace let herself out of the flat with a sleepy Harvey. He was worn out after all the socialising, so she didn't intend to take him far. It was a clear night with a full moon draping everything in silver light. There wasn't a soul about. She walked off the Esplanade right down to the water's edge where the moon had laid a silvery path across the still waters all the way to the horizon. Standing there she stared out to sea, feeling the tension from the evening ebb away and a sense of calm steal over her. Harvey sat at her feet as if he couldn't be bothered moving, no doubt enjoying the feel of the cool sand under his paws. It had felt good, if exhausting, to entertain again. She had been living like a hermit for too long. Her thoughts drifted to Tobias. He'd hinted over the course of the evening that he was interested in her and she had to admit it had felt good to be perceived in that way again. Although he was a good-looking man, she didn't feel drawn to him the way she had with Brodie. She certainly wasn't inclined to do anything rash. However, she acknowledged to herself that she might be starting to thaw ever so slightly and open herself up to the possibility of another relationship. *One day...*

Despite being tired to the very bones, she couldn't resist having a look at the camera footage that Sloan had pulled off the cloud when she got back in. After putting Harvey to bed with the obligatory treat and cuddle, she closed the door on him in the kitchen and took her laptop to bed. Opening up the file, she watched with curiosity. One of the things she'd always done in a murder investigation was try to get under the skin of the deceased, to get a real feel for who they were. In the course of this investigation so far, she felt she had barely scratched the surface of Paul Gordon. Seeing him on the footage, sat at his desk, she had to admit he'd been a handsome man. Grace looked at the time stamp. Two months and one day until his death. The door to the study opened and Xander Croft burst in. Paul Gordon immediately stood up as though expecting trouble. The first few words were missing, but Paul had clearly switched on the audio mode for what followed. The dialogue was audible but crackly.

'Are you out of your mind?' demanded Croft, his face contorted with rage. 'The college will lose all academic credibility if you persist with these preposterous plans of yours.'

'You're an insufferable prig, Xander,' snapped Paul, his eyes narrowed in anger. 'This TV show could catapult us into the big time. It's a recipe to print money. Who in their right mind would say no to this kind of deal?'

'You're nothing but a fraud and a charlatan,' said Croft. 'You're not even a good psychic. Admit it! You've never had the gift. You misled us all.'

'And you have? said Paul Gordon, leaning forward aggressively. 'You're as full of shit as the rest of us. Don't you get it? There's NOTHING THERE!'

Croft slumped into a chair on the other side of the desk.

'How can you even say that?' he asked, running his hands through his hair.

'Because it's the truth,' said Gordon. 'You're kidding yourself if you think otherwise. Don't forget I died on the operating table when I had my accident. Well, what do you know? There was nothing. No white light, no tunnel, no pearly gates. Just oblivion.'

'I've never asked you about it. I didn't want to pry…'

'You didn't want to know the truth, more like,' said Gordon with a challenging stare. 'Face it, man, there's just one life and this is it. All these notions of communicating with an afterlife? It's just a construct to stop everyone spinning out of their tiny minds.'

'You're wrong,' said Croft, getting to his feet. 'I don't know what happened to you on that table, but you've clearly lost your way. I can't allow you to embark on such a morally corrupt venture.'

'Oh?' Gordon sneered. 'And how do you think you're going to stop me?'

'With whatever it takes,' said Croft, his face contorted with rage. He stormed out, banging the door behind him, causing Grace to jump.

She hit pause and considered what she had just seen. Xander Croft certainly had a temper underneath that amiable façade. Had *whatever it takes* included murder?

Pressing play again, she jumped forward a couple of days to witness Regan Bradley entering. Her expression was serious as she sat down and leaned forward to speak.

'I've discovered some serious discrepancies in the accounts, Paul. There's a black hole in our finances. I hate to tell you this, but I think that someone has been embezzling funds.'

Paul Gordon sat back in his chair, his mouth sagging

open as he ran his hands through his hair, leaving it standing on end.

'Are you sure?'

'As sure as I can be. We need to get on top of this before questions are asked and the college suffers.'

'How much are we talking about?'

'Nearly sixty grand.'

'Bloody hell! How could this happen?'

'They've covered their tracks well. I haven't got my head fully wrapped around the ins and outs of it yet. Should we call in the police?' she asked.

Gordon screwed up his face as he considered her question.

'No. Definitely not. We have to avoid any taint of scandal, or it could jeopardise our TV negotiations.'

'But how are we going to plug the deficit?' demanded Regan Bradley. 'At this rate we will struggle to meet our payroll obligations in two months' time. Also, how are we going to stop whoever's robbing us blind?'

'Leave that to me,' he said grimly.

Bradley jumped to her feet and planted her hands on the desk.

'You know, don't you? Tell me who it is!'

'I don't know, but I have my suspicions. I'll get to the bottom of it and see if we can't get at least some of that money back where it belongs. In the meantime, don't mention it to a single soul.'

Grace realised she'd been holding her breath and let it out slowly. This footage was dynamite.

She watched Regan Bradley leave. Paul Gordon then gave a roar of rage and swept the papers off his desk.

Chapter Nineteen

Grace left her car in the car park and walked across to the college. It was sunny but cold and she was again dressed to impress lest she run into Regan Bradley. On the other side of the railings, she could see the motley crew of protestors and noticed Jean amongst their number, holding a placard aloft and chanting. She was proud of her staff for the way they had stepped up recently.

It hadn't been easy finding a way into this investigation. In her role as a police detective, she had been inserted into the heart of any case from the outset and all information such as bank statements, health info and phone records had been channelled her way. Operating on the periphery with no automatic right to information was a lot harder.

Walking into the college's impressive atrium, Grace headed for reception.

'I've a private reading booked with Xander Croft,' she said, trying not to wince as she handed over her credit card. Croft didn't share his otherworldly musings out of the goodness of his heart. Still, she hoped to get a feel for him and also some insights into his relationship to the deceased.

She was shown into a small anteroom. Helping herself to a glass of iced water from the refreshment tray, she casually inspected her surroundings. It wasn't long before she noticed the winking red eye. Knowing that she was most likely being scrutinised, she took a photo of her son out of her handbag and looked at it whilst dabbing her eyes with a tissue. She kept it facing away from the camera. No point in making it too easy for him.

The door opened and she felt Croft's presence before she saw him.

Grace stood up and he enfolded her hand between his.

'I'd like to welcome you to the college and before we begin, I'd like to say how very sorry I am for your loss.'

'Thank you,' said Grace. His touch made her feel overwhelmed in a way that she couldn't precisely put her finger on. His voice was deep yet soft and, above all, kind. Her reaction to him was unexpected.

Don't be fooled, her internal voice nagged. *He's a heartless conman – you saw it yourself the other day. Don't be taken in.*

He sat her down across from him at a small table.

'Have you had a psychic reading before?'

'No, although I did have a chat with Paul Gordon at one of your events some time ago. He gave me the courage to go on. What a great loss to the college.'

'Indeed,' said Croft, his jaw muscles tensing.

'When they said it was suicide, I was so shocked.'

'Perhaps the balance of his mind was disturbed. We can never truly see into the heart of another...'

'Has he communicated with you from beyond the grave?'

Croft looked surprised, as well he might.

'No, he hasn't. I appreciate that his passing has left you with questions, but we're here today for you and someone who was close to you. May I?'

Grace nodded and extended her hand as he reached for it. Tobias had warned her that he would already have gleaned the circumstances of her son's passing and also discovered that she was a private investigator from information online. She was to play along and not challenge him, to allay any suspicion.

'I see a young person close to you taken tragically soon. He had started to pull away from you before he crossed over and you felt like you were losing him?'

'Yes,' said Grace, her voice husky with unshed tears. Despite her best efforts, it was getting tougher to pretend – his voice and the sheer magnetism of his personality were battering down her brittle defences.

'The last words you said to him were harsh.'

Grace went very still. How could he possibly know that? Was it just an educated guess?

'I didn't mean it...' she whispered, just in case.

'He knows that. Things had been difficult between you. He had been pushing you away, trying to forge a different path from the one you wanted him to take.'

Croft looked at her with such compassion Grace felt like she was lost in his eyes.

'He's at peace now, and wants you to be at peace, too.'

'Did he drown?' asked Grace, hating herself for buying in to this crap, but unable to not ask.

'He's showing me a beach and removing his clothes by the waterline. He is standing by the edge of the sea, but refuses to let me see what happened next. He's now showing me a young woman. She was special to him and has a gift for you when the time is right. There's another voice coming through... an older man with a very gentle demeanour. Was he a poet, or perhaps a writer?'

Grace nodded, her heart beating faster. How could he have known that? Her father kept his writing private. It was never intended for public consumption.

'He wants you to know that he's proud of what you have accomplished. Oh, and he's happy that your mother has found another companion to accompany her through life. He says you are to stop giving this new man a hard time. It's all for the best and the union has his blessing.'

The words forced themselves out from between her lips.

'Is he with Connor?'

'I can't sustain the connection much longer. It's fading...' said Croft, looking suddenly pale and clammy.

'Please, try...' she begged, hating herself.

'He says... no, I'm sorry, the link has broken.' Croft slumped back, drained as if he'd run a marathon.

Grace quickly poured him a glass of water and sipped at her own. She had the beginnings of a migraine throbbing behind her eyes.

'Was that what you expected?'

'Yes and no,' she replied.

'Accepting the truth of the afterlife can cause a seismic shift in the psyche. I recommend you take things easy for the rest of the day. Don't dwell on the reading or try to force things to the surface. They'll bubble up when they're good and ready. I know that this can't have been easy for you,' Croft said, his eyes concerned. 'If you need any guidance on how to move forward, I would be happy to see you again.'

Grace thanked him and left the room, her mind in turmoil.

Chapter Twenty

She hadn't felt at all like heading out again once she'd walked and fed Harvey, but reluctantly she'd pried herself away from his warm cuddly body on the couch and, throwing on her thick winter coat, pushed herself out into the wind and rain. Sitting on the bus into town, staring out into the blackness as it neared the city centre, she struggled to separate her heart from her brain and regain control over the former. She used to pride herself on being level-headed and rational when she was in the force, never allowing her emotions to get in the way of the job. But since Connor's disappearance it felt at times as though her top layer had been flayed raw, leaving her exposed and vulnerable. As Grace saw the lights of Princes Street approaching, she rang the bell and stood up. She had to get a grip. The last thing she wanted was for Tobias to think her judgement had been compromised.

Battling across Princes Street against the throng of humanity heading for Waverley Station, she reached the haven of The Guildford Arms with a sigh of relief. Inside, the patrons at the bar steamed gently in the welcome heat and voices were muted as tongues were yet to be loosened with alcohol. She loved the quirkiness of this old-fashioned pub with its nooks and crannies tucked away from prying eyes.

A long bony hand waved languidly from a plush seat set into an alcove and she made her way across the crowded floor. To her relief, Tobias Sloan had already ordered her a hefty glass of red wine. Grace shrugged off her coat and squeezed in beside him.

'How did it go this afternoon?' he asked.

Grace took a large gulp of wine to steady herself.

'Not quite what I was expecting. I thought it would be like going to see one of those fortune tellers at Blackpool.'

'One you would find easy to shrug off?'

'Yes, I suppose,' she said, averting her gaze.

'He got inside your head,' he stated.

Grace thought about denying it but said nothing.

'Dammit, Grace! I warned you. This is what he does. I should never have let you—'

'Let me?' she snapped. 'Who made you the boss?'

'Sorry,' he sighed, running his hand through his hair. 'That came out wrong.'

'You think?'

'I know this man. He's smart, intuitive, he does his homework. Like it or not, you're vulnerable to his bullshit. That's not a criticism. I've walked in your shoes, remember? Had I not seen what this bastard did to my wife when we lost our child, I would have been taken in myself.'

'I was expecting him to use the techniques we'd discussed – to know things about me. That's not what threw me. I just didn't expect him to seem so... caring. He came across as a really nice guy.'

Sloan's face tightened.

'Look, the reading doesn't change anything. I'm a professional and quite capable of being objective,' she said.

'I hope that's true.'

'Given what you've told me about your circumstances, I would have thought that if anyone's integrity is going to be compromised then it's yours. Are you sure you aren't just scapegoating this man? I don't want to take part in a witch hunt.'

'I'm positive,' he snapped.

They both sipped their drinks. Sloan broke the awkward silence. 'Look, I'm sorry. I had no right to call you to account like that. Sometimes... I can be a little intense.'

'Apology accepted. When are you planning to expose him, anyway? I'm not quite clear on how you plan to do it?'

'Hopefully, not until we've got the answers you need for Sylvia Gordon. The college has a big open day coming up in May. He's going to do a reading. That would be the best time for me to do it to get maximum exposure and shut him down.'

'How exactly?'

'I've created a large number of sock puppet social media accounts which appear to be genuine people. I've dripped out their stories over many months online including snippets about the people they have supposedly lost. It's incredibly diverse and detailed, but it's all completely fake. These fake accounts have all joined Facebook groups attached to the college and joined any spin off groups and forums.'

'That sounds like a massive amount of work,' said Grace.

'You're not wrong. All these accounts will purport to be excited about the medium event and state that they are going to attend. The minute he reaches out to any of the fake accounts with any identifiable detail taken from the Facebook account then I've got him. It will prove he just looks them up online.'

'Wow, you've got it all figured out,' said Grace with a weak smile. Yet she couldn't help but feel a bit queasy inside. 'It'll be a brutal take-down if it works.'

'If it works, then he deserves it. Of course, if your investigation discovers that he also murdered Paul Gordon, then that would be even better.'

Grace felt uncomfortable. This was a personal crusade. She would need to ensure Sloan didn't corrupt the integrity of her investigation with his exposé.

'Have you had a chance to look at the memory stick I sent you yet?' he asked.

'Yes. There was clearly a schism developing at the heart of the college about the direction they were going in.'

'I thought it gave Xander Croft a motive to push Paul Gordon off that roof,' said Sloan.

'That's one possibility,' said Grace. 'However, it's also clear that the college has been haemorrhaging money to someone. It could even be Regan Bradley herself. Maybe she feared imminent discovery and was trying to get ahead of the curve and get her version of events in first.'

'Time will tell.'

Grace rose to her feet and fought her way through the crowd to get another round in at the bar. By the time she arrived back at the table, she no longer felt like talking about work. It had been a long enough day.

By tacit consent they spent the next hour talking about other things. It had been a while since Grace had enjoyed male company; Sloan was interesting to talk to once he had loosened up a bit and was distracted from his obsession with Croft. He had a wealth of stories to share about his previous journalistic exploits, some of which had her in stitches.

Eventually the conversation took a more personal turn again.

'This is the first time I've done this,' she said, looking around her at the convivial surroundings. 'It feels strange to be out in a pub again. Without Brodie, I mean. Even if it is sort of a work thing.'

'Sort of a work thing.' He winced. 'That's me put firmly in my place.'

'Oh! Er, what I meant was—'

'Relax, Grace, I'm just teasing.' He grinned.

'What about you? Have you started dating again?'

A shadow crossed his face and Grace wished she hadn't asked him.

'The truth is that I still feel married. I don't see that changing anytime soon.'

'I know exactly what you mean. I still feel like a mother even though I have no child.'

'Here's to holding on to what we have,' he said, raising his glass aloft.

'And boils and pestilence to those who don't understand,' she declared, clinking glasses.

'Boils?' He laughed.

'Nobody likes boils,' she said, mock serious.

The mood lightened, they stayed on safe topics like books and films for the rest of the evening.

Once back in her cosy flat, having been greeted by a sleepy Harvey who gave her an admonishing *what time do you call this?* woof, she drifted into Connor's room and sat down on his bed, the bed his feet had started to overhang the end of before he went missing.

Who am I kidding? she thought. Even the air sat heavy

from lack of use. This wasn't his room. He'd never set foot in it. Brodie was right. Had her son really been trying to communicate with her through Croft today? She'd thought starting the agency would be a new beginning, a way to forge a fresh life for herself. Taking on this case had been a catastrophic error. She could see that now. She could hear Harvey's nails clacking on the wooden boards as he came in search of her. Sensing her emotions, he sat close by and placed his heavy head on her lap, staring up at her with sad chocolate brown eyes and making comforting noises from the back of his throat.

'You miss him, too, don't you, boy?' she said as she stroked his velvety ears and patted his big head. It had been a blow seeing Julie so comfortable in Brodie's house. She hadn't realised their relationship had grown that serious. Grace knew she should be glad for him but a small mean part of her resented Brodie's ability to move on. He had been her whole life. She'd never so much as looked at another man.

Harvey thumped his tail hopefully. She dried her eyes and gave him a watery smile.

'Is that you hinting it's time for your last walk?'

An answering thump and he bounced to the door.

She got to her feet and went in search of his lead.

Chapter Twenty-One

Grace swung the golf club and the ball took off with a satisfying crack, coming to rest a credible way down the green.

'Not too shabby,' grinned Matt, the golf pro who was giving her a lesson. 'I think we'll leave it there for the day. Best to quit on a high.'

'Do you have time for a coffee?' asked Grace.

He glanced at his watch.

'I can join you for a quick one in the club house as I have half an hour before my next lesson.' He flashed a practised smile.

God, he thinks I'm flirting with him. Grace squirmed.

Twenty minutes later they were in the bright modern café bar, looking out over the fairway. Grace noticed a few envious glances thrown her way.

'You teach another woman I know, Regan Bradley. I was thinking of partnering up with her. How good is she?'

His face darkened. 'How well do you know her?'

'Barely at all really. Why? Is she too good for me?'

'No, it's not that. She's not much better than you but she's a complete and utter... never mind.'

'Cow...?'

He laughed. 'Hey, you said it, not me. She got the last pro fired. Said he'd been inappropriate with her. I happen to know the boot was on the other foot. She got him fired for turning her down. You might be better to find someone else, but it's up to you.'

'Wow! Thanks for the heads up. I'll steer clear.'

'She hangs around with that psychic, Xander Croft, sometimes. He's such a cool guy.'

'I had a reading at the college with him the other day,' Grace said.

'How was it? I'm not a believer myself.'

'Neither am I, really. It was... surprising.'

He glanced at his watch and drained his coffee. 'Same time next week?'

'Wouldn't miss it,' she said, as he rushed off.

She noticed Hannah had come on duty behind the bar and was busy serving hot drinks. About to head back to the changing rooms to get her stuff and see if anything had been nicked this time, Grace noticed a sudden movement. Xander Croft was swaying in the doorway, his face chalk white. Quickly she leapt up and moved to his side. He looked startled to see her there.

'Hey, you don't look well, let's get you sat down,' Grace said. She led him over to her table.

'Thank you,' he murmured. 'Most kind. Grace, isn't it?'

'Yes, are you feeling faint? Can I help in any way?'

'I'm sorry to have alarmed you,' he said, as though it was an effort to push the words out.

Grace sat down opposite him.

'So, we meet again?' A wariness had crept into his voice.

'I'm a member here.' She smiled. 'My mother's husband is on the committee. I'll go and get you a glass of water and some coffee.'

'Thank you.'

Grace walked to the bar and ordered. She was still waiting when the door opened again.

Sylvia Gordon stood framed in the doorway, her eyes snapping with anger, her face flushed. Grace was rooted to the spot.

Sylvia marched into the room and people started whispering behind their hands. She stopped in front of Croft.

'Why haven't you returned my calls?' she hissed.

Croft stood up, swaying slightly.

'Sylvia, this isn't the time or the place. I've simply been busy. Come outside and we'll sort out whatever is bothering you.'

Sylvia allowed him to take her elbow and guide her out, and they both disappeared from view. Grace thought about following them, but didn't want to blow her cover. As she sat back at the table, mulling over the ramifications of what had just happened, a shadow fell across her and she looked up as Regan Bradley slid into the seat opposite her.

'What was that all about?'

'I haven't got a clue,' said Grace.

'I thought you didn't know Xander Croft?' Regan said, staring at her with narrowed eyes.

'I don't! Well, I didn't until very recently. I had a reading from him the other day after you recommended the college. When I saw him looking faint, I led him to a seat and went to get him some water.'

Regan took in the glass of water at the table and nodded, apparently satisfied. Grace felt sick inside. Something was very wrong here, she could feel it. What on earth was going on?

'That woman he was with seemed angry,' Grace said, taking a shot in the dark. 'Is it his girlfriend?'

'Not anymore,' said Regan. 'She's a dreadful woman. He had the devil of a time extricating himself from her clutches. Making a scene in public is just so typical of her. Poor Xander, he must be mortified.'

'Didn't she used to be married to that other psychic, Paul Gordon?'

'Yes. It wasn't a happy marriage.'

'Oh, by the way, I had a lesson with your golf pro,' said Grace, thinking it best to steer the conversation into safer waters. She didn't want to arouse suspicion.

'Now there's someone who definitely does what it says on the tin,' Regan replied with an arch look.

'Oh, are you and he...?'

'No comment,' Regan replied with a satisfied smirk. 'Anyway, I'd better get to work, soothe ruffled feathers and whatnot.'

She left, a vapour trail of expensive perfume in her wake.

Grace felt the opening salvo of a headache. She was about to head back to the office herself when the door swung open for a third time and she saw young Hannah rush over to the bar manager, visibly upset. He immediately left in the direction she had come from, speaking into his phone as he went.

Grace made her way over to Hannah who had picked up a glass and begun polishing it, looking stressed.

'What's going on?' she murmured.

'A member of staff has been found dead in the changing rooms. It looks like she fell and hurt her head. The police have been called.'

'Stay here for now,' said Grace. 'I'll see if I can establish what happened.'

She walked out of the room casually, so as not to draw attention to herself. The female changing rooms had a closed sign on the door, but as no one was there to bar her way she slipped inside anyway.

Taking care to keep to the periphery of the room and not touch anything, she followed the sound of muted voices and came upon the bar manager and Matt, the golf pro, standing looking down at the body of a young woman who appeared to be in her early thirties. She was clearly well advanced in pregnancy.

'You can't be in here,' said the manager, turning to escort her out.

'Wait,' she said. 'I'm former police. I may be able to help. Has anyone checked for a pulse?'

'Yes,' replied Matt. 'I'm a trained first aider. She's still alive.'

Grace could see a pool of blood fanning out from under the woman's head. She leaned down to check her pulse for herself. It was weak and thready.

Suddenly the woman's belly moved under her baggy clothes.

'The baby might still survive if we're quick enough. Call an ambulance and explain the situation. Ask them to send the Medic One team if possible. Hurry!' Grace felt for a pulse again.

The manager got straight on to his phone.

'She's stopped breathing,' reported Grace.

Starting compressions, she shoved down her feelings of horror and revulsion and concentrated on what she was doing. There was very little hope for the mother, but if the baby was far enough along and she could get the heart beating again, it might make all the difference.

There was something else. The woman looked familiar. Where did she know her from? Then it came to her – this was the woman she had recently seen looking as if she had been crying in the changing rooms.

'They'll be here in a few minutes,' said the manager, turning back to them. 'Looks like she slipped and banged her head on the floor. A terrible accident.'

Grace wasn't so sure. The floor looked dry, and the woman was fully clothed. It would be interesting to see if she had any defensive wounds or DNA under her fingernails. If she hadn't slipped, then someone had most likely hit her with something on the back of her head.

She slipped effortlessly back into the authoritative tone she used to wield a few years ago. 'That's for the police to determine. You need to post guards at each of the doors into the changing rooms,' she said, gasping with her exertions. 'You also have to prevent people from leaving the club as the police may want to talk to them.'

'What if they refuse and leave anyway?' asked the young manager, who looked to be a nervous type.

'Make a note of their names; their contact details will have to suffice,' she said. 'Try and exit retracing the way you came in and without touching anything.'

The manager left. Matt got down beside Grace and together they took turns performing rhythmical chest compressions, trying to keep the baby alive.

Suddenly, she motioned to him to stop and felt for a pulse. It was faint but it was there. The woman was breathing again.

The door flew open and a team of paramedics with an attending doctor came in and took over. Grace staggered to her feet and leaned against the wall as they completed their observations, applied an oxygen mask and bore the woman away on a stretcher.

As the door banged shut behind them, Grace shuddered and exhaled. Matt was sitting on a bench white as a sheet. They stared at each other in silence, shaken by their shared ordeal.

'She's not going to make it, is she?' he asked, his voice struggling to stay steady.

'All we can do is hope,' replied Grace.

A few minutes later, Grace exited the changing rooms into the hustle and bustle outside.

Hannah came up to her, her eyes filled with unshed tears.

'She's going to die, isn't she?'

'It's too early to say.'

'I know her, her name's Maria Rossi. She's a massage therapist here. She came in for a coffee sometimes. Wasn't she pregnant?'

'Yes, she was,' said Grace.

'Do you think it's related to the missing stuff?'

'I doubt it. Try not to worry. Just go back to work and we'll talk later.'

A police car pulled up outside and two uniformed officers came through the doors towards her. She didn't recognize them and stood aside as they headed to her position after speaking briefly to the manager on the way in.

Grace felt overwhelmingly sad for the young woman, and the tiny baby inside her who was still clinging on desperately to life. She pitied her family, as yet unaware of the axe about to fall that would change their lives for ever.

Chapter Twenty-Two

Grace waited in the car park as she knew that Hannah was due to finish at two pm. Having given a brief statement to the police officers, she watched the comings and goings. This would most likely become a murder investigation, she thought, her heart aching for Maria and her unborn child. Two years ago, she would have likely been in the Major Inquiry Team on the case. It felt odd and not altogether pleasant watching from the sidelines.

Suddenly, a familiar car drew in and she wriggled down in her seat to avoid being seen. With his recent promotion to sergeant, she should have seen this coming. Brodie got out of the car and, with a brief word to the accompanying detective, he strode towards her, his face set in uncompromising lines.

'Grace, what are you still doing here? One of the uniforms flagged that you were at the scene. I can't have you sticking your nose in this one and interfering with a possible murder case.'

Her first instinct was to tell him where to get off, but she realised he was genuinely anxious that she was going to make trouble for him. Did he really think she would do that?

'Relax, Brodie. Just as well I was there to stop them stomping all over the crime scene. I take it that it *is* a crime scene?'

'It appears that way,' he said. 'I'm serious, Grace, you can't get in the middle of this.'

'I've no desire to. Though, if you need an unofficial sounding board you know where to find me. I've got your back.'

'I don't need your help, Grace. Just stay out of my way. I mean it!'

He strode away from the car, and she could see him giving commands as he went. If she was completely honest with herself, it felt a little uncomfortable seeing him issuing the orders rather than in the supporting role she was used to. She had been accustomed to being his superior in rank when she worked in the police.

Two hours later they were all sitting in the office at Portobello in the front room, drinking hot chocolates which Jean had ordered in from the café along the Esplanade. A tin of her homemade flapjacks were fast disappearing. Hannah had phoned her manager at the club and ascertained that, unfortunately, Maria had required to be intubated and put in a medically induced coma. She was awaiting a CT head scan to assess the extent of the damage. A baby girl had been delivered by Caesarean section and was still alive in the neonatal unit.

Grace was pleased to see the colour coming back into

Hannah's cheeks. Her youngest employee had done very well to maintain her cover and act professionally. Despite the horrible circumstances, it was very cosy in the office. Spring was almost upon them: the sun warmed the air in the room while the lightening skies turned the sea an inviting blue.

'Quite the day you've had,' said Jean to Hannah, squeezing her shoulder as she made her way round with the tin.

'It was horrible,' Hannah replied. 'At first I assumed she'd just slipped and cracked her head but to think that someone might have tried to kill her...'

'How often do you see her at the club?' asked Grace.

'I'd seen her a few times. The treatment room wasn't that close to the bar area, but she sometimes came in. Not long after I started, I completely mucked up her order and she was really cool about it. I liked her,' she said, with a slight wobble to her voice. 'That poor baby.' Her lips trembled with the effort not to cry.

'Who did she hang out with there?'

'I've seen her with Xander Croft and Regan Bradley, but not at the same time. She was a part-time student at the college. I've also seen her with the golf pro, Matt Turner. They had a big argument a couple of days ago. I was taking through her order and he was in the treatment room shouting at her. The door was open, but I didn't like to go in, so I waited round the corner until he left.'

'What were they arguing about?' asked Grace.

'I'm not sure. I only overheard snatches. If I'd realised at the time it was so important, I'd have got closer,' she said, her face distressed.

'You weren't to know,' said Tobias.

'It sounded as though she was breaking things off with

him,' said Hannah. 'I do remember she said she wanted nothing more to do him or his schemes.'

'Perhaps she was alluding to the thefts?' said Grace.

'I only know that she was crying and he stormed out in a temper,' said Hannah. 'I waited and then knocked on the door. I asked her if she was okay and she said everything would be fine, but it was time for her to move on. I went back to work.'

'What exactly did Maria do at the club?' asked Jean.

'She worked a few shifts every week offering sports massages,' replied Hannah.

'Yes, I had one with her that very morning after my lesson,' said Sloan. 'I'd pulled a muscle in my back. I never imagined such a fate awaited her.' He looked away and cleared his throat.

'Grace, you said that Xander Croft was there, too, and was white and faint,' said Jean. 'Perhaps he'd had an altercation with Maria and things got out of hand? He might have been in shock because he lost his temper and assaulted her.'

'I'm not ruling anything out at the moment.' Grace drained her hot chocolate then stood up and paced round the room, her mind grappling with what could have happened to Maria.

'Also, Regan Bradley was in the club, too,' said Hannah.

'Yes,' said Grace. 'She strikes me as the jealous type. She certainly can't stand our client, that's for sure. Sylvia was there this morning as well.'

'I didn't realise Sylvia was a member,' said Jean.

'Yes, she came over and had a go at Xander Croft. I was standing at the bar. I doubt she even registered I was there.'

'At least we've solved the mystery of stuff going missing from the changing room,' said Hannah, sounding glum. 'The manager told me before I left that the police found some stolen jewellery and a lady's watch amongst Maria's possessions at the hospital.'

'Hmm...' said Grace. 'Maybe. Or the items could have been planted there to frame her and distract the police from the real reason she was murdered.'

'So, you need me to keep working there?' asked Hannah.

'Yes, if you feel you're up to it. I'll fill Brian in. Okay, everyone, it's been a long day. Get off home and I'll see you all in the morning.'

They all left, and Grace busied herself signing a few background checks that Jean had typed up for her. They had a contract with a recruitment agency that specialised in supplying employees for domestic positions. She didn't make much money from it, but she also didn't have that many other clients. She opened the window to let the cool breeze flow in from the sea and laughed when she noticed Harvey's snout high in the air as he sampled the smells.

'You'll get a crick in your neck if you're not careful.' she said.

He grinned at her and thumped his tail, then stuck his nose up in the air again.

Stretching, Grace got up from her desk and moved to the window. The people on the Esplanade were thinning out but it was still fairly light. Her whole body felt knotted with tension.

She clipped on Harvey's lead and locked up the office. Walking down to the beach she slipped off her shoes, the tension leaving her body as she felt the cold damp sand beneath her toes.

Once she'd moved away from a few stragglers, she let Harvey off the lead, and he bounced away to sniff a clump of seaweed in the distance. She turned and stared at the sea, dark and turbulent. Would it ever give up her son so that she could lay him properly to rest?

A wet sandy snout nuzzled her hand, and she clipped Harvey's collar back on.

'Sorry, boy, all good things come to an end. Time for supper.'

Chapter Twenty-Three

The Esplanade was deserted as Grace neared the office. She must have been away longer than she thought. Looking forward to getting Harvey settled, her mind drifted ahead to the rest of the evening. A nice glass of red to warm her and some leftovers from last night's lasagne. It had been a long, upsetting day but she was done with dwelling on it.

Suddenly, Harvey started barking and straining on the lead. At first, she thought it must be a cat, but she soon realised he was warning her of danger. She tied him up to a lamp post as she knew he would be determined to get between her and any perceived threat. Commanding him to be quiet, she crept along to the office where she could see a curtain blowing through the open window. She was sure she had closed it. Normally, she was very security conscious. Had she simply forgotten and the wind had blown it open wider?

Grace slipped along the building until she could peer in the window. Now she could hear the sound of a filing cabinet opening. Squashing the rage building within her – she knew she needed a cool head – she retreated a few yards and phoned the police to report a burglary in progress. That done, she crept back to the open window. It was now quiet in the front office, but she could see the flicker of torchlight coming from the back room.

Grace knew she should wait for the police but there was sensitive information in her files, and she wasn't going to sit by idly whilst some low-life ransacked her place at his leisure. She hadn't reached the position she had in her career by shying away from conflict. Her body was turbo-charged with adrenaline and more than a little rage at this violation.

She shushed Harvey once more then jumped up on the window ledge and slid into the room. She could hear Harvey whine uneasily outside and hoped he didn't move on to full scale barking. Once her eyes had acclimatised to the gloom, she crept along a wall until she was looking into the half-open door to her office. Desperately she looked around for something that she could use for a weapon before settling on a hefty hole punch and a thermos flask. *Note to self: buy baseball bat for office.* From what she had seen so far, she was fairly sure it was just one person working on their own. Although she'd been well trained in physical combat in the police and felt she could usually handle herself, that would be useless if he had a knife. Worse still, a gun. Part of her knew she was allowing her anger and sense of outrage to get the better of her, but caution had never been her strong suit.

It was now or never. Bracing herself, Grace flung Jean's thermos into the far corner of the room then jumped forward with a bloodthirsty yell. Immediately she was grabbed in a choke hold from behind. So much for her diversion. She thrust back with her elbow and stamped her foot at the assailant's knee, then caught him on the side of the head with a blow from the hole punch. A muffled grunt and a yelp told her she had inflicted some damage. Grace dug her nails into the relentless fingers choking the life out of her, but they were wearing gloves so the grip didn't slacken. Struggling to breathe, she felt a curtain falling over her vision. Dimly, she became aware of the sounds of sirens. *They're too late. I'm not going to make it.* It had taken the near certainty of death to make her realise after all this time that she really did want to live. As she slid to the ground, the last thing Grace heard was the sound of furious barking and the last thing that she felt was a warm tongue licking her face.

Grace heard a bark. What was up with Harvey? She opened her eyes and squinted against the glare of overhead lights.

'She's awake!' a paramedic shouted over her, as memories started to pop into her oxygen-starved brain. A tail started thumping on the floor and a nose nuzzling her hand brought her to full consciousness.

'Grace! Thank God you're okay.'

She turned her head to see Brodie crouched by her side. The look of love and concern on his face made her tear up. She turned her head back to Harvey and raised a trembling hand to soothe his big head looming over her.

'Don't fuss! I'm fine,' she croaked. 'Have they caught him?'

'No, he'd scarpered by the time we arrived.'

'Is Harvey alright?' she asked, anxiously inspecting him. 'I tied him up before I came in.'

'He slipped his collar and was standing guard over you when we got here. He had a bit of material caught in his teeth which we're assuming came from the burglar.'

'Good boy,' she murmured. She pulled herself up to

sitting which caused the room to spin unpleasantly. Brodie's face came back into focus.

'Easy there,' said the paramedic. 'You need to get checked out at the hospital.'

'No, really, I'm fine,' she rasped, trying for a smile, but wincing as she moved her head.

'Grace, do what they say. You're far from fine. That bastard nearly killed you. Take a telling!'

'Now when have you ever known me do that, Brodie?' She summoned up a smile for the paramedic. 'Seriously, I'm fine. If I can get someone to stay with me overnight, can I just go home?'

'I can't stop you,' said the paramedic with a sigh. 'But it's against medical advice.'

'I'll phone my sister,' Grace said, pulling her phone out of her pocket.

'I'll stay with you,' said Brodie. 'That maniac might come back. You don't want your sister having to deal with that. Also, I can help settle Harvey down. He's had a shock, too.'

'Won't Julie mind?'

'Of course not!' he replied.

They helped her to her feet and slowly walked through the carnage of her office and out of the front door. Grace inhaled deeply as the cool sea air hit the back of her bruised throat.

Just as they were about to head up the stairs to Grace's flat, Jean arrived. Grace had asked Brodie to call her. Her face was a study in horror as she took in the scene. Practical as ever, she got straight to the point. 'What do you need me to do?'

'Can you secure the office after the police are done? Any tidying up can wait until tomorrow,' Grace croaked.

'No problem. Hannah and I will get it ship-shape in no time at all.'

Now that the adrenaline was leaving her system, Grace felt a deep weariness settle within her. Battered and bruised, she craved the comfort of a warm bath and her own bed. It felt good to relax against Brodie as he helped her up the stairs.

'Here's me thinking you would carry me up,' she grumbled.

'Are you kidding me?' He laughed. 'My back would never recover.'

'Charming.'

Chapter Twenty-Four

Grace woke up to the welcome sight of sun streaming through the window of her bedroom. Her throat and her neck were tender, and all her muscles ached from the struggle with her assailant. She hoped he was nursing a few bruises of his own. A hefty paw slammed up on the bed and a tail thumped against the wooden floor.

'Remind me to buy you some doggy mints, Harvey,' she groaned, staring into his lively brown eyes.

She tensed as the bedroom door opened, having momentarily forgotten Brodie was there. Hurriedly, she looked at the pillow beside her and was mortified when he clocked her doing it.

'Relax! I spent the night in... the spare room.'

'Thanks, Brodie, you're a star,' she said, smiling to cover her embarrassment and pulling the covers up further.

He deposited a tray with scrambled eggs, coffee and orange juice on the bed.

'I shouldn't really eat before I swim,' she said.

'Are you kidding me?' he almost shouted. 'I'm putting my foot down. No swimming today! Got it?'

Taken aback, she stared at him.

'Got it,' she said meekly. It was unlike him to throw his weight around.

He sat down on the edge of the bed and took his coffee off the tray. 'So, how are you? You look awful.'

'Gee thanks, Brodie. You say the nicest things.'

'You know fine well what I mean. You need to rest, take things easy for a couple of days.'

'I'll try,' she smiled, knowing that she had no intention of doing what he said. No way was she walking away from this fight.

'What do you reckon as to the burglary?' asked Brodie.

'I suspect it's linked to the case I'm working on. If it was your typically opportunistic burglary, then they'd have pushed past me and made a run for it. Whoever it was, they were searching for something important. Someone wanted to shut down this investigation.'

Brodie shook his head, looking worried.

'Anyway, you've got enough to worry about with your attempted murder case,' Grace said. 'How is Maria? Have you heard?'

'She's on life support still. The CT scan showed that she'd had a massive bleed on her brain, and they have pronounced her brain dead after the tests. Her life support is due to be withdrawn today after they have harvested her organs for transplant. She was carrying an organ donor card.'

'That's terrible,' sighed Grace. 'Have you any update on the baby?'

'Still alive but poorly. No one has enquired about her or been in to claim her.'

'Have you been able to contact the next of kin?'

'No joy, so far. Running the name of Maria Rossi through the system led to a brick wall. The personal details she gave the college and the golf club were false, but sufficient to stand up to casual scrutiny. Her clients paid her cash in hand, and she gave a proportion to the club for the use of the treatment room.'

'That's strange,' mused Grace. 'And it makes it trickier to establish a motive for the killing.'

'There had been some property stolen from the changing rooms. Several items were recovered from her body and also her handbag.'

'Yes, Hannah has been working at the club trying to flush out the thief at the request of my stepfather, so don't blow her cover if you see her there. It seems a bit too convenient, though?'

'Yes, I agree. I suspect that someone sensed the net was closing in on them in relation to the thefts and made her a convenient scapegoat by sticking a couple of items about her person and in her bag.'

'It'll be interesting to see if anything else is reported missing going forward,' said Grace. She cleared her throat painfully. 'Look, Brodie, I really appreciate you being there for me last night. How did you even get to hear about it?'

'It came over the radio so I got there as fast as I could,' he said.

'Thank Julie for lending you to me for the night.'

'Sure. Though... you do know that Julie and I don't live together?'

'But she—'

'She was waiting for the electrician as I had to go to work.'

'Oh, I see.' Grace felt inexplicably lighter.

'Tobias Sloan popped over earlier with those,' he said,

pointing to a vase of flowers on her dressing table. 'He'd heard what happened, but said not to disturb you. He's downstairs helping Jean and Hannah sort out the mess.'

'That was kind.' Grace managed a smile.

'You'll pop down later to give a statement to the attending police officer?'

'Yes, of course.'

For a moment he looked like he was going to kiss her goodbye then clearly thought better of it and left in a hurry.

Grace managed to force her breakfast down though she didn't really feel like eating. It was still early, and she felt somewhat at a loss without her usual swim to anchor her to the day. Padding along the landing in her bare feet, she looked in the bathroom mirror and flinched. The violence that had been done to her was plain to see in the mottled bruising to her neck. She hated the idea of being branded in that way and resolved to wear a scarf to work. She was going to find this guy and figure out what he was up to. *He picked the wrong woman to mess with*, she thought, glowering at her reflection. Still, it could have been worse. It could have been one of her staff in the firing line. Grace shuddered at the thought.

Instead of her normal icy dip, Grace had a steaming hot shower, trying to erase every last vestige of her attacker from her skin. She'd pulled muscles in her back and shoulders and wrenched a couple of fingers trying to prise away the hands from her throat. Whoever he was, he'd been strong and much taller than her. He'd also had a taste for expensive aftershave.

Grace hoped that she'd interrupted him before he'd found what he was looking for, but the trouble was she hadn't the first clue what that might be.

Chapter Twenty-Five

'Morning, all!' Grace said, throwing back the door to the office with a bright smile. Harvey started barking and pawing the ground.

'Easy boy, it's all right,' she soothed but he clearly wasn't happy and growled low down in his throat.

'Poor dog,' said Jean. 'He's probably remembering last night.'

'I've brought doughnuts,' Grace said, depositing the box on the table.

Jean and Hannah stared at her as she walked over to the pot of coffee to help herself.

'We didn't expect you in today.' said Jean.

'Why not? I had a minor scuffle with a burglar. I'm fine.'

'Grace, you're forgetting, I was there,' the older woman replied.

'We've tidied up your office,' said Hannah. 'I'm not due at the golf club till this afternoon.'

'That's brilliant, thank you.' Grace smiled, then winced in pain.

'We put any papers apparently disturbed by the burglar to the side of your desk, as requested,' said Tobias, walking through from her office.

'Brilliant, thanks everyone! Now let's have a cuppa and break out these doughnuts while we figure out where we're going next with this investigation.'

'Can I just ask about my case at the golf club?' said Hannah.

'Sure, fire away,' said Grace.

'Well, I don't really know if it's been solved or not?' said Hannah. 'I mean, they found a couple of the missing items in Maria's handbag, but she wasn't on my radar as a suspect at all.'

'I'll speak to Brian, but I'm hoping he'll be happy to employ you there a bit longer. He did say they were short-staffed anyway. I think that if any other stuff goes missing, we'll have our answer but otherwise it was either Maria Rossi or the real thief is going to quit while they're ahead.'

'What about the murder?' asked Jean.

'The police should be all over that one, at least. Brodie has been appointed senior investigating officer and, as it's his first major case since his promotion, there will be a lot riding on it for him. The press interest will be relentless because of the poor baby. If we uncover anything that might assist in the course of our own investigations, we should pass it on to him.' Grace helped herself to more coffee and turned towards Hannah. 'Can you try and get us copies of Maria's appointments diary? I'd like to know whether anyone associated with the college had booked in with her recently for a sports massage. No, scratch that, the police will already have taken it.'

Hannah gave a small smile. 'Well, it did occur to me that

might be useful, so I managed to get it on my phone when I was covering reception yesterday.'

'Get you!' said Grace. 'Can you email it to me?'

'Sure.' Her fingers tapped away.

Grace's phone pinged and she opened the message.

'On the day she was attacked, it appears she saw Xander Croft, Regan Bradley, and Matt Turner, the golf professional. Then you were her last appointment,' she said, turning to Sloan. 'How was her demeanour?'

'I didn't detect anything off with her. She wasn't that chatty, but then neither am I. For the most part I was lying face down, so I wasn't in a position to observe her. It's shocking to think I may have been the last person to see her alive apart from her killer.'

They all digested this in silence for a few moments.

'How are you doing after your ordeal last night? I don't know what you were thinking. You should have waited for the police, Grace,' said Tobias.

'Is that what you would have done?'

He considered for a moment then shook his head. 'Fair point,' he replied.

Forty minutes later, Grace sat back at her desk, weak and exhausted, relieved to close the door on them all. In truth she was far from fine. In all her years as a police officer she had never come quite so close to death as she had last night. The person who'd throttled her hadn't uttered a sound. Their silence had been all the more unnerving for the cold-blooded resolve it had shown.

What could have mattered so much that it was worth killing her? Most opportunistic burglars were after stuff they could pick up quickly and flog for easy money to get cash. Yet all the laptops remained. This man had clearly been looking for something specific. If he hadn't found it the first time, he might try again. The realisation sent a shudder through Grace's body. Responsive as ever to her moods, Harvey placed his head on her lap and she stroked it gently. Poor dog. Ever since they arrived, he'd been roaming around the office sniffing, a growl hovering at the back of his throat.

She worked her way through the pile of papers that had been scattered by the intruder, but nothing jumped out at her in terms of motive. She remembered she had heard the filing cabinet open and walked across to the corner. The key was still in the lock which surprised her as she normally kept it locked away in a drawer in her desk. Grace looked at the desk again and pulled on the drawer, but it was still tightly closed.

She opened the filing cabinet and noticed that the contents had been hurriedly rifled through and some were in the wrong order. The two that had suffered the most damage were the golf club file and the one marked Sylvia Gordon.

Suddenly, it hit her with a blinding flash where she had seen the dead girl before. Hurriedly she flicked through the thick file, but it was too late. The photos were gone.

Grace rushed through to the front office. 'The girl in the photographs, it was Maria Rossi!' she announced.

Hannah slapped her hand to her head and groaned. 'I'm sorry, Grace, I thought Maria looked familiar, but I couldn't place her.'

'Don't beat yourself up,' said Grace. 'It got by me, too.'

'I guess none of us wanted to peer at the photos for too long,' said Jean sheepishly.

'Yes, well, as investigators it's up to us to peer into all the dark corners,' said Grace, more cross with herself than anybody else. 'Where's Sloan?'

'He's gone to the golf club to see if he can pick up anything there,' said Jean.

Grace tutted in annoyance. 'He really doesn't play well with others, does he? He could have told me.' She sighed. 'There's no point in us haring all over Edinburgh at cross purposes.'

'Maybe he's taken Maria's death to heart,' said Jean.

'We're all a bit rattled. I'll catch up with him later and see what's going on with him.' Glancing at her watch, she was startled to see the time. 'In the meantime, I'm off to the college to attend one of Xander Croft's seminars.'

'I'll hold the fort here,' said Jean.

Grace glanced at her. She'd forgotten all about Jean's strand of the investigation. 'How are you getting on with the protestors?' she asked. 'Do you feel it's an angle worth pursuing?'

'I do. The majority of the group are completely harmless and protesting because the work of the college contravenes their beliefs. There are two or three of them that I have a bad feeling about, though. I suspect they have a hidden agenda and could possibly even be dangerous. They might be using the protests as a cover.'

'But you've no idea what they're actually planning?'

'Not yet. I get the feeling that three of them have been sussing me out. I've been trying to mirror their attitudes as much as possible and I feel they're starting to trust me more. I'm going out for more drinks with them tonight.'

Grace's forehead creased in worry. She hadn't really expected this part of the investigation to lead anywhere, thinking it was a safe area for Jean to just cut her teeth.

'Okay, that's great. Before you go out, text me the details. I'd also like to put an app on your phone so I can ascertain your location, if that's alright?'

Jean looked at her.

'It's alright, I don't care what you get up to in your private life, but if you're on the job, I need to know I can get back-up to your location.'

Jean nodded and passed it over.

'The same goes for you, Hannah.'

Hannah, too, looked reluctant but passed her phone across.

'I think it's time I got you all work phones, so this is just a temporary invasion of privacy,' she said.

They both brightened at that. They must lead far more interesting lives than she did if they were worried about her finding out what they were up to. She'd been living like a nun for so long she'd become comfortable with it. Anyway, she was so busy with work these days that particular can would have to be kicked down the road. This case was going to consume her time and energy for the foreseeable future.

Chapter Twenty-Six

Driving into the college Grace again felt swamped with fatigue. Perhaps she had been a bit too hasty coming in today. A pity you couldn't press the pause button on an investigation. The pressure was mounting to get some answers for Sylvia, but she had a sinking feeling that she wasn't going to be emotionally strong enough for today. The investigation was growing arms and legs and Grace didn't have sufficient manpower to keep on top of everything. Her staff were willing and enthusiastic, but inexperienced. She had hoped she would have longer to train them up before a case of this magnitude came knocking.

Grace walked into the seminar room not sure exactly what to expect. It was a free introduction into the courses offered by the college and had attracted a mixed bag of attendees. The people gathered seemed to be quite upbeat rather than the obviously bereaved that she had encountered before. There were only spaces for around twenty gathered round the seminar table and she made sure that she sat at Xander Croft's right hand.

The group was busy chatting and he turned to her with a smile.

'Welcome, I never got the opportunity to thank you for your kindness at the club the other day. I'm sorry we were interrupted.'

'The woman who came to the table, she seemed distressed?' ventured Grace.

'Indeed,' he sighed. 'Anger is one of the recognised stages of grief and she's rather stuck there.'

'I see. That must be difficult.'

He turned and stared directly into her eyes. He radiated warmth and compassion. It drew her like a moth to a flame.

'I suspect that is something you know only too well?'

'Perhaps,' she replied.

Croft glanced at his watch then called them all to order and started to outline the various pathways available for study within Merchiston College. His style was engaged and lively and he soon had them all responding. Some were there to extend their mediumship skills while others were therapists looking to explore different healing techniques.

When the introductions came to her, she felt it safer to stick as close to the truth as possible.

'My name is Grace, and I lost my son a couple of years ago,' she said, conscious of Xander Croft's eyes boring into her from the side. 'I'm here to look for ways to better come to terms with his death and perhaps take baby steps to letting him go.' She felt the truth of it as she spoke, tears springing up unbidden. Croft gently nudged her hand with a freshly laundered handkerchief, and she gave him a small smile in acknowledgement.

As Grace looked away in embarrassment, her eyes fell on the glass doors into the room. Standing there on the other side was Regan Bradley and she looked absolutely furious.

Confused, she took a sideways glance at Croft and saw that he was looking towards Bradley, his expression enigmatic. There was clearly some complicated dynamic between the two but for the life of her Grace couldn't figure out what was happening.

As she was filing out of the room with the others, she heard her name being called from behind. She scanned the crowd but could see no sign of Regan Bradley. She'd completely vanished.

But Xander Croft came walking towards her.

'I wondered if you might like to join me for a light lunch?' he asked with a smile. 'I found what you said in there very moving and I'd like to repay you for coming to my aid the other day.'

'Yes, that would be lovely.' Grace smiled. She turned towards the cafeteria, but he shook his head.

'It'll be jam packed in there. I normally phone in my order and they bring it to my private quarters. This way.'

Grace followed him, her palms sweating with unease as he led her to an unobtrusive wooden door, keying in a code. She immediately memorised it whilst appearing to stare elsewhere. Good peripheral vision certainly helped in this line of work. As soon as the door closed behind them the background noise disappeared. There were rich velvet drapes along the walls of the narrow corridor which felt rather claustrophobic.

'You needn't be nervous,' he said, as though he was reading her mind. 'Some of the mediums work along this corridor and it's vital that all background noise is cancelled to enable the ferocious amount of concentration required.'

Grace couldn't help wondering whether there were microphones behind those same curtains, snooping for clues.

At the end of the corridor, a walnut door opened into a

bright, welcoming room that was beautifully furnished with antiques. Croft invited her to sit opposite him in a wing-backed chair beside a massive bookcase overflowing with academic texts.

'Can I offer you a drink?' he asked, walking over to a modest drinks table.

'Thank you, a gin and tonic, please,' Grace said with a smile, keen to let him think she was letting down her guard. 'I must say, I didn't expect such a cerebral collection of books,' she added, as he handed her a drink and sat opposite her.

'Should I be offended?' he asked, raising an eyebrow.

'No, not at all. It's simply that I hadn't really considered the study of psychic phenomena as an academic discipline.'

'People have been studying divinity for years. What's the difference?'

'I suppose, when you put it like that...' Grace said.

'We also dip into quantum mechanics, neuroscience and spiritualist philosophy for those wishing to take their studies to the next level. It all has a bearing on the study of psychic phenomena.'

'I hadn't appreciated the breadth of study you can undertake here.' Grace sipped her drink and smiled at him.

'Have you been a member of the golf club long?' he asked.

'No, I've only recently joined. I have played before, though.'

'When you were in the police?' Croft said, with a slight tightening of his lips.

Grace's heart thumped unpleasantly. He'd clearly done his homework. 'Yes, that's right,' she said.

'Don't worry, I haven't been stalking you,' he said with a small wary smile. 'I was playing golf with Superintendent

Blair from your old station and he mentioned he'd seen you at the club.'

Uh oh, this was bad. She cursed the old windbag for gossiping about her.

'Nice to hear that he's as discreet as ever.' She frowned. Croft probably now knew that she'd had a breakdown, too. 'He's probably not my biggest fan,' she said, staring at him.

'I'm not his biggest fan either,' he said. 'What's that saying: my enemy's enemy is my friend?'

'Something like that,' said Grace, taking a slow slip from her glass. 'Anyway, as you no doubt know, the police and I parted company some time ago and I slammed the door on my way out.' The super hadn't come out of her case for unfair dismissal well and had suffered a career-limiting reprimand.

'I like a woman who knows her own mind.'

'Talking of which, Regan Bradley is quite a forceful character, isn't she? I've had a few coffees with her recently.'

A shadow passed across Croft's face, but he simply nodded.

'I can't get that young woman from the golf club out of my mind,' Grace went on. 'The thought of her poor baby struggling for life with no one to care for her is just awful.'

'It's very sad,' he said. 'I didn't know Maria well, but I had a few sessions with her to iron out the kinks in my neck and back.'

'When did you last see her?'

'It was the morning she died. We indulged in the usual small talk. There was nothing that would have led me to suspect that she was in trouble when I was with her.'

The same thing that Tobias had said, which suggested to Grace that Maria had been taken completely unawares by her attacker.

There was a knock at the door and a platter of sandwiches arrived.

'Apparently, she studied part time at the college,' said Grace, tucking in with gusto.

'Yes, she was interested in enhancing her massage techniques with the study of healing. Maria was a diligent student, though kept very much to herself. She always sat alone.'

'I gather she and Paul Gordon knew each other from the college – that they were quite close.'

'What do you mean by that?' Croft asked.

'Nothing at all. Why?'

'Sorry, you can't be too careful these days. Teacher-student relationships are a minefield.'

'Oh? I hadn't realised they were in a relationship.'

'They weren't!' he snapped, then tried to soften it with a smile.

Grace leaned forward to help herself to another sandwich. Glancing up, she saw Croft's horrified expression. Realising her scarf had slipped, she sat up abruptly and repositioned it.

'Grace, what happened? Tell me.' He reached forward and took her hand in both of his, his eyes fixed on hers. There was nowhere to hide.

She squirmed, hating to show vulnerability, especially to him.

'There was a break in at my office last night.' She shrugged. 'I got in a bit of a scuffle. No harm done.'

'It looks like someone tried to throttle you,' he said, sounding both perplexed and worried. 'What are you even doing out? You should be home resting.'

'It's not as bad as it looks. You should see the other guy,' she joked.

'Grace, you need to take more care of yourself,' Croft said, his voice gentle. 'Whatever you're working on, it can't be worth getting yourself killed. I'm worried that your grief might be making you reckless. Connor wouldn't have wanted that.'

Grace stood up, her eyes filling with tears, unable to hide her distress. 'I'm sorry, it's very kind of you, but I really need to go now. Thank you for lunch. I'm fine, honestly. You don't need to worry.'

He looked upset, too, now. He was either completely genuine or an amazing actor. All she knew with absolute certainty was that she needed to get out of there right now. He was getting under her skin and tearing down the protective wall she had built around herself. Part of it was his warmth and compassion – the way he looked at her as if he really saw her, warts and all. The other part was the exceedingly slim possibility that he might be able to connect her to her son. It was something that flew in the face of everything she had believed, but her beliefs no longer seemed as immutable as they had been before she met him.

'Grace, come back. Don't leave it like this...' His words floated down the corridor after her.

Grace rushed to the door and didn't stop until she made it to the sanctuary of her own car. With shaking hands, she switched on the ignition and turned the car towards home. She was positive she had never told him Connor's name.

Chapter Twenty-Seven

Hannah sat on the bus staring morosely out at the grey rain-soaked city. Her mum had been out on the town and brought some pals back in the early hours of the morning, waking up the whole household with her crappy music. It sometimes felt like Hannah was the one in charge while her mum made up for missing out on her youth. Admittedly, she had only been sixteen when she had had Hannah. Hannah's dad had stuck by her and kept them steady with his wages from the factory. They were managing fine until Hannah was five and he got stabbed trying to break up a stupid fight that had nothing to do with him. Her mum got in with the wrong crowd after that and that was it. She'd met someone else and had more kids – they'd just about been keeping their heads above water until her stepdad was put away for armed robbery. He'd been suckered into driving the getaway car and hadn't realised that two of the others were armed with guns. If it wasn't for her, the wee ones would go hungry and the oldest two would never hand their homework in on time. Hannah longed to move out and get her own place but knew that wasn't going to happen for the foreseeable future. In the meantime, it was up to her to cushion the chaotic household as much as she could. At least between the agency and the golf club she was earning decent money now.

Hannah liked Grace a lot, but at times she reminded her of her mum. Not for the partying: as far as she could work out Grace never went out. It was more that look as though she was coiled up tight inside, like a jack-in-the-box with only a thin lid preventing her from completely losing it. Sighing, Hannah pressed the button for her stop and trudged to the front of the bus.

Walking into the golf club she pasted a smile on her face, waving at one or two of her regulars. It felt like she was developing a split personality for all the roles she had to play these days. The attack on Grace had made her realise that her job at the agency was not without risk.

Working behind the bar, getting ready for the rush as the golfers headed back for lunch, she noticed Tobias Sloan tucked in behind a pillar with his back to her. She couldn't quite figure him out. Although he was always really nice to her, Hannah felt he took more from them than they received back. She wasn't a big fan of journalists.

Hannah was still devastated about what had happened to Maria. The thought of that tiny wee baby fighting for her life all alone in the hospital made her want to cry. It bugged her that the club had pinned all the missing stuff on Maria. Anyone could have planted it on her before her body was discovered. Matt Turner had found her body, she heard. He was always hustling. She'd watched him turning on the charm with all his clients. He flirted shamelessly with the women, even the really old ones, and a few of the men. She thought he was well dodgy but hid it beneath that clean-cut, sporty exterior.

Maybe she should look into him further and conduct a little side investigation of her own. If Hannah could prove that he was the thief, then Grace would be really pleased with her. It was time to show some initiative.

After the lunch rush was over, she took her break and sauntered casually into the network of rooms behind the dining area. She soon found the golf pro's modest office and, checking to see that she was unobserved, opened the door and slid inside, her heart hammering. He was teaching out on the green, so she should have a bit of time to snoop around. Heading for his desk she carefully rifled through all the papers there. Nothing interesting. Next, she opened his drawers. Three of them revealed the usual office rubbish of staplers and Post-its, but the big bottom drawer was locked. What was it they opened drawers with in the movies? A hair-pin. She didn't have one. Getting down onto her knees she inspected the underside of the desk. Gotcha! The small key was stuck there with Blu Tack. Fitting it into the lock with shaking hands, she pulled the drawer open. Inside was a bottle of vodka and some pills that definitely didn't look legal. She remembered her schoolfriends furtively passing stuff like this around at a party. Not so squeaky clean, after all. To her disappointment there were none of the missing items. *It doesn't mean anything*, she told herself. *He might have taken the stuff home.* She'd been stupid to think he would leave it lying around here.

Suddenly, Hannah heard the sound of muffled voices and approaching footsteps. She quickly relocked the drawer and stuck the key back then whipped around, desperately searching for somewhere to hide. There was only one option. She threw herself on her side behind the large leather couch at one end of the room just before the door opened. Hannah could hear a woman giggling and then kissing sounds. Her eyes flicked up in annoyance. As the couple sank onto the couch, squashing her painfully against the wall, she decided that this was it. She was officially in Hell.

'Drink?' Matt asked. 'I've only got vodka, I'm afraid.'

'Don't mind if I do,' the woman purred.

'Cheers!' They clinked glasses a moment later.

With a jolt she realised that his companion was Regan Bradley. Hannah cursed herself for hiding instead of brazening it out and making up some excuse for being in Matt's office. If she was discovered now, she'd be fired on the spot. Her break would be over soon, and someone would start looking for her. Hannah was aware that her mind was shutting down with stress when Regan Bradley's voice brought her sharply back to the present.

'Such a shame what happened to that massage therapist,' she said. 'You and she seemed rather friendly. You must miss her—'

'I barely knew her,' he replied, his voice more distant now. 'I was no more friendly with her than anyone else on the staff. Can we talk about something else?'

'Sorry, dead tarts *are* rather a buzzkill.'

'Don't talk about her like that,' Matt snapped.

'Oops, have I hit a nerve?' Regan said, her voice malicious.

Behind the couch Hannah shivered.

'Of course not,' he said, his voice softer now. 'It's just not something you expect to happen to a work colleague, you know? She was on her own. No family and no friends to speak of. Nobody to miss her.'

'Apart from you?'

He was silent.

'I saw you together, you know. In Princes Street Gardens.'

'You should have come over and said hello,' he said, his voice tight.

'You were rather busy at the time...'

'Have you mentioned this to the police?'

'Of course not, Matt,' she said, drawing the name out possessively. 'It can be our little secret.'

There were sounds of more kissing. Hannah felt the dust getting up her nose and panicked she was going to sneeze.

'I've got to go,' Matt said when he came up for air. 'I've a client waiting.'

'Don't be getting too friendly,' Regan warned, her voice sharp.

The door closed and Hannah assumed they had both gone. She was just gathering herself, ready to wriggle out of her hiding place, when she heard the drawers of the desk being opened. She froze, scarcely daring to breathe.

Ten minutes later, the door closed for the second time, but it was another ten minutes before Hannah dared extricate herself and flew back to the bar.

Regan Bradley was clearly possessive and controlling. Could she have been so angry about Matt's relationship with the dead girl that she'd killed Maria in a jealous rage?

Chapter Twenty-Eight

Grace looked away from her laptop, a perplexed frown on her face. She was thoroughly confused as to where the investigation was headed. Instead of progressing in a linear fashion it was sprouting offshoots and it was difficult to work out where to apply her limited resources. She was no further to establishing whether Paul Gordon's death was down to suicide or murder.

Her objectivity in relation to Xander Croft was becoming clouded by the inexplicable attraction she felt towards him. It was so unlike her. Why now? And to someone so patently unsuitable? She wouldn't let it compromise her professionalism. He made her feel completely exposed, like a hermit crab without its shell. It was uncomfortable to be seen like that when she was used to hiding from people. Even though Tobias had warned her about the psychic and his tricks, it was becoming more difficult for her to resist the idea of an afterlife. The conviction on the faces of those at the college was starting to get to her. Grace sighed and forced all thoughts of her son from her head for now.

Normally, in a murder investigation she would try to find out everything she could about the murder victim, yet Paul Gordon was as much an enigma to her now as at the beginning. She needed to start afresh and track down new witnesses who had no hidden agenda or axe to grind.

Standing up, she stretched out her aching muscles and pressed her forehead to the bay window. Her throat and neck were still really tender, and it unsettled her to see the fingertip bruises from her assailant reflected back at her. The rain slanted against the window and the wind had whipped up the waves to jagged points. Harvey lifted his head and watched her sleepily from his position by the fire. Even he had no notion to go out. Grace had been working upstairs for a couple of hours to get some peace and quiet from the phone ringing and Jean's hands flying over the keys as she typed up details of another case – background checks on some new employees for a private residential home for the elderly. The home had wanted them to investigate their social media accounts as well and Grace had uncovered some rather disturbing posts on an old Facebook account for one of the applicants. Jean wouldn't want that one looking after an aging relative of hers, to be sure.

Grace wandered out into the hall and pushed open the door to Connor's room with a tentative finger. She sniffed the air and picked up undertones that weren't there before. It smelt slightly different since Brodie had slept there. Traces of his presence remained, and she suddenly missed them both with a fierce visceral longing. She knew it was only a matter of time until he moved in with Julie and then there would be no going back. He would be lost to her for good.

Not liking the direction in which her thoughts were heading, she decided to head back down to the office.

'Coming, boy?' she asked.

Harvey thumped his head down between his paws.

She stroked his ears, turned off the living flame fire and left him where he was for now.

Jean shivered as Grace walked through the door, preceded by an icy draft of sea air.

'Hannah phoned to say she's on the bus heading back here,' said Jean. 'She sounded quite excited, so I suspect she may have some news for us she couldn't share on the phone.'

'Are you all sorted for protester drinks tonight?' asked Grace.

'Yes,' said Jean, her face alight with excitement. 'I've even invested in a new wardrobe so I look a bit edgier and blend in better.'

'You're meeting in Bannerman's at the Grassmarket?'

'Yes, at eight pm. I'm hoping to get the full measure of them tonight. It's not the whole group, only the three troublemakers.'

'Well, just so we're clear: no unnecessary risks and keep your phone switched on at all times. Don't accept an invitation to go anywhere other than a public place. I want to know what they've done and what they're planning, but it's not worth you getting hurt.'

'Got it,' said Jean, looking ten years younger all of a sudden.

Hannah arrived in a flurry of raindrops, shaking out her sodden umbrella to protests from both Grace and Jean.

'Sorry,' she said, collapsing on a seat, then she swiftly updated them on her adventure.

Grace was a little troubled to hear that Hannah had gotten herself into such a tricky situation. She would have to keep a closer eye on her youngest employee.

'So, Matt, our golf professional, gets around,' she said. 'Regan hinted as much to me, and now you've witnessed it first-hand. We also know he knew the dead girl, Maria, better than he let on – there was the argument you saw, now this.'

'You said he was first on the scene when Maria was found,' said Jean. 'He could have killed her then framed her for taking the missing items?'

'Or, for that matter, Regan could have murdered her and done the same,' said Grace. 'She's very intense and doesn't strike me as being too burdened with a conscience. She doesn't need the money, but I could see her doing it for the thrill.'

'I wonder who the baby's father is?' mused Jean.

Now that the adrenaline had faded in the young girl, Grace noticed that Hannah was looking completely worn out. 'Good job today, Hannah, you've confirmed two links in the case that might be important.'

Hannah beamed.

'However, I don't want you taking a risk like that in the future.'

Her tired face sagged.

'The people that we're investigating are dangerous and it would appear can't be trusted. I need you to bear that in mind from now on.'

Hannah nodded, her eyes drowsy with fatigue.

'Come on, grab your coat,' said Grace. 'I'm driving you home. You can go too, Jean, as you've got a big night tonight. Again, I don't want you taking any risks. Clear?'

'Crystal,' said Jean.

Grace put Hannah's address into the satnav and headed towards Niddrie, only two and a half miles from Portobello.

Her youngest employee never mentioned her family which, given her age, was a bit of a glaring omission. Glancing sideways she noticed Hannah had fallen fast asleep, her mouth slack. Grace was cross with herself for not realising that the kid had been overdoing it.

Pulling up alongside the kerb at the given address, Grace saw the garden of the rundown council house was overgrown and choked with weeds. Undeterred, there were a number of kids in it playing together. They were all skinny and scrappy looking, like they had to fight to get their share of what little was going around.

She nudged Hannah gently and noticed shame and embarrassment cloud her face when she saw Grace looking at her home.

'That's you,' Grace said. 'Try and get an early night and I'll see you tomorrow.'

'Thanks,' Hannah mumbled as she hurriedly got out of the car.

From the way the children pounced on her, clamouring for her attention, Grace doubted that Hannah's work was finished for the night.

Chapter Twenty-Nine

Grace glanced at her watch. She wasn't that far away from Brodie's house. Before she had time to talk herself out of it, she pulled over and fired off a quick text asking if she could pop round as she had some information that he might be interested in. Grace went hot and cold after she'd pressed 'send', worrying that he might think she was chasing after him and trying to get between him and Julie.

'Stop overthinking,' she admonished herself. She didn't want him to fall flat on his face during his first murder case in charge. Time seemed to slow down as she drummed her fingers on the steering wheel. *He isn't going to reply*. Sighing, she started the engine and was about to indicate and pull out in a U-turn when she heard a ping.

Come straight over. I'll order pizza.

What the heck did that mean? She fretted. Was he on his

own or was she going to have to sit and play Happy Families with Julie?

Fifteen minutes later she pulled into the neat housing estate. It had 'conventional living' stamped all over it and she felt she would lose the will to live if she had to live somewhere so dull and monotonous. Immediately, she felt guilty, thinking of the sub-standard home of young Hannah. God, her brain felt like a hive of bees tonight.

She'd grabbed a bottle of red on the way over although even that had her in paroxysms of indecision. What had happened to the crisp decisive woman she had once been? Back in the day she used to despise dithering idiots.

She rang the bell and pasted on a bright smile.

Brodie came to the door wearing faded jeans and a t-shirt. His familiar scent drifted over her. Her face melted into a frown and she thrust the bottle at him.

'Judging by that face I reckon we're going to need this,' he said with a grin.

'Is Julie joining us?'

'Like I said, she doesn't live here.'

Grace wandered through the living room into the kitchen, her eyes taking in every detail. Julie might not live here, but she was clearly exerting her influence. Grace would bet good money that Brodie hadn't been spending his days off in Ikea selecting scatter cushions and picture frames. She noted with wry humour that there were no pictures of Grace, though she was pleased to see a large one of Connor in the centre of the mantelpiece. *Nice one, Julie.*

'What did you need to tell me?' Brodie asked, as he sliced up the pizza.

'Regan Bradley and Matt Turner, the golf pro, are connected romantically, though he's keeping it quiet. He was also in a relationship with your murder victim, Maria Rossi. I'm guessing he hasn't mentioned that in his statement.'

'No. He said they were only work colleagues and that they hadn't seen each other outside work.'

'Regan Bradley mentioned that she'd seen them cosying up together in Princes Street Gardens. She strikes me as the jealous type.'

'That doesn't surprise me after interviewing her,' he said.

'If she's got the hots for Golf Boy and discovered he'd been stepping out on her with someone she considers her social inferior, that might provide a motive for murder,' said Grace.

'They could have got into it in the changing rooms and Regan lost her temper, walloping Maria on the head with something,' Brodie said. 'How long before the murder did Regan see them together?'

'We're not sure,' Grace replied.

'What about the missing items?' said Brodie. 'She was found with a watch, a gold necklace and a pair of pearl earrings in her handbag. Items Brian said had gone missing from the female changing rooms. It feels a bit too neat.'

'I agree. I think that Brian has been too keen to pin it on a staff member and quietly get shot of them. Anyone could have got wind of our investigation and decided to frame the dead woman and cut their losses.'

Sitting opposite each other, scoffing pizza out of the box, Grace felt overcome with nostalgia. Was it really too late for her and Brodie? Pushing those uncomfortable thoughts away, she focused back on her case. It was tricky.

'I'll expect a quid pro quo for that tip, Brodie.'

'Of course,' he said. 'As long as it doesn't involve me completely selling my soul to the devil.'

She could tell that he was feeling the pressure of running

his first murder investigation and longed to smooth away his worry lines and the tense set of his jaw. However, that was Julie's job now, not hers, and she had to respect the careful lines they had drawn.

'So, your turn to spill the beans,' Grace said. 'I need to know what the crime scene and pathology reports on Paul Gordon and Maria Rossi said.'

'Obviously, I don't have them here with me... look, don't tell me any more now. You can swing by the station to offer up some more information relevant to the investigation – I might need to answer a call of nature while you're there. I trust I can rely on you *not* to look at the papers on my desk if that happens?'

Grace nodded and smiled, though the thought of returning to the office where she was once held in such high esteem was painful.

'We haven't discussed divorce for a while,' Brodie said suddenly.

'No...' said Grace, striving to keep her voice and expression neutral.

'I didn't want to rush you when you were still... well... a bit fragile.'

Her heart swelled painfully, but she owed it to him to be fair. Brodie had moved on because she asked him to, and she had to face that and deal with it.

'Shared custody of Harvey?'

'Always,' he said. They had already divided up their finances some time ago without the need for lawyers. As they no longer had a shared child and had been separated for some time, only a simple form lay between them and the dissolution of their marriage.

'Well, send me the paperwork and I'll sign it,' she said.

'If you're sure,' Brodie said, his face inscrutable.

A chill descended and Grace shivered, suddenly swamped with fatigue. It had been a long day and her bruises throbbed more at night.

'I'd best get back,' she said, aware that a new awkwardness had sprung up between them.

He stood up to see her off. 'Take care of yourself, Grace,' he said. He hugged her to him before letting her out into the dark night.

She turned back to wave as she got into her car and he remained silhouetted in the doorway as she drove away.

It felt as if she was leaving safe harbour and sailing out into a choppy and uncertain sea without him by her side.

Chapter Thirty

Jean stared at the unrecognizable woman in the mirror. Her hair was caught up in a messy bun and her eyes glittered with darker makeup than she was used to. A bold red lipstick finished the look and contrasted well with her biker jacket and skinny black jeans. The heartbreak diet had caused the weight to drop off her.

If the kids could see her now, they'd have a complete fit. And what would Derek make of it? she wondered. Would he like the new confident, feisty woman she was becoming now she'd been released from the straitjacket of their marriage?

Her tummy grumbled with nerves and her hands were clammy. Jean had never felt more alive. Grabbing her phone and keys she shut the door behind her.

She was desperate to prove herself to Grace. Although she'd been taken on primarily to provide admin support, Grace had given her a strong hint that her role might be expanded someday, and this could be the first step.

Approaching the pub on foot, Jean noticed there were already a few drunk people lurching about. She pulled the strap of her small bag tighter to her before pushing through the door. *It's only a drink*, she told herself as she elbowed past the heaving crowd.

Jean spotted Beverley waving her over from the bar and headed in her direction.

Seeing that the other woman was ordering pints, Jean said that she would have a pint of lager, though she could have murdered a gin and tonic. They made their way over to a table in the corner and joined Leo and Helen who were deep in a whispered conversation.

Jean felt a bit uncomfortable as they both stared at her, clearly weighing her up – not yet ready to trust her despite Beverley bringing her into the fold.

'Hi,' she said, sitting down and taking a deep glug of her lager. The talk was about preparation for a forthcoming demo, and she offered to make some new placards, writing down the proposed wording in her notebook.

Several rounds of beer later, Jean was struggling to keep up with them. Her head was spinning, and her eyes were losing focus. She told the others that she was going to the bar but instead headed for the toilets. After splashing her face with water, she locked herself in one of the cubicles and took some deep calming breaths. About to head back into the throng, Jean suddenly froze as the door banged opened and she heard Beverley's voice.

'I'm telling you, she can be trusted. You've seen how she feels about what they're doing at the college. I think she's looking for a more active involvement in the cause.'

'If you're wrong about this and she shops us to the police...' said Helen.

'Even if she did, how are they going to prove it?'

'I guess. We barely know anything about her, though,' Helen replied nervously.

'We know enough. That beer is running right through me tonight.'

Two cubicle doors banged on either side of her as Jean stood frozen, her heart thumping in panic.

Terrified, she flushed the toilet and ran out. Putting her head down, she thrust her way over to the bar and ordered another round, taking care that her own was non-alcoholic lager.

When she'd got the job with Grace, she hadn't imagined that she'd end up running with criminals. Surely, they must be if they were worried about her shopping them to the police? She was getting seriously out of her depth.

Once back at the table, there were a few covert glances, but the chat meandered on. Just as Jean thought that nothing was going to happen after all, the conversation took a more philosophical turn.

'What do you think about activists that break the law, Jean?' asked Beverley.

'Well... I think that sometimes the end can justify the means. I mean, I'd condone anything, short of murder, to prevent animal suffering.'

There were nods of approval.

'I completely agree,' said Helen.

'Sometimes direct action can get into places the law hasn't been able to reach,' said Jean, wondering whether she'd have to leave the pub and flag down the nearest police car.

'We have to allow the word of God to lead the way,' said Leo. 'It's about what is right.'

There was a tense silence as they awaited her response.

'Sometimes we need to defer to a higher law?' she said.

Beverley looked at Leo and smiled. 'I told you she was one of us.'

'So, what are you talking about?' asked Jean.

Beverley looked at Leo and he shook his head slightly. 'I'm afraid that's going to need to wait for another day,' she said. 'In the meantime, welcome to our newest recruit!'

They all clinked glasses and the conversation quickly moved on, leaving Jean in turmoil. She still had no idea what they had planned, but she had a feeling that she wasn't going to like it.

Chapter Thirty-One

Grace woke early after a restless night. She stepped into her swimming suit and pulled on joggers and a fleece before feeding Harvey, making a mug of coffee, and padding over to the bay window. Blowing out the candle in the storm lantern, she wondered how long it would be before she felt able to relinquish this tiny beacon of hope and accept that her son was gone for ever. Sitting deep within her armchair, looking out over the Esplanade to the sea below, she wondered how many dispossessed souls floated beneath the waves in a watery grave. Shivering, she took a gulp of hot coffee and patted Harvey as he ambled over to sit at her feet. Fortunately, he had a big tank, so she had a few minutes grace before he started nagging for his morning walk. As if he had heard her, he leaned his big head on her foot and gave a single thump of his tail. Grace really didn't know how she would have come through the last two years without his comforting presence and the reciprocal need to take care of him.

The light was advancing across the sky now as though someone had swept a canvas with a wash of colour. Draining her coffee, she picked up the lead and secured her bouncy dog before heading outside. The cold salty air, with undertones of seaweed, soon woke her up and she revelled in being out before the rest of the world had properly woken up. Setting foot on the beach and checking no one was around first, she let Harvey off the lead to run free. This was his time as much as hers. She loved to watch the joy with which he greeted each new day as he pranced about, the wind whipping his coat upright and causing the hair round his ears to curl into ringlets.

Once he was starting to tire, she called him to her side and deposited her clothes on their usual spot, telling him to stay. The cold wind gave her goosebumps as she plunged her toes into the white froth of the sea. Faster now, not wishing to prolong her agony, she kicked her legs out and once the water reached her waist she dived underneath a wave, her skin first tingling and then numb before the burn flared in her hands and feet. Striking out strongly she emptied her mind until the pain receded and all she was aware of was the mechanical action of her arms scything through the water and pointing towards the horizon. As she settled into a comfortable rhythm, she felt Connor's presence flow all around her as though he was keeping her buoyant. *Why*? her mind shrieked. *Why did you leave me? Was I such a bad mother?* As usual, her questions went unanswered.

How many times had she tortured herself with her very own 'Sliding Doors' moment. Grace remembered her last words to him. He'd stayed out all night and she'd been out of her mind with worry, knowing full well the horrors that could befall a boy his age in the city. She'd lost her temper and yelled that he was a disappointment and ruining his life and hers with his out-of-control behaviour. He'd stared at her in shock then turned on his heel and walked out of the house without a word. She'd let him go, figuring they both needed time to calm down. The regret had eaten away at her ever since. *If only...* She paused, the salt from her tears indistinguishable from the sea water.

Her shoulders ached. She had swum out further than she intended. Flipping on to her back she allowed the sea to take her where it chose, still tempted to succumb to its chilly embrace. Her life was a mess. Her agency was swamped with this investigation, and she had no idea when or if she would be able to bring it to a successful conclusion. Brodie was leaving her behind and growing further and further away from her. At the end of the day, what was it all for? This continual struggle. Why was she battering herself against the indifference of the universe? It's not as though anyone would miss her if she was gone. *Was that what Connor had thought?* she wondered, startled, as her mind absorbed the direction it was heading in.

She turned back onto her front as she realised how far she had floated out on the outgoing tide. A frantic barking carried to her on the air. Harvey! She had to get back to him. Her body was now being buffeted by the waves and she realised that the wind had increased while she had been lost in the dark room of her thoughts. This wouldn't do. Gritting her teeth, she took a deep breath and plunged ferociously into the waves, battling to get back to shore. Her feet cramped alarmingly but she ignored the pain and simply stopped kicking, letting her arms do all the work, clawing her way back to shore, knowing that for now, she wished to live.

Harvey kept barking as though willing her on and she

aimed for the sound, focusing on the need to get back to him. Her stroke began to slow as fatigue set in. She wasn't going to make it. She'd pushed it too far this morning. A wave caught her the wrong way, causing water to flood up her nose and down her throat. Spluttering and coughing, treading water, she felt her body sink lower. Her shoulders were on fire. She was close enough to see the beach clearly now, but there was no one to come to her aid. The sight of Harvey running back and forth at the water's edge spurred her on. Poor dog, she had to get to him. She plunged into the waves once more, grunting with determination, blowing out water with every stroke. Finally, she felt her feet touch down on the sand. Harvey swam out to her despite his aversion to the water, determined not to let her out of his sight. His soft mouth closed on her wrist and he turned around, tugging her with him as she lurched forward, her teeth chattering now.

As Grace finally struggled free of the water, a figure ran down the beach towards her and when her eyes cleared, she realised it was Tobias Sloan. To her intense chagrin she tripped and fell flat on the sand, unable to feel her feet, gasping like a fish out of water.

'Grace!' he yelled. 'Are you alright?' He skidded to a halt and sank down beside her, careless of his cream chinos in the wet sand.

'I'm fine,' she said, her voice hoarse and rasping. 'Just overdid it a little.'

'A little? I was on the verge of calling the Coastguard. I don't know what possessed you...' He tailed off, clearly realising that now was not the time.

He quickly put a resistant Harvey on the lead and helped her put her fleece and trousers back on. A small crowd was starting to gather, and Grace groaned inwardly as she saw the inevitable bright spark filming her. Forcing a brittle smile, she grabbed onto Sloan's arm and stumbled up the beach with him, turning away from the onlookers' avid gapes. Risking a glance behind her she saw the group had begun to disperse, no doubt disappointed they weren't going to star in the drama of her life. *Imagine if this got back to Brodie or, even worse, my mother!* She shuddered and Sloan put his arm around her and held her close as he marched her up the Esplanade to her flat with a bemused Harvey following at his heels. He was a dog who liked his routine and was no doubt bewildered at this recent turn of events. Her free hand snaked behind her, and he nuzzled it, giving her a warm wet kiss with his tongue.

As they reached the door to her flat, Grace glanced sideways at Sloan. His face was unreadable.

'Er, thanks.' She inserted the key in the lock with shaking fingers. 'I'll catch you at the office later...'

'Aren't you going to invite me in for a coffee at the very least?' he said, looking down with horror at his ruined trousers.

'Oh, of course,' she replied, with a distinct lack of enthusiasm. 'I thought you'd be wanting to shoot off back home.'

'That can wait. I want to make sure you're sorted first. And it's non-negotiable,' he said as her mouth opened to protest.

'Fine,' she said instead and waved him through.

Once upstairs she started a bath running and gave Harvey a vigorous towel dry and a treat whereupon he trotted off to his basket. She also gave Sloan a clean damp cloth to repair the damage to his trousers as best he could.

'I'll sort out the coffee while you have a hot bath,' he said, heading for the kitchen.

She wasn't about to argue.

Even sitting submerged in a steaming hot bubble bath her teeth still chattered. It was happening again. She was losing control. Today she had turned back just in time. Somehow, she had to pull herself back from the brink, but first she had to want to...

Chapter Thirty-Two

Grace entered the lounge in her work clothes. She stood inside the door watching Tobias Sloan pour the coffee into two mugs.

'I'm ready for that,' she said. 'I can't imagine a world without caffeine.' A thought occurred to her. 'What were you doing out on the Esplanade so early?'

'I wanted to catch up with you before the office opened. I feel I can't speak quite as freely in front of the others at times.'

'What's on your mind?' she asked, buttering a piece of toast that Tobias had offered her.

'I need to know how close you are to nailing Xander Croft for the murder of Paul Gordon. I want to get in with my exposition of him as a fraud before he's dragged off to stand trial and every other journalist is switched on to the case.'

'We don't even know that it was him yet.'

'What do you mean?' he asked. 'Who else could it possibly be? He had both opportunity and motive.'

'I'm not going to fit someone up to collect a fee,' snapped Grace. 'If you think that, then you really don't know me at all.'

'I knew it!' Sloan barked. 'Croft's got to you, hasn't he?'

Grace flushed in anger. 'I don't know who the hell you think you are telling *me* what to think and feel, but I'm nobody's puppet. I'm a bloody professional with years of high-level investigative experience behind me.'

Sloan reeled back as though she'd slapped him. 'Grace, I only meant—'

'I've said all I'm going to on the subject for now so, if you don't mind, I need to be getting on.'

He opened his mouth to speak but then seemed to change his mind. Turning on his heel he left, shutting the door rather too firmly behind him.

Grace made herself another cup of coffee with shaking hands and loaded it with sugar.

This was shaping up to be a hellish day and she hadn't even started work yet. Sinking into a comfortable armchair, she soothed Harvey who had bared his teeth at Sloan's retreating back.

'It's okay, boy, nothing for you to worry about,' she murmured.

Sloan could be so inflexible sometimes. His obsession with exposing Croft as a fraud was blinding him to other possibilities in the case.

He had managed to land one shot though, and she needed to pay it some mind. Just as Sloan was becoming more intent on proving Xander Croft had murdered Paul Gordon, she was becoming more reluctant to accept that he might be guilty. Had Croft worked his charm on her or was her experienced instinct telling her that he was innocent? Was it possible that her growing suspicion that he might have some genuine psychic ability was getting in the way of her investigation? Just how far would she be prepared to compromise her investigative integrity for a connection to her son? Truthfully, she didn't know. She had never felt so frustrated with a case in her life.

The doorbell rang.

What now? She assumed Sloan had decided to have another go at her. She stabbed the buzzer and waited at the open door, feeling her features settle into a scowl.

'Brodie!' she exclaimed, her grimace dissolving as he rounded the corner. 'I thought it was someone else.'

'Clearly,' he said. 'I met Tobias Sloan outside. Good night, was it?'

Grace drew herself up to her full height. The nerve of the man!

'I don't kiss and tell,' she said, too stubborn to correct his false assumption.

'Sorry, that was out of line. It's none of my business. He just doesn't seem your usual type.'

'I don't have a usual type, Brodie. I had one type.'

The air crackled between them.

'Anyway, come on in. There's coffee in the pot.' A furry tornado pushed past her and took Brodie's wrist in his mouth, making happy noises at the back of his throat.

'Hey, boy, been swimming this morning? Weirdly, I miss the smell of wet dog.' He grinned, turning to Grace, and the tension between them dissolved.

Once seated with their drinks, Grace waited for Brodie to state what was on his mind.

'Maria's baby is doing well. She's still in the neonatal unit, but she's breathing unaided and there's no cause for concern. The father still hasn't made himself known to us, despite the press coverage.'

'Maybe he doesn't know he is the father?' she said.

'Possibly.'

A thought struck her.

'I've seen photos showing Paul Gordon in a sexually compromising position with Maria Rossi. Whether one or both of them were ignorant of being filmed, I can't say. It could be that they were being used for blackmail, but I have no direct evidence of that yet.'

'You're only telling me this now?'

'Well, he died over six months ago so it's not like the affair was ongoing.'

'Can I see the photos?'

'That's the reason I didn't tell you. There was only one set, and it was stolen from my office.'

'But you told the police nothing was taken?' Brodie frowned.

'I didn't discover they were missing until the following day. If she'd got pregnant and told Paul Gordon before he died, then that could explain why he killed himself,' she pondered.

'It could also give his wife a motive for murder,' said Brodie.

Grace said nothing, though the thought had, of course, occurred to her. The problem was, the only evidence she had was gone.

'We'll be able to get Paul Gordon's DNA from the records of post-mortem. Did he have any family apart from his wife?'

'No, both his parents are dead, and he had no siblings,' Grace replied. 'I imagine Maria's baby is headed for foster care until she can be adopted. What about statements from friends and co-workers?'

'By all accounts she kept herself to herself.'

'That's certainly what Hannah picked up from the other staff. Anyway, I'm still planning to drop by the station for those files.'

Brodie sighed. 'Of course.' Grace expected him to get up but he continued to sit there.

'What's going on, Brodie?'

'We're starting to get hung out to dry by the press. It's not exactly ideal cutting your teeth on such a high-profile case.'

She hated to see him so despondent. 'Don't worry, you've got this,' she said.

'I hope you're right,' he said as he got up to leave.

Chapter Thirty-Three

Grace was shattered by the time she walked into the agency. Her shoulders were aching from her battle with the sea and her heart was aching, too. She had to grit her teeth and get on with it. She had employees now, people who were depending on her to keep it together.

'There's coffee in the pot,' said Jean.

Grace did a double take. Jean looked different today. Her clothes were more fashionable and she was sporting a chic new hairdo. The staid, mumsy look had gone. But it wasn't only the way she looked, it was the energy she was giving out.

'Love that skirt,' Grace said.

Jean blushed. 'I thought it was time I had a bit of a makeover,' she replied.

'I'll have to up my game.' Hannah grinned.

Grace looked at their cheerful faces and felt a rush of positive energy.

'Right, you guys. Grab a coffee and come through to my room so we can all catch up with any developments and plan where we go from here.'

'Is Tobias coming in?' asked Jean.

'No. I saw him earlier but he... er... slipped and got his trousers all muddy. He's nipped off home to get changed.'

'When's he planning to expose Xander Croft?' asked Hannah.

'Last I heard, he wanted to publicly expose him as a fake at the College Open Day demonstration in May. But you're right. I need to clarify what's happening with that. Jean, can you text me Sloan's address? If he hasn't checked back in by the end of today, I might have time to pop round after work.'

'I saw Tobias at the golf club yesterday having coffee with Sylvia,' said Hannah.

Grace felt a stab of irritation. She hoped he hadn't been indiscreet.

'How is the golf club going?' asked Grace. It had been agreed with Brian that Hannah would continue working there three mornings a week. Hannah was happy as it meant she was effectively being paid double for that time.

'Well, nothing else has gone missing but I still don't think Maria Rossi was the thief. I'm sure someone framed her, I just need to prove it,' said Hannah. 'What's going to happen to the baby, Grace?'

Grace looked at her youngest employee. The murder had been tough on her.

'I don't know,' she admitted. 'I imagine she'll be fostered.'

'I took her a present yesterday,' said Hannah. 'I left it with a nurse.'

'That's a lovely thought,' said Grace, as she exchanged a worried glance with Jean. Maybe it was time to pull Hannah out of the golf club. She was still a kid herself, after all.

'I know what you're thinking,' said Hannah. 'It's fine, I can handle it. I need to do this.'

'Okay, but keep me fully in the loop,' said Grace.

'Will do,' said Hannah.

'So, Jean, how did your pub jaunt go last night?'

'Well, I don't mind admitting I felt horribly out of my depth for much of it. However, I feel I'm getting somewhere. I think last night was some sort of test. Beverley seems to be the spokesperson for the group, but she runs everything past Leo who is quieter but in charge. It's possible that they may even be using the group as a wacky front to mask some serious criminal intent.'

'How serious?' asked Grace, worried. She'd thought that this strand of the investigation would turn out to be a dead end.

'I'm not sure yet.'

Hannah's eyes were nearly popping out of her head. 'Wow, Jean, get you!' she said in admiration.

'Hannah, this isn't a game. This type of work can be dangerous,' admonished Grace.

'I know that!' said Hannah, reddening.

'Are you happy to keep playing along, Jean?' asked Grace. 'I don't want you to do anything you're not comfortable with. We can find another way.'

'No, really, it's fine. I want to find out what they're up to and if it takes our case any further forward...'

'Okay then, safety precautions.' She unlocked her bottom drawer and removed a locked metal box into which she inserted a key. Reaching inside, she removed two personal alarms disguised as lipsticks and also pepper sprays disguised as perfumes. She distributed printed sheets of instructions.

'I want you to keep these on your person at all times. We don't yet know how all these things are connected, but the people we're chasing have a lot to lose. We need to be vigilant until these cases are solved. Hannah, you'll need to lock your stuff away securely when at home.'

'What do you mean?' she asked with a tilt of her head.

'I noticed you had a number of younger siblings when I dropped you off.'

'Oh... right, no problem,' Hannah mumbled.

'Excellent work, everyone. Sooner or later we're going to catch a break that will blow this case wide open. I'm sure of it.'

Her phone pinged. It was Tobias.

> Sorry about earlier. I have signed up for a few lectures at the college so I can chat to students and staff about Croft without raising suspicion. One of them is quantum mechanics! Thought I should take one for the team.

She was heartened to see that he was making an effort.

Chapter Thirty-Four

Grace ordered her usual double shot espresso and bacon roll at the golf club and sat herself down in a corner where she could observe the comings and goings as the morning crowd swirled and eddied around the wood panelled bar. She focused her attention on all the snippets of conversation she could hear around her but caught nothing of any interest. She'd have thought the members would still be agog about the murder, but they had clearly moved on. Grace felt a little disturbed by the fact that a young woman's death clearly had so little impact on the rich clientele. The only ones showing any sign of strain were the staff members who were not as inclined to chat, huddling together at every opportunity as though there might be safety in numbers.

A shadow fell across her and Grace looked up to see Xander Croft, just as she'd sunk her teeth into her bacon roll.

'Hello, won't you join me?' she managed, waving to the empty chair in front of her once she'd managed to swallow without choking.

'I gave up caffeine years ago,' he said, sitting down. 'Best thing I ever did.'

'Without caffeine, I would be like a burst balloon,' she said, smiling. 'You don't want to talk to me before I've had my morning fix.'

'I'll bear that in mind,' Croft said, with an amused smile. His expression changed to one of concern. He gestured to her neck. 'How have you been since I saw you last? I haven't been able to get what happened to you out of my mind. You could have been killed!'

'It was something and nothing. Probably just someone looking to score stuff they could sell for a fix.'

'Grace... when are you going to learn to trust me?' Croft said, pinning her in place with the intensity of his gaze. It felt like she was being hypnotised.

Yanking her eyes away from his, Grace lifted her coffee cup and sipped it. 'Who says that I don't?'

He laughed and sat back in his chair. 'Prove it. Come out for dinner with me tonight? It sounds like you could do with some downtime.'

Grace wasn't sure she could trust herself, never mind him. Now was definitely not the time to muddy the boundaries between her professional and private lives. Yet, she knew that if she could catch him off guard, she might well learn something to progress the investigation.

'I can hear you thinking.' He grinned. 'It sounds like an Enigma machine.'

'Very funny,' Grace retorted. 'I'll happily join you for dinner.'

'How about I pick you up at seven?'

'I'll meet you there, text me the details.' She wasn't about to tell him where she lived, although it wouldn't surprise her if he already knew.

Grace saw Regan Bradley enter the bar and order a coffee. Grace waved but Regan blanked her.

'Charming,' she said in a low voice. Croft noticed and his expression darkened.

'Don't take it personally, she can be a bit temperamental.'

'Forgive me for saying this but she seems rather territorial where you are concerned. Are you and she...?'

'No! We're work colleagues, nothing more. She's very good at her job.'

Regan Bradley walked over to join Matt at a table for two.

'She also seems very friendly with the golf coach.'

'I can't stand him.'

'Why's that? He seems fairly inoffensive.'

'He's nothing but a parasite preying on vulnerable women with more money than sense.'

'I heard he might have been involved with the young woman who died last week?'

'It wouldn't surprise me.' Croft grimaced. 'If there's an angle to work, he's right in there.'

'I'm sure Regan can take care of herself,' said Grace.

'She's not as tough as she looks.' Croft shot her a sidelong glance. 'Anyway, we were discussing dinner. How about the Lone Piper at seven?'

'I'll see you there,' Grace replied, wondering what on earth she was letting herself in for.

As Xander Croft left she looked across at the tactile young golf professional. He was clearly both driven and charming with an eye for the ladies. How far would he go to prevent someone derailing his ambitions? Could it be that behind the smiling mask there lurked a cold-hearted predator who would stop at nothing to remove someone he saw as standing in his way?

Chapter Thirty-Five

Grace rang the doorbell and waited. It was time she delivered another update to her client. She noticed a curtain twitch upstairs. There was the sound of hurried footsteps on the stairs and the front door was flung wide.

'Grace! Did we have an appointment?' Sylvia's face was flushed and moist as though she'd been sweating.

'I thought I'd swing round and update you on the investigation,' she replied with a smile.

'Great, come in then,' Sylvia replied.

As Grace entered, she heard the back door close.

'Dratted wind,' said Sylvia.

Why was she being so secretive? wondered Grace. *I'm not exactly the morality police.* There was a faint scent lingering on the air, but it dissipated before Grace pinned it down.

'Please, sit,' said Sylvia, hurriedly clearing away two mugs and an ashtray into the kitchen. 'Coffee?' she shouted over her shoulder.

'Please – black, no sugar,' Grace yelled back. She took the opportunity to glance around the room. There were no photos of Paul Gordon here.

Sylvia returned with the coffee.

'I'm afraid that someone broke into the agency,' Grace said, watching Sylvia's reaction closely. 'The intruder took those photos of your husband and... the woman.'

Sylvia exhaled and turned to straighten one of the cushions. 'What a strange thing to go for!'

'You know who she was,' said Grace, in a tone that brooked no argument.

For a moment she thought that Sylvia was going to try and brazen it out, but then her client simply sighed and nodded.

'Yes, it was that girl who worked at the golf club.'

'Why didn't you tell me when I asked before?' demanded Grace.

'I didn't want it to get out.'

'If you want me to solve this case, you can't pick and choose what information you give me. It's for me to determine what's relevant to my investigation. Now, tell me again, when did you find out your husband was having an affair?'

'Like I said before! Not until after he died and I looked in the safe. When I saw those photos, I was so shocked and upset I just shoved them back in there. I should have got rid of them straightaway.'

'Then why didn't you?'

'I don't know. I worried they might have had something to do with his death.'

'You thought that someone might have been blackmailing him?'

'Yes.'

'Those payments from his bank account, that you

confirmed to Jean were charitable donations to a good cause, were actually going to his blackmailer?'

'I didn't know for sure, but I suspected as much.'

'I'm still having trouble understanding why you didn't tell me about all of this from the start,' said Grace, allowing an edge to creep into her voice.

'I didn't want you to suspect me of having killed him.'

It was a good point. Blackmailers didn't usually murder their victims: it would cut off their income stream. But a wronged wife might have no such qualms.

'You were at the golf club the day that Maria Rossi was murdered.'

'So were a lot of people. It doesn't mean I killed her.'

'You had motive, means and opportunity.'

'You're barking up the wrong tree,' said Sylvia, her eyes wary now. 'I didn't blame Maria. She was a free agent. I do blame Paul for cheating on me, but I didn't find out until after his death. I swear to you.'

Grace really didn't know what to think. 'I'll carry on with the investigation if you want me to, Sylvia, but I can't ignore evidence that implicates you. And if I find out you've lied to me again—'

'I won't. Paul was murdered. It's not just about the money. I want whoever did it brought to justice.'

'When did you find out Maria was pregnant? Was it the day she was murdered?'

'Yes, I suppose so. Why?' Suddenly, the penny dropped. 'You think the baby was Paul's!' Sylvia said, her face draining of colour.

'It's a possibility,' Grace said, watching her client closely. Sylvia had seemed genuinely shocked, but Grace had been around long enough not to take things at face value.

'I desperately wanted a baby of my own. We tried and

tried for years. Unexplained infertility, they called it. If he got another woman pregnant, that would be the ultimate betrayal...' she said, her voice choked with emotion.

Chapter Thirty-Six

Hannah was exhausted. Her stomach was growling with hunger. Her mother had pinched the last slice of bread. Hannah gave her what money she could afford, yet somehow the cupboards always remained bare. The baby had kept them up screaming all night long and her mother had been cranky. Sometimes she wondered why she'd even had kids. The way she looked at them sometimes was enough to sour milk.

Walking into the golf club, all she could see were miserable, discontented faces, their frowns tugged into smiles by Botox. Her stomach rumbled again as she cast her eye over all the plates on the tables with food carelessly pushed aside.

Moving behind the bar, she hitched a smile onto her face and went to serve Matt. She recognised that, like her, he was dragging himself up by the bootstraps. He had a hungry look about him at times and she had caught the revulsion in his eyes after he was accosted by yet another over-stuffed rich person wanting a piece of him.

'Hey, Matt, the usual?'

'Hit me up, Hannah. I need my caffeine fix today.'

She turned towards the coffee machine, then clutched at the counter as she felt a sudden onset of dizziness... then everything went dark.

When Hannah came to, she was lying on a couch in Matt's office. Startled, she burst into tears and struggled to a sitting position.

'What happened? How long have I been here? I need to get back. My job—'

'Relax,' he said, gently pushing her back down. 'I've arranged for Bob to cover for an hour. Here, eat this. It'll make you feel better.'

Her cheeks flamed. 'How did you know?'

'Been there, got the T-shirt. Official version is that you ate a dodgy kebab last night.'

Her eyes filled at how kind he was being. Hannah wasn't used to that in her life. Grace and Jean had been lovely, but she was in awe of them still. And she had her own reasons for wanting Grace to think she had it together. Hannah let herself relax and attack the sandwich. It felt freeing for someone to see the real her for once.

When she had scoffed it down and completed her mortification with a gentle burp behind her hand she looked directly into his eyes and smiled.

'That's better,' Matt said, grinning back. 'So, Hannah, tell me what you do when you're not working here?'

The urge to unburden herself and tell him everything was almost overwhelming. She had lost all her friends from school a while back. They'd disapproved of her life choices.

'I have another job as well as this one,' she said.

'Very mysterious, tell me more,' he said, waggling his eyebrows comically.

She was about to start talking when she remembered that Regan Bradley had said Matt had been involved with Maria, the dead girl. And, of course, she'd heard him fooling around with Regan.

'Nothing exciting! Typing reports and general admin.'

'Hey, we all have to do what we can to get by. How about we meet for a bar supper at the Crown down Leith later? On me! It's time I got to know the latest recruit to this hellhole.'

Hannah chewed her lip in indecision. Her mother would go mental if she was late home to help her with the kids and make tea. But it was the fact that she might learn something that would help the case that swayed her. She so badly wanted to impress Grace.

'The fact that it's taking so long to make up your mind really isn't flattering,' Matt said, with mock offence.

'Sorry! You're on,' she laughed. 'I'd love to.'

'Pick you up at seven?'

'How about I meet you there?'

'It's a date,' he said, giving her a slow look that made her think she might have bitten off more than she could chew.

Back behind the bar, fuelled by her sandwich, Hannah went into turbo mode and it was soon time to serve lunch to those coming off the green after their morning round of golf. She noticed Tobias nursing a whisky in the corner and he beckoned her over.

'I heard you fainted this morning. Are you okay now?' he asked.

'I'm fine.' She smiled at him and went about her work. Tobias was actually quite kind underneath that crusty façade, she decided.

Regan Bradley wandered up to the bar. Hannah pasted on a cheerful expression. She couldn't stand the woman.

'A skinny latte and a Caesar salad, please,' Regan said, her ice-cold eyes raking over Hannah like she was something the cat dragged in. As Regan put her hand up to tuck her hair behind her ear, Hannah noticed a unique and expensive-looking gold and amber bracelet flash on the woman's wrist. *Imagine what I could do with something like that*, Hannah thought. *It might be a trinket to her but to me it could be the deposit on a flat with change left over to get the kids a whole new wardrobe and a slap-up meal out somewhere.*

'What are you smirking at?' demanded Regan.

'Nothing,' said Hannah, dragged back to the present. 'I'll bring over your salad. You have a good day.' She forced herself to smile as she put down her coffee on the counter.

Regan shook her head at her and went off.

That woman is the absolute limit, Hannah fumed.

Chapter Thirty-Seven

Grace approached the police station on Leonard Street with a feeling of dread in her stomach. A curious mix of nostalgia and anger made her feel somewhat off kilter. As a DI in a busy Major Investigation Team, she had been first in and last out. All that had mattered back then was the thrill of the chase. Putting bad people behind bars had been her drug of choice. Nothing gave her more of a buzz. When Connor had gone missing, she realised she'd sleepwalked through parenting and paid the worst price imaginable. Her marriage had been collateral damage from the fallout. She hoped that she didn't bump into any of her old team. She'd shown weakness to them, and they'd thought less of her for it. The last thing Grace wanted now was their pity.

Pushing open the familiar door, she spied a young constable behind the front desk.

'Hello, I've arranged to come in to see DS Brodie McKenna.'

'Name?' asked the officer.

'Grace McKenna.' Not a flicker of recognition. Grace didn't know whether to be relieved or insulted. It had only been two years, after all.

The young PC looked up from her computer.

'He'll be with you shortly, if you'd like to take a seat?'

Grace sat down and looked around her. Nothing had changed and yet everything had.

Brodie stuck his head round the door and she jumped to her feet. 'Is this the first time you've been back?' he asked as they marched along the corridor.

'Yes,' she acknowledged. The reality of Brodie being here, business as usual, in fact, enjoying a big promotion, made her feel snappish and upset. How had he been able to carry on when she had fallen apart?

'I know what you're thinking. You have to let it go. Neither of us should be blamed for the choices we made,' he said.

She gave a tight nod of acquiescence. They'd almost made it to Brodie's office when a loud, slightly nasal voice stopped them in their tracks. 'Grace McKenna! Well, this is an unexpected pleasure.'

Gritting her teeth, she swung round, chin tilted and fire in her eyes.

'Superintendent Blair. How lovely to see you,' she said, with a lazy smile that bordered on insolent. He had no power over her now, so she wasn't going to take his crap.

'Grace has some information that might be of assistance in our murder investigation,' Brodie said, looking so anxious to please that she cringed for him.

'Yes, I've noticed you hanging round the golf club,' Blair said to Grace. 'Didn't have you pegged for the golfing type. Your little agency not keeping you busy enough?' he asked with a combative gleam in his eyes.

Before she could reply, to Grace's disbelief, Brodie's girlfriend Julie came haring along the corridor. *Could this day get any worse?*

'Dad, here's that file you left on your study desk. Oh, hi, Grace! Got to dash, I'm still on my break!'

'Thanks for bringing it in,' Blair said, a rare smile flickering across his face.

Julie waved at Grace, blew a kiss at Brodie and turned on her heel to race back along the corridor.

Grace was frozen in shock. Julie was the super's *daughter*? She didn't even know how to begin to process that. Why hadn't Brodie told her?

The super had deflated, having been distracted. 'I'll leave you two to get on,' he grumbled and retreated to his office.

They walked a few more steps in silence and turned into Brodie's small office, flopping down into chairs on either side of the desk. Brodie looked at her warily.

'So, that just happened,' she said. 'Why on earth didn't you tell me?'

'Why do you think? I know how you feel about him. I'm not his biggest fan either.'

Grace gave a short laugh. 'Julie is his daughter? I did *not* see that coming.'

'She's her own person and I admire her for it,' Brodie said, looking so exhausted she suddenly felt sorry for him. It really was none of her business.

'It must add to the pressure, though,' she said.

'Tell me about it. Anyway, what have you got for me?'

She rattled off everything she had on Maria Rossi including her previous relationship with Matt, the golf professional, and those persons that had been present in the golf club on the morning of the murder that might be pertinent to his enquiry. 'Remember those monthly withdrawals from Paul's account?'

He let out a low whistle. 'So, *was* he being blackmailed?'

'I don't have any hard evidence, but there's no other explanation for what they are, so it would appear that way. Another thing: I suspect Matt Turner might try to deny he had a relationship with Maria, but Hannah overheard Regan Bradley mention it to him. He seems to be involved with her as well, so possibly jealousy could be a motive?'

'Duly noted. We're interviewing everyone she gave a massage to in the last few weeks. Quite a few of them seem to be associated with the college, too. Tobias Sloan was the last name in her appointment diary the day she died.'

'I know,' said Grace. 'He didn't try to hide it.'

'I'd watch your back there if I were you, Grace. He might be using you to further his own agenda. I don't trust him.'

Grace wondered whether that distrust was linked to Brodie's assumption that she and Tobias were sleeping together. She couldn't put him straight on that now without making a big thing of it.

'Right, Brodie, that's enough show and tell from me. Aren't you going to offer me a coffee?'

There was a tense silence as Brodie removed a bulging file from the cabinet. This dancing around each other at work felt so strange when they used to be on the same team.

'Black?' was all he said, as he came out from behind the desk.

She nodded, staying where she was until he exited the room, then pulling the file towards her, praying for both their sakes that the super didn't come barging in. He was never one for the social niceties.

Flicking through the post-mortem report on Maria Rossi, she discovered that the murder weapon still hadn't been found, but that she had definitely been struck by an object rather than merely hitting her head during a fall. Hurriedly, Grace flicked through the statements taken so far, noting down some details she hadn't yet obtained in her own investigations. A sheaf of Maria's bank statements were there and she rifled through them, looking for anything of interest. Surprised, she noticed a payment of five hundred pounds from her client Sylvia's account. Hurriedly, she took a photograph and snapped the file shut. She pushed it back across the desk as Brodie returned after a decent interval with two steaming cups.

Grace gulped her coffee down as quickly as possible, wanting to get away now she had got what she came for.

'You'll burn your tongue,' he said, watching her with quiet amusement.

He wasn't wrong, but she wasn't going to admit to it.

'Thanks, Brodie. See you later,' she said and rushed from the room. It wasn't until Grace had pushed her way out the door from the station that she realised she'd been holding her breath.

Chapter Thirty-Eight

Grace was a bag of nerves, pacing up and down her flat. Even though Harvey had been walked and fed already, he was alert to her mood and hadn't settled down for his normal post prandial nap.

'Everything's fine, boy,' she soothed him, pausing to give his massive head a pat and stroking his silky ears.

But was it? *It's not as if this is a date*, she argued with herself. *It's a work event. I'm trying to further the investigation.* She knew she was kidding herself. She wouldn't have got worked up into this state and tried on half her wardrobe if that was its only significance.

Sighing, she went into her bedroom and looked in the mirror for the umpteenth time. The red dress she had decided on was looser on her than the last time she had worn it, but still skimmed her curves. Her eyes glittered with makeup. The woman in the mirror looked somehow unfamiliar. It was like a snapshot from her past. Losing Connor had pushed her into a monochrome existence, but tonight she had dialled up the colour. She didn't know if she should be clapping or weeping.

Grabbing her bag, she threw on a dark wool coat and picked up her keys.

'I'll see you when I get back, Harvey.'

He dropped his head between his paws and refused to look at her. The usual guilt trip.

The restaurant Croft had selected was in Rose Street and not one she'd been to before. It took a moment for her eyes to adjust to the discreet lighting. Handing her coat to an attentive waiter, she finally spotted him at a table in the corner. He looked as nervous as Grace was and stood as she approached, greeting her with a kiss on the cheek. The admiration in his eyes was palpable and she was glad of the candlelight as she felt her cheeks redden.

'I was worried you wouldn't come,' he said with a wry smile.

'I'm a woman of my word,' she replied, then instantly felt guilty as she was mostly here to mine him for information.

After they'd ordered and exchanged a few pleasantries, Croft sat back in his chair and looked her straight in the eye. 'So, tell me Grace, what's it like being a private investigator? Is it as interesting and intriguing as it sounds?'

Her heart missed a beat, and she shoved a forkful of food in her mouth, playing for time as her mind raced. She had known it would only have been a matter of time until he asked about what she did for a living.

'I'm fairly new to it but loving it so far.' She smiled, once her mouth was empty. She sat back in her chair and looked at him. 'You've done your homework.'

'I like to know who I'm getting into bed with.'

'I'm sorry?' she asked, incredulous.

'Sorry, bad turn of phrase. I mean, I'm considering hiring you on a professional basis in relation to a private family matter.'

Grace felt mortified that she'd jumped to the wrong conclusion but also wrong-footed on every possible level. How could she answer him without tipping her hand? Could Croft be trying to muzzle her by placing her in a conflict of interest situation? Yet, how could she tell him he couldn't be her client while he was a person of interest in her investigation into Paul Gordon's murder?

Weighing up the pros and cons at lightning speed, she came to a decision.

'Okay, I'm going to be frank with you,' she said. 'Someone has already engaged me to look into Paul Gordon's death. That person has a strong suspicion that he was murdered.'

Xander Croft looked shocked. He opened his mouth then closed it again as though he'd been temporarily robbed of speech.

'I see,' he finally managed. 'Some psychic I am, as I did not see that coming. Paul, murdered? I just don't see it.'

'So, he's not been protesting about his untimely demise from beyond the grave?' Grace said with a small smile.

'Well, no. Not all spirits choose to come through. Hang on, he went off the roof – if he was murdered, that would mean someone pushed him off. It doesn't bear thinking about.'

'How did you get on with Paul?' she asked.

'Less well, latterly. We both had a lot of money invested in the college, but at times we disagreed on the direction it should take. He wanted to concentrate on the commercial side and develop a network TV show and our own YouTube channel. I was more interested in the spiritual and academic side. I wanted us to fund research studies and engage with the mainstream rather than be seen as some kind of freak show. However, he persuaded me to let him run with it.'

'Now that he's gone, are you still proceeding with the show?'

'I'm afraid so. Although Paul was going to be fronting it, the contract was with the college, so I have little choice in the matter. At least it will give the college finances a welcome boost.'

'In your opinion did Paul have any kind of psychic ability?'

'When we first met, I formed the impression that he did, but then I think his chaotic personal life got in the way of that. I think by the time he died, he was making it up as he went along.' A brief expression of disgust distorted Croft's handsome features.

'You mentioned his personal life was spinning out of control. In what way?' asked Grace.

'Well, I know that he was having an affair in the months before he died.'

'How did you find out?'

'His wife told me.'

Grace schooled her expression to remain neutral, but the knowledge that Sylvia had lied to her again made her deeply uneasy. 'When was this and did she mention the name of the woman?'

'It was a few weeks before he died. She didn't give me a name and I didn't want to pry. At the time Paul and his wife were working together at the college. I did wonder if it might have been Regan Bradley?'

Grace hadn't even considered the possibility that he may have been involved with more than one woman. 'It's tricky for everyone when someone dies, and the circumstances are unclear. The police still don't seem any closer to catching Maria Rossi's killer,' she added.

'Such a tragedy. That poor young woman and her baby.'

'No clues to her killer over the ether?' Grace asked, trying and failing to sound open-minded.

'I can tell you're not a believer,' he said. 'It doesn't matter to me.' He reached over the table and placed his hand over hers and she felt the warmth infuse her skin. She forced herself to gently slide her hand away on the pretext of reaching for her glass of wine.

'I would like to believe,' she hedged. 'What's it like for you?'

'You mean am I deluded or simply a cunning mentalist exploiting the bereaved for my own personal gain?'

'I didn't say that,' she protested.

'You aren't the first and you won't be the last. It's not a path I would have chosen for myself. I do have a connection to the spirit world. I will also admit to you that I use acquired mentalist skills to enhance readings where necessary.'

His honesty took her by surprise.

'Tell me about it then,' Grace said, meeting his eyes with a small smile.

'I've always been aware of the spirit world. As a young child I failed to understand how others in the family couldn't see my friends on the other side. When I grew older, I hid it from my living friends. No one wants to star in their own freak show when you're a teenager.'

'That must have been quite alienating,' Grace said.

'You have no idea. My parents couldn't accept my gift and tried to beat it out of me. They saw it as a shameful aberration.' Grace placed her hand over his, this time, as the pain he had experienced was clearly etched on his face. 'I left as soon as I was sixteen and they cut off all contact with me.'

Grace squeezed his hand and released it.

'I changed my name and managed to block out the spirit world for years. I studied science. Perhaps I felt its rationality would give me armour.'

'Did it help?'

'At first. I constructed a narrative that I must have been mentally ill, even psychotic. Then in my final year, my girlfriend's brother died, and his presence made itself felt. I'd only met him a couple of times, but he wouldn't leave me alone. He kept harping on about something he wanted to give Janie. Well, I couldn't tell her what was going on in my head, could I? Eventually, one night when we were over at her parents' he told me to go into his room and showed me a loose floorboard. Under there was a box with a memory stick on which he had recorded a video message for her. He'd hidden it because he didn't want their parents to see it as it would be too painful for them. In it he revealed he'd been hounded to death by bullies at his school.'

'How did Janie react?'

'She dumped me.' Croft gave a bitter laugh. 'You attract a lot of female attention in this line of business, but most can't handle the reality.'

This successful, powerful man is lonely, Grace thought incredulously. She could feel the aching void within him and wondered how she hadn't seen it before. Then, she was stunned to realise that he wanted her to see it. He was letting her in. *Things are getting complicated*, she fretted. She couldn't discount that he could be exploiting her sympathy and manipulating her.

. . .

After dinner, Croft insisted on accompanying her home in a cab. Walking slowly along the Esplanade they perched on the low wall in front of her office, huddling deep into their winter coats. He placed his arm around her, and Grace huddled into him for warmth as they inhaled the chill salty air and watched the waves crash against the shore in a flurry of salty spray. Despite everything, she felt at ease in his company.

'I don't know if you want to hear this, but I can sense your son is here.'

She stiffened but said nothing.

He paused, waiting to see if she objected.

'He wants you to know that he's sorry and that he's at peace in spirit. He wants you to forgive yourself and let him go. Nothing you could have said or done would have changed the outcome.'

Grace became aware that her cheeks were wet. It felt as though a howl of grief and loss was trying to force its way out of her throat.

His face turned grave and he lifted up her chin, gazing deep into her eyes. Grace felt completely naked as though he could see into her soul.

'He knows about your swimming and wants you to stop. He fears you might not make it back one day soon. He needs you here. Someone he was close to needs your help. He has a gift for you and will show you when the time is right.'

Grace desperately wanted to believe him, but still felt conflicted as she remembered everything Sloan had told her about this man. What he had done.

'The connection has gone,' Croft said, turning to her with a sad smile as if he could read her mind. 'He was a wonderful young man, I could see that most clearly. I'll leave you now.'

Grace stood up and faced him. Their earlier closeness had turned awkward. Her mind was a maelstrom of emotion and she needed to be on her own to process things.

'Goodnight,' she said. 'Thank you for a wonderful evening.'

He bent down towards her, and she didn't turn away, but he kissed her on the cheek.

'Goodnight, Grace.'

Grace watched him walk away from her, already missing the comfort of his presence. Sighing, she unlocked the door to her flat and trudged upstairs.

Chapter Thirty-Nine

Hannah didn't get out much. Usually, she had to stay in and babysit for all the kids while her mum was out working. Not that she minded. She loved the kids to bits, so it was no hardship. Her Auntie Carol had stepped in tonight so she could have a much-needed taste of freedom.

Matt the golf professional was older than anyone she had been out with before. Although a bit wary that he might be a player, Hannah was determined to enjoy her night. She might even get something out of him that would throw light on Maria's killer, which would please Grace.

Spotting Matt in the busy bar, Hannah waved and made her way across to him. He'd ordered a bottle of white wine in an ice bucket which made her feel very sophisticated. She'd have to watch her alcohol intake. The last thing she wanted to do was end up blabbing all her secrets.

An hour later, Hannah was feeling pleasantly woozy but still in control. Matt had her in stitches with his impersonations of some of the trickier characters at the golf club.

'You should do stand up,' she gasped.

'Nope,' he said, his expression turning serious. 'No distractions. It's golf all the way for me. I'm aiming for some of the larger tournaments next year. I want to land a sponsorship deal and have my own high-end club by the time I'm forty.'

'Blimey! You've got it all figured out. I can barely see past the end of my nose compared to you.'

'Don't be so hard on yourself, Hannah. You and I – we're alike,' Matt said, staring into her eyes. 'We've had nothing handed to us on a plate. We have to find a way to take what we want from life, or we'll end up existing only to wipe other people's arses.'

Hannah said nothing but felt the prickle of tears.

'Sorry, I didn't mean to upset you,' he said.

'You didn't. Not really. And you're right. My life is tough sometimes... though I try not to let it get me down. Something happened. It changed me, I suppose,' she said. Things were getting heavy, and she wasn't sure how she felt about it. The stuff she was keeping in rose up like bile, threatening to choke her, but she swallowed it down. 'You were friends with Maria, weren't you?' she said, trying to change the subject.

'Yes, she was a mate. I tried to help her – you know, financially. She was really grateful but, you know, she was terrified of someone – wouldn't tell me who. I figured it was most likely an old boyfriend. She told me that if he saw us together, he'd kill her.'

Hannah froze.

'I didn't believe her,' Matt said, his face twisting.

'Was he the baby's father?'

'No idea. All I know is that the baby wasn't mine. Like I say, we were just mates.'

Hannah didn't believe him. She'd heard Regan say to

him she'd seen them getting frisky in Princes Street Gardens. Also, she'd overheard him arguing with Maria. If he was even slightly worried about the possibility the baby could be his, then they'd been a lot more than just mates.

'Did you tell the police?'

'About the ex? No! I didn't want him coming after me next.'

'But what if he gets the baby?' blurted out Hannah.

Matt glanced at her. 'You can't control everything in life, Hannah.'

Hannah made her way home on the bus feeling vaguely dissatisfied. The evening hadn't gone as well as she hoped. Although Matt was great to look at and could be really good fun, he had a selfish streak that she hadn't warmed to. All he cared about was himself and his stupid ambitions. She wished she'd had the nerve to ask him more about Maria. Would her killer ever be brought to justice?

Chapter Forty

Grace stood nursing a mug of tea, staring out of the bay window over the beach as the sun came up. Harvey was regarding her suspiciously, his head cocked to one side. His human had deviated from the normal routine therefore something was clearly afoot.

She glanced down and laughed at his quizzical expression.

'Don't look at me like that, Harvey. So, I didn't go for a swim this morning. You still got your walkie, didn't you? I thought it would be nice to take you to Figgy Park for a change. You weren't complaining when you were romping about with that chocolate lab!'

He hummed in the back of his throat and thumped his tail.

Grace had tossed and turned all night, going over Croft's words. She so desperately wanted to believe what he had told her. The alternative was that he was guilty of levels of manipulation she could scarcely countenance.

How could he have known about her daily swims? The

thought that her son might be watching over her had shamed her into not going this morning. Grace knew that she pushed the envelope sometimes, but had never quite admitted to herself what her motivations might be. She didn't know what to do about Croft, but she knew one thing for sure. Nothing could happen between them until the investigation was wrapped up. Grace was discovering, to her cost, that boundaries had been much easier to maintain in the police. Her new role was a lot less defined, which brought its own problems. Her gut was telling her that Croft was innocent, but she would follow the evidence regardless. Grace was still missing crucial pieces of the puzzle. However, she was sure that the death of Maria Rossi and the death of Paul Gordon were connected in some way. If only the people of interest would all be straight with her, she would be able to figure it out.

Grace slipped Harvey's lead on and locked the door. It was only just gone eight, but she liked to have some time to gather her thoughts and catch up on the core work that every agency needed to survive. Background checks for her handful of commercial clients were her bread and butter and she wasn't about to start neglecting them.

By the time Jean and Hannah arrived just before nine, she had already emailed across a few more background reports and a couple of credit checks for them to type up, and fresh coffee was brewed. Harvey was snoring gently under her desk and grunted sleepily as the front door shut with a bang.

'Coffee's in here,' Grace said, poking her head round the office door.

Hannah and Jean had just settled themselves when the door banged again.

'Only me!' yelled Tobias.

'Come through!' shouted Grace. He hadn't been into the agency since their tiff in her flat though they had exchanged a few texts. She was surprised to realise that she was happy to see him. Recently, she had been hoping he'd given up on his plan to expose Croft at the open day. Though maybe that was wishful thinking. Grace really wanted no part in it now, but didn't know how to tell him that. 'Glad you could join us,' she said, pouring him a coffee and pasting on a welcoming smile. 'A lot has happened recently. Why don't you fill us in on what you've learned this last week?'

'I'm still liking Xander Croft for Paul Gordon's murder,' Tobias said.

Grace's heart sank. 'Oh?'

'Croft was seen in a passionate clinch with Sylvia Gordon a few weeks before Paul Gordon went off the roof.'

'What? By whom?' snapped Grace.

Sloan looked surprised at her tone and raised his eyebrows.

'Sorry, I'm just a little tired of our client not being completely frank with us.'

'Regan Bradley told me. I caught her drinking in the bar one night and she let it slip that she'd seen them canoodling on the roof terrace at the college when she went up there for a smoke. I've been spending my time between the college and the golf club, trying to strike up conversations where I might learn something.'

'And you believe her?' asked Grace.

'That Croft was fooling around with his business partner's wife? Yes, I totally believed her. It's exactly the kind of thing he would do.'

Grace closed her eyes and leaned back in her chair. 'I

don't trust Regan Bradley as far as I can throw her,' she said. 'If ever there was a person out for number one, it's her.'

'And Xander Croft? What about him?' Tobias challenged, zeroing in on what she hadn't said.

'Truthfully, I don't know,' she admitted. 'The more I speak to him the less likely I find it that he's a cold-blooded killer.'

Sloan stood up and paced around the room. 'He's got to you, hasn't he?'

'Nobody has got to me. I just prefer to base my accusations on something more substantial, like concrete evidence. Which we don't have.'

'I went out with Matt from the club last night,' piped up Hannah, clearly trying to diffuse the rising tension between them.

'He's a fair bit older than you,' clucked Jean. 'Not to mention that he's a potential suspect in Maria's murder.'

Hannah rolled her eyes. 'I'm not a kid, Jean.'

'Says the one with the My Little Pony pencil case.'

'That belongs to my sister!' Hannah protested, going a little pink.

Grace held up her hand and smiled through gritted teeth. 'Let's concentrate on the matter in hand. Hannah, did you learn anything of interest?'

'Yes, I did as it happens,' said Hannah, glaring at Jean. 'He said that he'd tried to help Maria financially.'

'Did he say how?' asked Grace.

'No, I didn't want to make him suspicious by seeming too nosy. He also said she'd been terrified of someone finding out where she was. He thought it was maybe a jealous ex, but he didn't know for sure.'

'Great work, Hannah,' said Tobias with a warm smile.

Hannah beamed at him, looking pleased with herself.

Grace frowned. 'You'll need to tread carefully, Hannah. You heard him arguing with Maria not that long before she was killed. He could be dangerous.'

Hannah considered Grace's words. Then she brightened. 'I bet I can get him to tell me more about their relationship, you know – he was really opening up to me.'

'I commend your enthusiasm, but from now on if you're seeing him outside the golf club, I want to know about it in advance so I can put measures in place to keep you safe.'

Hannah acquiesced but didn't look happy. Jean passed her the cake tin in silent sympathy and Hannah took a Mars Bar slice with a small smile of thanks. Harvey innocently wandered over and collapsed on her feet.

Grace wished she was still of an age where the world could be improved or righted by a piece of cake.

'Right, if no one needs me for anything else, I'm heading over to the college.' She grabbed her bag, stroked Harvey and headed out the door, thankful to escape. It was a bit crowded when they were all in there together.

Chapter Forty-One

Grace decided to head for the college via the golf club where she could recharge her depleted battery with another bacon roll and double espresso. Hannah wasn't working today, so Grace thought she might try and have a crack at Matt Turner and see if she could get anything further out of him. She'd managed to book him for a lesson using the online system.

After she'd scoffed her snack, Grace changed and made her way out on to the green where Matt was waiting for her, looking crisp and professional. Once they'd played a few holes she insisted on a quick break, and they stepped off the green into rougher ground.

'Watch your step,' said Matt. 'It's easy to twist an ankle on here.'

Grace pulled out a silver hip flask from a side pocket on her bag and took a sip, trying not to screw up her face. Then she offered it to Matt.

'Fancy a wee snifter?' she said with a grin.

Matt folded his arms and stared at her, his lips tightening.

'I don't drink on the job.'

'I didn't have you figured for such a straight arrow,' Grace said. 'That's not what Maria told me. She didn't mention that we were friends?'

'No,' Matt replied, giving her a hard stare.

'Look, I get it. It can't be easy charming these rich women and their fat slob husbands. Some people are dripping with money and here you are, the one with all that talent, having to sell little pieces of yourself for pennies in comparison.'

'You have no idea. Look, we should get back on the green.'

'They've got so much that they can't even keep track of their own stuff. Hardly surprising bits go missing.'

The mask slipped. Even Grace was startled by the venom displayed underneath.

'I don't know what Maria told you, but whatever it was it was all lies. Why would I be interested in a stupid gold and amber bracelet? You'd best not be trying to pin this on me, lady.'

'Is that a threat?' asked Grace.

'Of course not!' he said, going back into his professional performance, flashing a wide grin, his eyes like chips of ice. 'Are you ready to continue?'

'Actually, I've a bit of a headache,' Grace said. 'I reckon I might head back to the club house.'

'As you wish.'

Grace smiled, confident at last that she had found her thief.

. . .

Back at the club house, Grace spied Regan Bradley sipping coffee and headed over to her table.

'Mind if I join you?' she asked, quickly sitting down before Regan had a chance to reply. By the scowl on her face the answer would not have been an emphatic yes.

'I've just seen a list of items stolen from the club over the past few months. Someone has been busy.'

'What's it to you?' asked Regan. 'You've only been a member for five minutes.'

'My stepfather is on the committee. Did you have anything stolen?'

'Me? Of course not,' she retorted. 'If you leave expensive stuff lying around you deserve what you get.'

Grace reached across and lightly grabbed her arm.

'Let go of me,' snapped Regan.

'Just admiring your bracelet,' Grace said.

Regan flushed.

'A gentleman bought this for me as a gift.'

'That gentleman wouldn't be Matt Turner, by any chance? We had a lesson about an hour ago. He seemed awfully knowledgeable about a bracelet that bears a striking resemblance to that one – one that was previously stolen from the locker room of the club. The funny thing is, police haven't released any information about it, so how could he have known what it looked like?'

Grace saw the penny drop almost comically as Regan's eyes widened. She took the bracelet off and threw it across the table to Grace. 'That cheapskate! I had no idea,' she said, looking so genuinely cross that Grace didn't doubt her.

'Will you tell the committee where you got the bracelet?' Grace asked.

'Yes, of course,' said Regan. 'I had nothing to do with the

thefts. But... wait a minute, the dead girl, didn't she have some missing items on her?'

'Yes.' Grace said nothing further.

'Working together, were they?' Regan said, looking sick.

'I'm sorry, I'm not at liberty to say anything more,' Grace replied as she got up to leave. She scooped up the rejected bracelet and popped it into an evidence bag. 'I'll make sure that this gets back to its rightful owner once the police are done with it.'

Grace had spotted her stepfather Brian wandering about self-importantly earlier and managed to track him down quickly. Grace reported the result of her investigation. He looked so shocked she got him to sit down in the wood-panelled hall.

'Matt Turner? I would never have believed it,' he said. 'It's beyond the pale, it really is. You don't think he...?'

'Killed her? I don't know, that's for the police to determine.'

'Have you called them?'

'Yes,' she said, glancing out of the window to see a police car nudging up the driveway. 'Here they are now.' She'd phoned Brodie on his mobile the minute she left the fairway. 'I know that the golf club would have preferred to simply have him leave and sweep it under the carpet, but this could provide new evidence in Maria's murder. He has to answer for what he did.'

Brodie came rushing in with a couple of DCs. 'Grace, where is he?'

'On the fairway heading for the twelfth hole, I should think. He also has a locker here in the staff room.'

'I'll show you to the locker,' said Brian, heaving himself

up out of the overstuffed chair. The other officers went out to the fairway to arrest Matt Turner and Brodie came with Grace and Brian to the staff room.

They waited until the two officers returned with Matt in handcuffs. When he saw Grace standing there, he lunged at her angrily, but she stood her ground and remained expressionless.

Brian opened the locker with a pass key and the police removed and bagged up the contents. There were several men's watches and some women's jewellery underneath the regular golfing gear.

'That bitch planted it!' he yelled, pointing at Grace. 'She's got the hots for me and I turned her down. This is her twisted idea of payback.'

Grace didn't give him the satisfaction of a response, but her heart was racing. Brodie waited behind with her while the other officers led the still-ranting golfer out to the car.

'You okay?' he asked.

'Of course!' Grace retorted. 'It's not my first arrest. Though I kind of miss slapping on the handcuffs myself.'

'Now that I believe.' He laughed. 'Do you think he killed Maria?'

'I don't know,' said Grace. 'From what Hannah said – they could have been working together. I take it you guys are finished with her flat?'

'Yes. Why?'

'I could really use a look inside. Maria's connected to my investigation into Paul Gordon by virtue of being in those photos with him.'

Brodie looked reluctant.

'Look, I know the drill. Gloves on and leave everything as I find it. Worst case scenario and someone catches me, you can say you hired me as a consultant or something. Please, Brodie, I need this.'

'Fine,' he said with a sigh. 'But don't think for one minute I'm going to make a habit of it.'

'Course not,' Grace said, looking as innocent as she knew how.

Chapter Forty-Two

Grace let herself into the small airless flat. By road it was a short distance from the leafy avenues of Morningside, but it was a long way away in aspiration. She kept away from the windows as she surveyed the interior. The contents of the flat were sparse and utilitarian, as if the occupant had no interest in making a home or laying down roots. The rental company who managed it for the owner had many similar flats on their books. It looked like the living space of someone who had been on the run. No personal knick-knacks or photos. No cushions or little touches of comfort. A place from which she might disappear into the night, leaving very little trace behind her.

Snapping on a pair of disposable gloves and overshoes, she carefully examined every inch. Even as a police officer, visiting the home of someone recently deceased had always felt a little creepy to her, even if the death wasn't suspicious. There was a winking light on the ancient answer machine in the lounge. Pressing play, Grace waited to hear if it would afford her a clue. It must have been recorded after the police had processed the scene or they would have taken the tape with them.

The new message was just a spam call. Grace tutted and rolled her eyes.

There was an old message as well. At first there was just static, but then a loud distorted voice made her jump.

'I'm coming for you, bitch.'

It was impossible to tell if the voice was male or female but there was no mistaking the malevolence.

Grace played it again and made an audio recording of it on her phone.

Moving on, she searched through the kitchen drawers and pulled a kitchen chair over to the units so she could search on top of them. Not only were they empty, but impressively clean, thought Grace, guiltily recalling her own. There was a pregnancy book on the table and, pressed inside its pages, an ultrasound photo. This child would grow up with the knowledge that her mother had never once looked upon her face.

Heading for the only bedroom, she noticed the photo of a young girl aged around eleven in a solid silver frame beside the bed. There was a scented candle in front of it. *Who was she?* wondered Grace. She gently opened up the frame but there were no clues inside as to the child's identity or when the photo was taken. Taking a photo with her phone, she turned to the inside of the bedroom drawer. There was a small makeup bag with the barest essentials and some cheap hand cream. There was a small, framed picture on the wall of a sampler which said, 'There's No Place Like Home.' It looked as though it had been made by a child, perhaps the little girl? Carefully, she removed it from the wall and opened the back of the frame. Inside, there was a photo. Drawing it out, she saw that it was a photo of Paul Gordon.

He was sitting at a pavement café and his eyes were warm, loving even, as he stared into the camera with a smile on his face. So, this was more than just a casual hook-up to Maria. And what were the odds that two people involved in a romantic relationship would be murdered within six months of each other unless they had a killer in common?

Moving over to the wardrobe, Grace was surprised to find not only work uniforms neatly pressed and hanging up but also a range of expensive, chic clothes that did not correspond with Maria's basic digs. They were all shrouded in plastic as if they had been cleaned and never worn again. She quickly checked through the pockets, but they were all empty. Who exactly had Maria been and what had she been running from that was so terrible?

Once she was back in her car, Grace fired off a text to Brodie to update him on what she had discovered and confirmed she would drop the key back to the front desk at the station. He didn't need to know that she was going to have a copy made first.

The unclaimed and motherless baby girl had been preying on Grace's mind. Stopping in Portobello, she bought a small white teddy and a little sleepsuit and drove to the Royal Infirmary to hand them in at the nurse's desk.

'I was there just after the mother was found,' Grace said to the nurse on duty.

'I heard it was touch and go,' the woman said, shaking her head. 'Thankfully, a woman gave the poor mother CPR and got her heart going again which kept the baby alive until she could be intubated and safely delivered. I don't suppose that was you?'

Grace smiled and nodded, a touch embarrassed.

'Do you want to see her?' the nurse asked. 'I shouldn't really, but seeing as you saved her life, I'm sure no one would mind. Come with me.'

The nurse walked up the corridor with Grace following behind and went into the neonatal unit. Grace walked after her over to the cot and her breath hitched in her throat as she saw how vulnerable the baby looked, surrounded by machines monitoring her with bleeping efficiency.

'Has she been given a name yet?'

'No, we're still hoping that she'll be claimed by a family member,' the nurse said. 'I'll make sure she gets your gifts when she's well enough. She should be moved to a ward fairly soon.'

Grace thanked her and with a last, lingering look left with a heavy heart.

Chapter Forty-Three

Jean's feet were killing her, and her nose was numb from the cold. In fact, if someone was inclined to give it a good twist it would probably snap off. Switching the weight of the placard she was hoisting to her other arm, she thought longingly of her comfy sofa where she should be perched right now reading the Sunday papers, something tasty from M&S cooking in the oven. The turnout was sparse today. Beverley, Leo and Helen had disappeared off somewhere without telling her. She was getting nowhere with them, and she needed to go to the loo. Slipping to the back, Jean put down her placard and cast around desperately for a public convenience. As suspected, there was none. There was only one thing for it: she was going to have to sneak into the college canteen and use theirs. It was open to the public, but she imagined that Beverley would have some rousing words to say about consorting with the enemy.

Ten minutes later Jean was sitting in a corner of the college cafe nursing her frozen hands back to life by cupping a mug of steaming hot chocolate. She'd thrown in a piece of carrot cake for good measure. To heck with the calories. She was jolted from her thoughts by the sound of raised voices in the reception hall. Peering forward from her vantage position, she saw Beverley being escorted from the building by two security guards. A white-faced Xander Croft stood watching.

'You're nothing but the Devil's pawn!' Beverley shouted at him as she was dragged away.

'Well, I guess you'd know all about that,' he replied, his fists clenched by his side as he strove to regain control.

'You killed him!'

'Hurry up and get her out of here,' Croft said and, turning on his heel, he strode away.

'Enjoying the show?' said a voice in her ear.

Jean jumped as Leo slid onto the seat opposite her.

'No! Of course not! I only came in because I was desperate for the loo and needed to warm up for a bit. What's going on? What are you doing here?'

'Same.' He laughed. 'Don't worry, I won't rat you out to Beverley.'

'What was all that about?' asked Jean. 'I mean, I know she's against the college. We all are. What did she mean? Who did he kill? I don't understand.'

'There's some things you're better off not knowing,' Leo said, the shutters coming down once more.

'I thought you guys trusted me?'

'We do,' he said, his face still closed. 'Your chance will come. Anyway, I'd best head off and find her. Wait here for ten minutes before you come after me. I don't want her to know you saw that. She'll freak out.'

Jean returned to her hot chocolate, her mind spinning. What on earth had Beverley meant? Had Xander Croft killed someone? Could it be Paul Gordon?

. . .

After a few minutes she quietly re-joined the protest. There was no sign of Leo or Beverley. Perhaps she could go round to Beverley's house with some flowers. They'd all gone round there a few days ago to collect extra placards from the garage so she knew where she lived. But then she'd have to admit what she'd seen and Leo had told her not to. However, if he himself told Beverley and Jean didn't confess herself that would also land her in bother. Longingly, she thought of the warm office and coffee machine with all those files to organise and bend to her will. She wasn't cut out for all this stress.

Her phone rang. Seeing it was Beverley she accepted the call, her heart banging against her chest.

'Can you come round?' Beverley said, her voice thick with tears.

'Yes, of course,' said Jean.

Twenty minutes later, she drew up outside a rundown mid terraced house in Polmont. As she was about to leave the car, she remembered Grace's instructions to report where she was at all times. She pulled out her phone to text her, but it was too late. Beverley was standing in the doorway watching her. Instead, Jean gave her a little wave and climbed out of the car.

'Beverley! Are you okay?' she asked. 'I came as soon as I got your message.'

Her heart jumped as Leo silently stepped out from the shadows, joining Beverley in the open doorway. *What had he told her?* She had no idea how to play this.

Feeling sick, she followed them both inside and the door shut behind her.

'What's happened?' she asked, once inside. 'I saw you leaving the college. There were two security types with you who didn't look very friendly.'

Leo nodded and gave her a thumbs up behind Beverley's back.

'They were brutes!' Beverley exploded.

'What were you doing there?' Jean asked, hoping for more information to help her walk this tightrope.

'I went to see Xander,' she said, her voice muffled by the handkerchief she was sobbing into.

Jean's heart skipped a beat as she registered the use of his first name.

'I don't understand...' said Jean with a quick look at Leo who slid his eyes away from hers.

'I needed him to repent before it's too late,' Beverley sobbed.

'Why? What is he to you?'

Beverley told her.

Jean was shocked. 'I'll make tea,' she said, squeezing Beverley's shoulder on the way to the kitchen.

Passing the cups round, she sat down beside Beverley and patted her hand. The woman might be up to goodness knows what but right now she was in pain and Jean could relate. For over an hour, she made soothing noises and offered Beverley biscuits, which the other woman waved away.

Finally, Beverley rallied. The fire returning to her eyes, she hissed, 'He needs to be stopped! Peaceful protest has got us nowhere.'

'Um... what do you have in mind—?' asked Jean.

'All in good time,' interrupted Leo, shooting Beverley a warning look.

'Right. It's getting late anyway.' Jean smiled. 'I really need to be going. Take care of yourself, Beverley. Let me know if there's anything else I can do to help the cause.'

'Thanks for coming,' Beverley said, grasping her hand and squeezing it.

Jean gave Leo a small wave and departed, relieved to be out of such an intense atmosphere.

She drove back to her home in Portobello, but before she went inside, she fired off a quick text to Grace. She had no idea how this would affect the case, but she had to let her know at the earliest opportunity.

Xander Croft is Beverley's son.

Chapter Forty-Four

Hannah lay on the single bed in her room, trying not to wake the sleeping baby in the crib or the toddler in the cot. They were all shoehorned into a three-bedroom terraced house and the feeling of claustrophobia could be overwhelming at times. Her mother was entertaining a man in the room next door, and she winced as she heard her laughter. The other kids were outside playing, bribed by the prospect of a visit down the chippie later.

'Just get it over with already,' she hissed, unwinding her headphones so she could try and block them out. Unbeknownst to her mother, Hannah had already saved a fair amount for a rental deposit from her two jobs, though she suspected that the one at the golf club would soon be coming to an end.

Her phone rang, startling her and causing the baby to grizzle in protest. It was Matt! Sliding off the bed she managed to slip down the stairs and out of the back door into the street to take the call.

'Hey, how are you?' she said.

'How do you think?' he snapped.

There was an awkward silence.

'Sorry, it's not your fault. It's that bitch, Grace McKenna. She had the hots for me and shopped me to the police when I turned her down.'

Hannah's mind was racing. Grace had told her what happened at the club and not to take his calls, but Hannah was sure she could get him to open up to her more about his relationship to Maria.

'They've let you out?' she asked.

'I've been released on police bail. It's a bloody joke, that's what it is. The golf club has fired me, and everything has turned to shit. All because of that stupid cow poking her nose in.'

'I'm sorry, Matt. That's rubbish. Do you want to meet up, take your mind off things a bit?' Biting her lip, she waited for his reply.

'Yes, that would be good. I can come and pick you up?'

Quickly she told him to pick her up at the chippy. She toyed with the idea of texting Grace first, but knew that she wouldn't sanction it. Best to tell her in the morning when she would hopefully have some new information to go with it. Grace might even pay her some overtime if she played her cards right.

Hurriedly, she popped back inside and checked on the sleeping kids who didn't stir. She gave her thirteen-year-old sister a fiver to say that she was sleeping and keep an eye on all the kids until her mother re-emerged. Kylie was a bit of a wild child, but her heart was in the right place. A bottle of milk was already made up in the fridge, should the youngest wake up. She only expected to be gone a couple of hours.

. . .

Hannah didn't have to wait long for Matt's Alpha Romeo to pull up to the curb. As she slid into the passenger seat, she felt a moment's panic which she forced back down. She was pretty sure he had nothing to do with Maria's death. He might be a bit shady and an opportunist, but he wasn't a monster. He'd been so kind to her when she fainted.

'Where are we going?' she asked as the car roared away.

'I thought we'd get a takeaway and go back to mine. That way I can have a few drinks.' Seeing her expression cloud over, he reached over and patted her knee. 'Don't worry, I'll get you a taxi home. I fancy blowing off a bit of steam with a mate. Okay?'

She nodded, flashing him a smile. He lived in one of the new flats down by Leith, near Ocean terminal. She could walk home from there if push came to shove, she thought, a tiny bit reassured.

Looking round the swanky, if small, bachelor pad, she had to admit that Matt had good taste. He'd shown her around when they got here, and she'd blushed as he opened the door to his immaculate bedroom.

'Relax,' he said with a wry grin. 'I've never forced anyone into bed with me in my life.'

I'll bet, she thought, trying to keep her eyes away from the six-pack outlined by his tight T-shirt. They'd picked up a Chinese takeaway on the way and she smiled as Matt came out of the kitchen bearing a glass of white wine for her and a beer for him. Although she didn't usually drink much, nerves made her gulp it down. She attacked the food with gusto – there'd not been enough to go round at home, so she'd just grabbed a yoghurt.

It was *so* good! She closed her eyes in bliss and opened them to find him watching her, his dark eyes curious.

'You're still not getting enough to eat at home. How come?'

Hannah started to protest, but fell silent. What was the point? Yet again she had a strong desire to unburden herself completely to him, sensing that Matt wouldn't judge her, but her instinct for self-preservation kicked in so she decided to tell him only part of the story.

'I earn enough,' she said. 'But I have responsibilities. My mum had me when she was only sixteen. My dad died a few years later and she didn't handle it well. I got taken off her for a few years.'

'That must have been tough,' he said, reaching for her hand. She let him take it.

'It wasn't great,' she admitted. 'She eventually got herself clean and met somebody in rehab. They got me out of care and started having their own kids. I liked him, he was pretty decent and treated me the same as the others. Then...' She gulped at her drink.

'Go on,' he said, squeezing her hand.

'He made a stupid mistake and got banged up for years.'

'I'm sorry, Hannah. That must have been shit.'

'My mum couldn't cope and went to pieces again. She does work from time to time, but if I didn't give her practically all my wages the kids would starve. Basically, I'm trapped.'

'If I'd known what you were dealing with, I'd have cut you in to my side hustle,' Matt said.

'The jewellery?' she asked, looking him straight in the eye.

'Yes,' he said, staring back unflinching. 'I like to think it was a victimless crime. It's not as if any of those rich bastards at the club would be uninsured. You have to be loaded to even be a member there.'

'So Maria was in on it, too?'

'Nah, I tried to convince her, but Maria was a proper goody two-shoes.'

'But I thought some stuff was found in her bag?'

For the first time he appeared defensive. 'Yeah, well, that was me. I found her lying there. I could see that she wasn't going to make it. There was too much blood. I had a couple of things in my pocket that I dropped into her bag. It was a spur of the moment thing. I knew it couldn't go on and that way I was free and clear. I was only on my own with her for a few minutes before the manager arrived.'

'I thought she was your friend...' said Hannah.

'She would have understood,' he said, his voice becoming colder. 'Like you, I was dragged up, Hannah. No one handed anything to me in this life. Sometimes if you want something you have to take it.'

Hannah nodded in agreement, but his comments had made her feel sick to her stomach. *I will never be like him*, she decided.

'I still can't believe she's dead,' Hannah said. 'She was one of the few people at work who treated me like a human being.'

His face softened. 'She was the real deal,' he said. 'I liked her. Then she got in with that slimy psychic guy from the college. Fancied himself something rotten, he did, despite being well past it.'

'Paul Gordon?'

'How do you know about him?' he asked, shooting her a suspicious look. 'He was before your time.'

'My mum was into him. She loved all that mumbo jumbo,' she replied, rolling her eyes. His face relaxed once more. 'You've had such a mental time, what with losing your job and Maria, too. It must have been terrible finding her there like that. If only you'd been a few minutes earlier, you might have saved her. You've no idea who killed her?'

'No, the room was empty when I got there. She was on the run from something. I asked her about it a few times, but she said it was safer for me if I didn't know. I should have forced her to tell me. I could have done something. More than that loser Paul Gordon ever did for her.'

He had done something, she thought in disgust. He'd framed her for a crime she didn't commit. And to think she'd once quite liked him! Looking at him now made Hannah's skin crawl.

'Look, sorry to be a buzz kill. Let's change the subject,' he said as he filled up her glass again.

Hannah was starting to worry. She'd been gone for a couple of hours already and God knows what state her mum would be in when she got home. She picked up her glass and started drinking it quickly, not wanting to seem rude. Unfortunately, he got the wrong idea and drew closer to her on the couch. She was getting out of her depth here.

'I need to use your loo,' Hannah said, jumping up and startling him.

'Along the hall and second on the left,' he said. As she turned to go, he grabbed her hand.

'Don't be long,' he said with a lopsided smile, confident of his charm.

Hannah smiled as her stomach lurched. Her head felt woozy from knocking back that drink. She had to get out of here. And soon. Once she was in the bathroom, she locked the door and reached for her phone. It wasn't there. It must have slid out of her pocket onto the couch. Splashing her face with cold water to help her sober up she glanced at the mirror, taking in her pinched, anxious appearance. Her head was throbbing. Hurriedly she flushed the loo, her mouth set in determination. She was going to get out of here right now.

Unlocking the door, she screamed to find him waiting there, holding her phone aloft.

She tried to close it again, but he jammed his foot in it.

'Matt, you're scaring me. Let me go! I want to leave,' she shouted.

Still blocking her way, he turned her phone round to face her. There was a text from Grace about work on the screen.

'When were you going to tell me you work for that bitch Grace?' he asked, his voice laced with menace.

'I don't,' she said, her voice sticking in her throat. 'Give me that!' She lunged at him, but he held her off with one arm, raising the phone out of reach.

'I thought we were mates,' he snapped. 'Then I find out you're a double-crossing little cow. To think I felt sorry for you. You're scum, that's what you are.'

Hannah burst into angry tears and pulled out the pepper spray Grace had insisted she keep on her. She sprayed, and he immediately dropped her phone, clawing at his eyes, the air laced with expletives as he pushed past her into the bathroom to wash them out.

'If I see you again, you're dead!' he screamed.

Hannah grabbed her phone from the floor and scooped up her coat from the hall. She wrenched the door open and fled down the stairs, gasping with relief when she stumbled out into the fresh air.

Chapter Forty-Five

Grace sat quietly, looking at her youngest team member as she sat wrapped in a blanket, both hands round her mug of hot chocolate. Harvey sat at Hannah's feet, his head in her lap. Despite the heat blasting out from the fire, Hannah's teeth were still chattering. She'd had a nasty shock. Grace had received a panicked call from her an hour ago and had immediately gone to pick her up.

'Have you let your mother know where you are?' Grace asked.

'I texted my sister. She's thirteen and will keep an eye on the little ones until tomorrow. She told Mum I'm at a friend's house. Mum won't be bothered.'

Grace looked at her in consternation. Hannah's home life seemed impoverished in more ways than one.

'You don't need to talk about it anymore tonight. The main thing is that you got out of there unharmed.'

'Thanks to your pepper spray,' Hannah said with a weak grin. 'I think he had a real thing for Maria, way more than he let on to Regan Bradley. He hated Paul Gordon, too, and knew she was seeing him.'

'That's enough for tonight,' Grace said. 'It's time you got some sleep. You can lie in tomorrow. I'll leave Harvey with you when I go to work. He likes having a guest to fuss over.'

Harvey thumped his tail in agreement as Hannah got unsteadily to her feet.

Grace quickly showed her where everything was and then opened the door to what she still thought of as Connor's room. Hannah's eyes widened but she said nothing for which Grace was grateful.

'Goodnight,' Grace said as she closed the door behind her. Maybe it was time to pack up Connor's stuff for good – she was a private person and it felt too public a manifestation of her pain.

Pouring herself a hefty glass of red wine she exhaled gently and sank into her usual armchair beside the fire with Harvey padding over to settle by her feet.

She pondered over Jean's text about Xander Croft which had come in earlier, remembering what Croft had said about how his parents beat him when he was a child. Perhaps Jean was right, and Beverley Thomson was more dangerous than she had hitherto thought. Then, another thought popped into her mind, this time about Matt.

If Matt had been romantically involved with Maria – what if she had thrown him over in favour of Paul Gordon? He was not a man used to being scorned. Might he have had it out with Gordon and killed him in a jealous rage?

'What is it, boy?' she said to Harvey who suddenly sat up, listening with his head cocked to one side and facing the door to the hall.

Quietly, she opened the door and then closed it gently – still, she could hear the sound of muffled sobs. These cases were taking a toll on Hannah; Grace couldn't let it continue. She'd have a word with Jean in the morning and work out a way they could put her onto lighter duties for a while until she found her feet again.

'She'll be okay, boy,' she whispered in Harvey's ear as she clipped on his lead. 'Time for your walk.'

Grace walked along the promenade deep in thought. As she doubled back, she viewed her office with a heavy heart. How could something that had filled her with joy a few short months ago now be dragging her and her staff into such dark places? Couples passed her, murmuring softly to each other, their arms entwined, and she suddenly felt an aching sense of loneliness. Harvey nudged her hand with his nose. He always seemed to pick up on her moods, bless him.

Her phone pinged. It was Xander Croft.

Been thinking about you. Fancy a nightcap?

Where are you?

Outside your office.

Grace looked up and waved to him along the Esplanade. As she walked towards him, she agonised over whether to bring up the subject of his mother, but decided not to mention it. He had already shared the story of his upbringing with her and the wound from today would still be fresh.

As she reached him, Croft gave her a peck on the cheek and made a fuss of Harvey who was putty in his hands.

'I can't invite you to my flat,' she said. 'I've got someone staying with me who's already in bed. How about we go to The Espy? It's dog friendly.'

'Fine by me,' he said.

They found a quiet nook with two green leather wing-backed chairs and a small table which Harvey wriggled under, watching the comings and goings with his head between his paws. She passed him a treat and he gobbled it up, then contented himself by making eyes at the springer spaniel under a table nearby. The conversation flowed and after a while Grace realised her jaw was aching. Seconds later she realised why, and a cloud danced across her face. Intuitive as ever, Croft leaned across the table.

'What is it, Grace?'

'It's nothing,' she said, trying to laugh it off. Then she decided to be honest with him. 'I had a pain in my jaw, and I suddenly realised it was from laughing so much. Something I've not done a lot of lately.' She felt a little embarrassed at bringing the conversation to such a personal level.

His blue eyes crinkled. He had a face that oozed character, she realised, studying it across the table with her chin resting on her hand.

Croft reached over the table, laying his hand on hers.

'That's the nicest thing anyone has ever said to me,' he said. 'It shows that you are starting to heal, which is something to feel glad about.'

'And guilty about,' Grace added.

'It's fine to feel what you're feeling.' He smiled. 'All of it.' He swiftly switched the conversation on to safer topics. 'How is your investigation going? I heard that Matt was arrested. It's tragic that he chose that path when he had such a bright future ahead of him.'

'You don't know the half of it,' she said, thinking of Hannah asleep in her flat.

'I think about Maria a lot. We spoke on various occasions when she was sorting out my back.'

'When was the last time you saw her?' she said, not wanting him to know that she already knew the answer and praying that he would tell the truth. Grace was starting to trust him but wasn't totally sure yet.

His face twisted in what looked like genuine anguish. 'It was the morning she died. We chatted away as normal while she was working on me. But, looking back, she seemed rather tense and jumpy. I remember someone knocked on the door to bring in more towels and she let out a small cry. It sounded a lot like fear.'

'Did she ever say what she was afraid of, or mention her personal life?' asked Grace, feeling bad that she had switched into professional mode rather than simply relaxing and enjoying his company. Croft didn't seem to mind. Maybe he needed to talk about it.

'Not much and I didn't like to pry. Intentions can be misconstrued. She did tell me she had lost a child some time ago.'

Grace's heart ached, thinking of the photo of the young girl in the flat. Poor Maria. Another mother left with only a flickering candle.

'That morning you saw me at the club, I had a communication from the spirit world. It came through with such force, it all but knocked me off my feet.'

Grace stiffened, wondering what was coming next.

'It was a voice shouting in my head. *Save her*! Then you came over to help me and I thought it was related to you.'

Grace didn't know what to say. She opened her mouth and then closed it again.

'It's alright,' he said. 'I don't expect you to believe me.'

'I want to,' she said, suddenly realising it to be true. 'But

I'm afraid I'm not quite there yet,' she added, giving him a small smile to cushion the blow. 'It's not that I think you are lying—'

'No,' he finished for her. 'You think I'm deluded or psychotic.'

Grace leaned back in her chair and threw her hands in the air. 'Honestly? I don't know what to think.'

Croft leaned towards her, trying to reconnect. 'You could try trusting me and see where that leads us?'

'Blind faith is for fools,' said Grace, knowing her words would push him away.

The conversation faltered after that and they both finished their drinks quickly. Grace cursed herself for ruining the mood, but she couldn't do what he was asking of her.

Leaving the pub with a sleepy dog in tow they parted outside her flat with a brief hug that might as well have been a handshake.

Chapter Forty-Six

Grace tossed and turned all night, waking up with a tension headache. She listened at Hannah's door, but there was no sound. Back in the lounge she exhorted Harvey to pipe down by shushing him with a finger to her lips. It had no effect, and she gave in as he zoomed about the living room, trying to kill his fluffy teddy by shaking it violently from side to side.

There's something so joyful about the way a dog greets each new day, thought Grace as she sat down with her usual coffee and toast. Really, she needed to be more 'dog'. She wondered if Harvey found her a bit of a drag at times, moping around the flat, but looking at his smiley face and waggy tail she realised he loved her anyway.

Before Grace took him out for a walk, she prepared a breakfast tray for Hannah.

Knocking lightly on the bedroom door she entered.

Hannah struggled up to a sitting position, yawning. She looked about twelve with her long straight hair hanging in curtains around her face.

'Morning,' Grace said with a smile. 'I've brought you some breakfast.'

Hannah teared up. 'Thank you, no one's ever done that for me before.'

'All part of the service at Casa Grace.' She grinned, though her heart suffered a pang at the lack of nurturing Hannah appeared to have had in her life.

'Connor was lucky to have had you as a mum,' said Hannah, her eyes travelling round the room that was a homage to her only son. 'This room... it's... how I remember him. It's like he never left.' Her bottom lip wobbled.

Grace paused. This was the first time Hannah had mentioned knowing Connor. Why had it taken her so long? She had to tread carefully.

'You knew him?' she asked gently, sitting at the bottom of the bed.

'Yes, we were... friends,' she said, looking away. 'I was very upset... when, you know... I heard.'

Grace got to her feet. Now clearly wasn't the time to talk about it. Hopefully, Hannah would open up to her when she was good and ready.

'We all were,' Grace said simply. 'I'll leave you to enjoy your breakfast. Stay and sleep for as long as you like. You're having a paid day off.'

Hannah started to protest, but her heart clearly wasn't in it.

'I've been working you relentlessly,' said Grace.

'Thank you,' Hannah said in a small voice, again looking as though tears weren't too far away.

Grace was so busy worrying about Hannah that she'd forgotten to put her swimming costume on before going out.

After Harvey had frisked about the beach for long enough, she decided to stop by The Espy for a coffee and cooked breakfast. Harvey sat at her feet on the wooden floor, looking at her like she had taken leave of her senses. Then the cooked breakfast arrived and a line of drool snaked on to the curly hair of his chest.

'Can't take you anywhere, Harvey.' She grinned as she swooped to wipe it away with the napkin. Surreptitiously she slipped him a sausage and made his day. Once she'd demolished the rest, she ordered more coffee and grabbed a paper from the rack by the bar. Glancing at the headline, she froze in horror.

Normally, she'd have looked at the news on her iPad by this time, but she'd been jolted out of her routine by Hannah staying over so hadn't bothered. Pulling out her phone she anxiously scrolled for more information. There was precious little on offer. She phoned Brodie, hoping to catch him before he left for work.

'Hello?' answered a cheerful female voice.

Grace realised she was grinding her teeth. She might have guessed Julie would be a morning person.

'Hi Julie, it's Grace. Is Brodie there?'

'I'll get him,' she said.

Seconds later, Brodie picked up the phone. He sounded tense.

'Grace, I take it you've heard?'

'Just now. Have you any leads? Can I help in any way?'

'Meet me at the café on the corner across from the station in half an hour. We can catch up before I head in. I can use all the help I can get,' he said.

'See you then,' said Grace, hanging up, not wanting to detain him further.

She drained the dregs of her coffee, paid the bill and

clipped the lead on Harvey. Still smacking his lips from the sausage, he happily trotted back to the flat with her.

The door to Connor's room was ajar. Hannah must already have cleared out. Sticking her head in the open doorway, Grace noted she had made the bed and left the room immaculate. Hannah was a special kid and it warmed her inside to know that she and Connor had been friends.

'Sorry, boy, I've got to go out again,' Grace said, bending down to make a fuss of the dog. Harvey dropped his big head between his paws and gave her the look which twisted her heart every time. 'Don't give me that,' she scolded. 'You know you're going to be asleep in five minutes dreaming about that big juicy sausage.' He licked his lips and thumped his tail. 'See you when I get back,' she called as she opened the door. *People would think I was barking mad if they heard the way I talk to him*, she thought with a small smile as she sped down the stairs.

Chapter Forty-Seven

It was a gorgeous sunny day by the time Grace took a seat at the pavement café. From here she could watch the traffic in and out of St Leonard's Street Station. In her previous life she would have been charging in there, head bent, her brain already churning information round and round, the beauty of the day lost on her. Who was she kidding? She still missed it.

Her eye was drawn to Brodie walking towards her. He looked stressed and she felt a pang of anxiety for him. Even though he was no longer her responsibility at work or at home, her stomach tightened in concern as he flopped into the seat across from her.

Grace pushed across a large latte as the waitress arrived with scrambled eggs and bacon.

'Eat,' she commanded.

Wordlessly he wolfed it down, then pushed his plate away.

'Thanks, I didn't have breakfast,' he said.

'So? Tell me.'

'The baby went missing from the neonatal unit yesterday evening. A woman visited last night wearing both a hospital visitor badge and a lanyard with an Edinburgh City Council logo proclaiming her to be a social worker. The unit had been expecting a social worker to arrive as the ward Charge Nurse had been phoned in advance. They'd been told a foster care placement had been found. The woman had a newborn car seat with her. She asked if she could get the baby organised while they processed her discharge papers. She strapped the baby in and gathered up her things. Once the paperwork was done, she calmly left with the child. It was only when a real social worker turned up this morning that the alarm was raised.'

'CCTV?'

'We've had people going through it all night. It's like looking for a needle in a haystack. The lens of the main camera pointing along the corridor to the ward exit was sprayed with some kind of film, so is useless. It's a busy hospital with relatives and patients coming in at all hours of the day and night. We're going through the motions of tracing them through the CCTV, but it could well be a dead end.'

'Possibly someone who lost a baby themselves?' said Grace.

'We've put out a call to local GPs to keep an eye out for new baby registrations and check each one thoroughly. The birth hadn't even been registered yet.' He sighed.

'It's not even as though you can track down the father,' said Grace. 'I assume it was Paul Gordon, in the end?'

'Yes, we had his DNA on file. It was a match. Keep that to yourself for now.'

'Does Sylvia Gordon know?'

'Officers went out to speak to her early this morning.'

'What a mess!' said Grace, shaking her head. She felt a wave of sadness sweep over her. That poor baby, dragged into the world before she was ready and already an orphan. 'People who abduct babies don't usually want to harm them. Often there's a strong psychological motive. It's going to be a waiting game by the sounds of it, in the absence of any credible leads.'

'We've set up a hotline for members of the public to phone in so, as you can imagine, that's going bat-shit crazy,' Brodie added.

'It only takes one nosy neighbour to blow the case wide open,' said Grace, patting his hand. She longed to give him a comforting hug, but held herself in check. She didn't want to jeopardise the fragile détente between them.

'Are you cross-referencing those at the golf club on the morning Maria was murdered with anyone who visited the hospital when the baby was last seen until after she disappeared?'

'No, but that's a good idea. Are you thinking it's the same person?'

'Impossible to determine without more information.'

'Thanks, Grace,' said Brodie, taking a final slug of coffee and getting to his feet.

'Any time, keep in touch.'

He turned to head back to the station.

'Fake it until you make it,' she whispered to his departing back.

Chapter Forty-Eight

Grace left the café feeling on edge. This business with the baby was really getting to her. She couldn't help but feel invested in the tiny girl's fate. If only the media hadn't covered the tragic story of Maria's death so intensely, then the baby girl might have slipped under the radar and not attracted the attention of the sick person who had stolen her away. Mind you, the police had had little choice but to encourage the media interest in the hope that family might be discovered, to give the baby the happy ending she deserved. Since the story had aired there had been a relentless parade of nutters and opportunists trying to lay claim to her, but nobody from her actual family. It was as if Maria Rossi had existed in a vacuum. She hadn't trusted anyone with her true identity. Paul Gordon had no living family himself. It was impossible to know if Maria had even told him about the pregnancy.

Grace suddenly had a troubling thought. If Sylvia Gordon had suspected that the baby was her late husband's, could she have flipped and abducted the baby herself? She'd said they had tried for a family. Maybe it was time Grace paid her client another visit.

Her phone pinged. It was Tobias Sloan. Finally! She'd left him a message about what had happened to Hannah last night and he was only now getting back to her.

> How is she this morning? You need to keep a better eye on her. Anything could have happened, Grace. Is there anything I can do? I can stay in the office working all day if that helps? I'm only revising my article.

Grace felt rebuked but he wasn't wrong. She needed to keep better tabs on all of them. She wasn't yet used to operating like this. Things had been so different in the police when she always worked alongside professionals.

> Thanks for the offer but not necessary. I've given her the day off. Feel free to do your own thing. Jean will manage and I'm out of the office anyway.

Grace pulled up a little down the street from Sylvia's house. She wanted to approach unnoticed. As she walked up the drive to the stunning detached house, she listened intently for any sounds that might indicate Sylvia had a baby on the premises. It was as quiet as the grave. The thought instantly made her stomach churn.

Remembering the sound of a quickly shut back door during her previous visit, Grace had enlisted the assistance of Jean, who was slouched down in the car, keeping an eye out for anyone leaving via the back of property.

Grace paused to listen on the front step. All was quiet. She was probably being ridiculous in her suspicions, she acknowledged. She rang the bell and heard it reverberate through the house. It certainly hadn't triggered any crying. Maybe Sylvia was out? She was about to turn and leave when she heard the sound of footsteps and the door was opened.

'Grace! I wasn't expecting you,' Sylvia said.

'There have been quite a few developments with the case, so I thought that I'd better give you an update.'

Sylvia showed her into the lounge where the TV was set to the news channel. She switched it off and went to make some tea.

Grace quickly scanned the room, but there was no sign of any baby paraphernalia. Mind you, the police had already been round, and she was unlikely to leave any clues in plain sight.

After a few minutes, Sylvia came back with the tea tray. The cups were rattling in the saucers and her face was taut with stress. After she'd poured the tea, Sylvia perched on the edge of the couch. Grace took up her cup and deliberately settled back into her chair, subtly signalling to her client that she intended to be there for some time.

'I understand that the police have already been to see you?' Grace said.

'Yes,' said Sylvia, twisting her hands in her lap. 'I'm still trying to wrap my head around it, to be honest.'

'Did you know that Paul was the baby's father?' asked Grace, looking directly at her client.

'No! I swear to you. I had absolutely no idea,' Sylvia protested. 'I told you before, I only found out about his affair when I went in the safe after he died. If I'd known about any of this, he would have been out on his ear. A tawdry affair is one thing, but fathering a baby with another woman is a whole other level of betrayal.' Her face twisted in disgust.

Grace studied her. Sylvia seemed to be on the level, but if her career in the police had taught her anything it was how accomplished liars could be. She only had Croft's word for it that Sylvia had known about her husband's affair with Maria in the months before he died. One of them was definitely lying to her. Of course, if Sylvia had known that Maria was expecting Paul's baby before he died, that would give her an even greater motive to murder her cheating husband.

'I hope they find that poor baby soon,' Sylvia said. 'She's had a bad enough start in life.'

She sounded convincing, thought Grace, but she still resolved to keep an open mind.

'Could I use your bathroom?' she asked, putting her teacup down.

'Yes, of course,' said Sylvia.

Grace closed the door behind her and ran lightly up the stairs. Pausing to listen she quietly opened each door in turn. There was no sign that a baby had been here. When she reached the master bedroom, she paused. There was a pair of male slippers on one side of the bed and a gent's watch on the bedside table. Her heart racing, she ran lightly across to the ensuite and peered in. Two toothbrushes. Leaving hurriedly, she found the toilet and flushed it before racing back downstairs to the lounge.

Sylvia was standing waiting for her with her arms folded, her lips compressed in a thin line. She'd been rumbled.

'Find what you were looking for?' she asked sarcastically.

Grace held her hands up in surrender. 'Okay, you got me. I had to check if the baby was here, especially in view of what you told me. If I put keeping a client over a baby's safety, I wouldn't be able to live with myself.'

Grace picked up her bag to leave, but Sylvia stopped her.

'It's fine,' she sighed. 'I suppose I can't blame you in the circumstances. I wouldn't steal the baby – it would only be a permanent reminder of my husband's infidelity.'

'The kidnapping is not necessarily connected to our case,' said Grace. 'The most probable scenario is that someone has seen the coverage in the press and hatched a plan then. The lengths people will go to for a baby are extreme.'

'Yes, I'm aware.'

Grace cursed herself for being so tactless. 'Anyway, we should focus on Paul's murder. We've been going over the footage taken from his study. It would appear that someone may have been embezzling money from the college. Do you know anything at all about that?'

'No,' said Sylvia, shaking her head. 'Paul never said anything to me.'

'You told me that you used to work at the college before Paul's death. What exactly was it that you did there?'

'Well, officially, I was an administrative assistant. I dealt with course enquiries, prospectuses, all the run-of-the-mill stuff really. Paul wanted me in there as his eyes and ears. He never really trusted Xander Croft. Not deep down. Turns out he was right.' She sighed.

'Why do you say that?' asked Grace, leaning forward.

'It's nothing,' Sylvia said, looking down.

'Please, let me decide what's relevant,' Grace said.

'He was... a bit too friendly at times.'

Grace was surprised, but then Sylvia was undoubtedly a very attractive woman. 'To what extent?'

'At first, I thought he was simply being welcoming. But one night we were all at a party and he wouldn't leave me alone. I went out into the garden to get away from him and he followed me out there. He'd been drinking and wouldn't take no for an answer.'

Grace didn't know what to think. She would have sworn that Xander Croft was not that type of man, but how well did she really know him? Regan Bradley could have lied to Tobias to stir up trouble.

'Did you tell your husband at the time?' asked Grace.

'I didn't dare,' Sylvia admitted. 'They were already at loggerheads by then. I put it down to a drunken episode and tried to forget it. Xander was always jealous of Paul and wanted what he had. Maybe my rejection pushed him into action?'

It wouldn't exactly be the first crime of passion and there had been seething professional jealousy between the two men. Grace couldn't tell if it was her head or her heart holding out against believing it.

'At what point did you realise that Maria was carrying your husband's child?' she continued.

Sylvia's eyes widened in alarm.

'The police only told me about the baby being Paul's this morning. Okay, I admit that I had occasionally wondered if he was having an affair before his death. There'd been some signs. He often worked late, and I caught him in a few lies about where he'd been. But I didn't know the identity of the woman involved until this morning when the police told me they had matched his DNA to her baby.'

Grace watched her through narrowed eyes.

'So you're saying that you didn't know that the woman in the photos worked at the golf club?'

'That's exactly what I'm saying,' her client retorted, more confident now. 'I only started going to the club again recently. The newspaper said that she was a sports massage therapist. Well, I never went for a massage, so I never came across her. In real life she looked nothing like those photos in the safe. Much beefier.'

'So you *did* meet her?' said Grace.

'Stop twisting my words. I didn't meet her as such. I knew that she was the massage therapist. She came in to order something from the bar when I was in there and I asked someone what she did at the club. I certainly didn't put two and two together at that stage.'

'You were at the club the day she was murdered. Yet, strangely, the police don't have you on their witness list as being present?' Grace could see Sylvia waging war with herself by the contrasting expressions flicking across her face like a slideshow. *Probably trying to reconcile all her lies,* Grace thought, feeling a wave of fatigue. Finally, Sylvia came to a decision.

'Yes, I was there that morning but not for long. I would prefer you don't mention it to the police. I didn't see anything. There was no point in leaving my details. I slipped out the back way.'

Grace knew that she was pushing Sylvia to the extent she might get kicked off the case, but she decided to press on regardless.

'I was at the bar. I heard you having a go at Croft. Care to tell me what that was about?'

A flash of anger passed across Sylvia's face as she jumped to her feet. 'What is this, Grace? You're supposed to be working for *me,* not trying to fit me up for a crime I didn't commit.'

Grace remained seated, keeping her voice calm. 'You haven't been straight with me from the start. I've been told that you were seen in a passionate embrace with Xander

Croft prior to your husband coming off that roof. Were you also having an affair at that time?'

There was an awkward pause then Sylvia exhaled and sat back down. Again, a number of conflicting emotions tripped across her face in rapid succession: anger, confusion and then... relief?

Grace relaxed her jaw, suddenly aware she'd been grinding her teeth again.

'I admit that I may have kept some things from you, but I had my reasons. None of it is relevant to the case. I'm entitled to a personal life. I asked you to look into my husband's murder and that's all that matters to me. Everything else is surely irrelevant.'

'You're the one who has been pointing me in the direction of Xander Croft throughout this whole investigation,' said Grace. 'I need to know what that exchange in the bar was about and whether it impacts on this investigation.'

Sylvia remained silent.

Grace got up to leave. 'I'm sorry but this isn't going to work,' she said.

'Wait! I'll tell you.'

Grace turned round to face her once more.

'I wanted him to try and contact Paul for me... on the other side.'

'But you told me that you are psychic, too,' said Grace. 'Why would you need *him* to do it?'

'I thought that if Croft really had shoved him off the roof, Paul might come through and condemn him in front of me. I was going to record it.'

'You do know that wouldn't stand up in a court of law?' said Grace.

'I might have been able to trap Croft in an admission of guilt.'

'I see,' said Grace, though she didn't really. There were so many conflicting versions of events she was no longer sure what to believe.

Chapter Forty-Nine

Grace awoke with a start, drenched in sweat despite the chill in the room. She'd been dreaming about the baby again. She could still hear the frantic cries reverberating around her head as she tried to shake the feeling of helplessness and dread the dream had evoked. Sighing, she dragged herself out of bed. Throwing on her jeans and a fleece, she left the flat with Harvey and trudged down onto the sand with leaden feet. A storm had whipped up the tips of the waves into a creamy concoction and the rain battered against her face relentlessly as she bent her slight figure into it. Even watching Harvey frisk about the shore with his fur standing on end wasn't enough to lift her mood. It had been a week since the baby went missing. She was so small and fragile and there hadn't been a single credible sighting. She was worried about Brodie and how he would be coping. The police had been coming under heavy fire in the press for making no progress in either solving the murder or locating the baby. She had better check in with him today. He would be trying to present a strong front to his team, but he could let off steam to Grace. *He's got Julie for that*, a little voice niggled in her head. But it probably didn't help that her father was the super and his boss.

Grace had decided not to go for a swim today. It somehow felt like an indulgence rather than a penance at the moment, for reasons she didn't want to look at too closely. She had a formless feeling of dread that the next few days were going to be critical in the investigation and she could not afford to let her guard down for a single minute. Lives might depend upon it.

Back in the flat she gave Harvey a rigorous towel dry then heaped blankets on his bed to avoid it becoming soggy as he dried out. Shaking his food into the bowl and seeing his delight as he scarfed it down, she marvelled, not for the first time, about how dogs exist almost entirely in the moment. Her stupid brain, on the other hand, ricocheted from the past to the future and back again, rarely stopping in the present. Once he'd forensically examined his bowl for leftovers with both his nose and his tongue, she bent down to give him a hug, wincing at his meaty breath and damp coat fumes.

'Once this is all over, you and I are going for a holiday together to make happy memories again,' she promised him. Grace forced herself to eat a piece of toast with her coffee though it tasted like cardboard. Hurriedly, she got dressed, remembering to paper over the cracks with some makeup. She left Harvey nodding off in his basket and closed the door behind her. He'd sleep for a couple of hours and then she'd pop back up for him.

Entering the office, she was pleased to see the whole team assembled including Tobias. He immediately marched over and thrust a newspaper into her hands.

'Have you seen this?' he demanded, a nervous tic twitching at the side of his mouth.

'Good morning to you, too,' said Grace, scanning the front of the newspaper, her eyes widening as she took in the headline.

Local Psychic to Try and Connect with Missing Baby's Mother.

'Crikey,' she murmured, turning to Jean. 'Can you get a couple of tickets?'

'Already done.'

'I'm coming with you,' said Tobias, his face like granite. 'He's gone too far this time.'

'He'll be totally discredited,' said Grace. 'It's a crazy stunt. I don't know what's possessed him.'

'But what if he actually succeeds?' asked Hannah.

'No chance of that,' said Tobias. 'Unless he's got the baby stashed away somewhere. Nothing that man could do would surprise me.'

His words sowed a tiny seed of worry in Grace. How far would Croft go to put Merchiston College on the map and attract funding to enhance research and development? She was also concerned about his contact with her client. If what Sylvia had told her was true about his unwanted advances, then Grace had been completely deceived as to his nature. However, if it wasn't true that meant Sylvia had been blatantly lying and trying to misdirect the investigation.

A thought occurred to Grace. Clearly her client was seeing someone as evidenced by the toothbrush and slippers and that faint whiff of aftershave. Was there any chance that she might be colluding with Xander Croft? The thought was painful to her for all sorts of reasons, but she forced herself to examine it. Could they be trying to throw her off the scent by demonstrating such an obvious public antipathy towards each other?

'Grace?' Hannah's voice intruded on her reverie. She snapped her focus back to the room.

'What if Matt stole the baby? He and Maria were clearly involved as Regan saw them kissing. If he discovered that she was pregnant he might have panicked, thinking it was his, and killed Maria, hoping the baby would die with her.'

'That's definitely one possibility,' said Grace. 'He'd gambled everything on being a golf pro and thought he had a shot at making it big. The last thing he would want is being financially tied to a kid.'

'He might have paid someone to go back for the baby to finish the job,' said Jean with a shudder.

'I wouldn't put it past him,' said Tobias.

'I can't even imagine how evil you would have to be to murder a baby,' said Jean.

'Oh, Matt's evil all right,' said Hannah. 'Framing a dead woman for his crimes? Despicable.'

None of them could argue with that.

'We haven't considered another possibility,' said Grace. 'What about Regan Bradley? She's been intimately involved with Matt Turner and became aware that he'd been involved with Maria. What if she discovered that Maria was pregnant and thought that Matt was the father? Regan could have killed her in a jealous rage.'

'I'm not sure,' mused Hannah. 'When I was hiding in the room with them that time their relationship seemed more flirty than emotional. It sounded to me like she was only having a fling with him.'

'Maybe that was just the impression she was trying to give?' piped up Jean.

'She doesn't have children either,' said Grace. 'It's impossible to know if that was her choice or not. She's bold enough to pull off a stunt like taking the baby, although it's difficult to see her as the nurturing kind. As to whether she could murder someone? Put it this way, the shock wouldn't kill me.'

'If Regan Bradley took the baby, that wouldn't bode well,' stated Tobias. 'That woman is stone cold.'

'She seems to have a very intense relationship with Xander Croft as well.' Grace got up to pour herself more coffee.

'Yes,' said Tobias, 'I've noticed that. She stares at him as though she wants to devour him.'

'There's a peculiar dynamic to their relationship that I haven't been able to figure out yet,' Grace added.

'Anyway, don't you think you're all getting rather distracted from the main event?' Sloan frowned.

'What do you mean?' Grace questioned as she returned to her desk.

'Well, all this speculation about who murdered that woman at the club and/or stole her baby isn't getting you any further in relation to the case you were hired to solve.'

Grace's hackles went up at his tone, but he wasn't entirely wrong, she conceded.

'You have a point but it's still possible that the two murders are connected either directly or indirectly. I don't want to narrow our focus at this stage in case we overlook something crucial. Paul Gordon was having an affair with Maria Rossi and now Maria's baby is missing. It's not a huge leap to speculate that these events are connected,' said

Grace. Remembering that Brodie had asked her to keep it quiet, she refrained from mentioning that the baby was unquestionably Paul's.

'I still think you're overcomplicating things, but don't mind me. I've got to head off now to do some research. I'll see you at Xander Croft's pitiful charade?'

'Wouldn't miss it,' Grace said, though really she'd rather pull out her own fingernails than go to the wretched thing.

Chapter Fifty

Grace arrived early and secured seats right at the front of the impressive auditorium. A couple of minutes later, Brodie appeared and sat beside her.

'I'm really not comfortable with this,' hissed Brodie in Grace's ear.

'You and me both,' she whispered. 'However, you can't ignore anything that could lead to the baby's safe return.'

'As far as the press is concerned, I'm damned if I do and damned if I don't,' he said. 'There's no way Croft is going to find that baby. And have you considered the possibility that he may be involved in this somehow? Perpetrators can sometimes try to insert themselves into the investigation in some way—'

'Look, I'm aware, but that's not the case here,' snapped Grace, edging slightly away from him.

Looking round for Tobias Sloan, Grace saw him filing into the room. She waved to him to join them. The two men nodded brusquely to each other as he sat down. In just a few minutes, the auditorium was packed full. The sense of excitement was palpable. Grace felt disturbed and conflicted. She was usually a decisive person, but she still hadn't made up her mind about Xander Croft. Had he really tried to force himself on Sylvia or had they simply been caught out in a secret affair? Could he really be the heartless conman Tobias believed him to be? She was normally a good judge of character, but how much was she being propelled by her still unresolved grief towards someone who held out the enticing prospect of connecting her with her son? Having experienced an alleged message from Connor once, she could not help hoping for more. It had hit her nervous system like the high of a forbidden drug.

The voices swelled with excitement as the stage lit up and then died away as Xander Croft walked on, his hand raised in greeting.

'Thank you for coming,' he said, his voice rich and melodic. 'Today is not about me. It is about a vulnerable baby girl who has been ripped prematurely from the womb of her murdered mother and deprived of that most sacred bond, the love between a mother and child.'

Croft's eyes alighted on Grace and the warmth and compassion on his face were tangible. She felt her cheeks redden as she became aware that the men on either side of her were staring.

'Now I can't promise that I will be able to shed any light on what has tragically happened to the child, but I couldn't live with myself if I didn't at least try.'

'He's full of it,' grumbled Tobias beside her. She could feel the heat of anger coming off him and hoped he would be able to contain it until Croft was done.

'I've been given these items by the police for the purpose of this demonstration and will use them to help me establish a link to the spirit world.' Grace glanced at Brodie. She hoped this was worth it, as the press were no doubt waiting in the wings, ready to crush him if it wasn't.

Croft opened a clear plastic bag and removed an item which made the audience gasp. It was the maroon uniform tunic that Maria had worn in her role at the golf club. Sitting right at the front, Grace could see the darker bloodstains. The other items he took from a different bag were a blanket and a small white rabbit.

The mood had become sombre and a few of the women in the audience were quietly weeping now. Grace shivered, startled at the sudden chill that had crept into the room. The lights dimmed once more. There were a few nervous coughs. Croft sat in a wingback chair beside a small occasional table on which he placed the items. As he picked them up and handled them one by one, he seemed to shrink into himself, his eyes imperceptibly sinking into their sockets.

He sat like that for what felt like an eternity. The audience gradually became more restless, shifting in their seats. Grace stiffened, both fascinated and repelled. The light over the stage became silvery, almost ethereal.

Suddenly, Croft let out a visceral howl that made Grace's hair stand on end. Reflexively, she grabbed for Brodie's hand in the dark.

'I can't listen to this bullshit anymore,' said Tobias, getting up and swiftly walking out. Grace barely noticed him go. All her attention was focused on Xander Croft. A woman a few rows back slumped to the floor with a small moan and was helped out by a couple of young women.

'Find my baby!' shrieked Croft, his voice high-pitched and shrill.

'What can you tell us?' he whispered next, as though forcing the words out.

'I see a grandfather clock. The baby's growing weaker. She's hidden in a drawer.'

'Who killed you, Maria?' said Croft, his lips loose and floppy as though he was struggling to articulate the words.

'My husband.' He quivered. 'Hurry! Find her... before it's too late...'

Croft slumped forward in his chair. A man and a woman wearing Merchiston College T-shirts and carrying first aid packs rushed over to him and he was revived. They helped him to sit up and sip some water. His body was trembling uncontrollably, and his eyes were dark pools of suffering, a world away from the confident man who had strode onto the stage earlier.

Brodie jumped up and moved to the stage with another officer who Grace vaguely knew. They recovered the items and resealed them in evidence bags, countersigning the labels.

Regan Bradley walked onto the stage as the lights went back on at full strength.

'Thank you for coming, ladies and gentlemen. If you could all file out calmly, as directed by our members of staff.'

All the pent-up emotion in the room exploded then into a high-volume clamour of voices that finally receded as the space emptied.

'You need to leave, too,' said Brodie in Grace's ear, his face set in uncompromising lines.

'Please,' said Croft. 'Let her stay. There's no need to fuss. I'll be fine in a while.'

Brodie crouched down beside Croft, his expression carefully neutral. The other detective stood to the side.

'I need to question you in relation to what just happened,' he said.

'Of course,' said Croft, still an alarming shade of grey. 'Can we do it in my office?'

Brodie turned to Grace. 'I'm sorry, I'm afraid you'll need to leave.'

'No! I want her to stay,' Croft said, struggling to his feet.

'But I can stay,' piped up Regan.

'Thank you, but I need you to deal with the press, Regan,' he said, pressing her arm. 'I know that you have my back.'

With a poisonous glare at Grace, Regan stormed off with a brittle smile and a nod to Croft.

Brodie threw her an exasperated look, but capitulated.

After they had all moved to Croft's office, and Brodie's officer opened his hand-held device to type in what was being said, the questions began. Grace sat motionless to one side, not wishing to be a distraction though she would have killed to be the one asking the questions. Looking at both men she had rarely felt so conflicted.

After attending to the formalities, Brodie got down to business.

'Can you describe to us your experience of what happened today on stage?' he said.

'When I handled the maroon item of clothing, a spirit claiming to be the dead woman, Maria Rossi, made contact.'

'Did she give any indication of how she died?'

'She was hit on the back of the head, she doesn't know what by. It was her husband who killed her. She doesn't care about that. All she wants is for her baby to be saved.'

'You got the feeling the baby is still alive?'

'I'm sure of it,' Croft stated. 'She showed me an image. The baby is lying in the bottom drawer of a chest of drawers. She's weak but she's alive.'

'What else did you see? Any detail at all would be helpful.'

'The room was quite dark. The curtains were drawn. I heard a train go by. It sounded like an intercity one, really fast. There's one other thing. She showed me a photograph of a wedding. A date flashed up. It was 7th October 2011. You have to hurry! The baby's life is in danger.'

Brodie glanced across at Grace. His frustrated expression mirrored her own. It wasn't a lot to go on, even assuming it wasn't a complete fabrication.

'Thank you for your time, sir,' said Brodie. 'Please get in touch if anything further comes to mind.'

'There's one more thing. She told me the baby's name is Isabella.'

Grace squeezed Croft's shoulder. 'I'll be back,' she said, as she followed Brodie and the other detective out of the room. Brodie nodded to his colleague to go on and took Grace to one side.

'To find the baby, we need to ascertain Maria's true identity. She was obviously on the run from something.'

'Or someone,' said Grace. 'The wedding date – it was most likely an abusive husband who tracked her down. Why else would she have shown it to Croft?'

'If she even did,' said Brodie, running his hands through his hair. 'I'm worried about sending the investigation off at a tangent on the say-so of some psychic. Can you imagine what the press will do to me if it's all complete and utter bollocks?'

'You have to cover all bases anyway,' said Grace. 'If it were me, I would circulate Maria's photo on social media and the press as widely as possible asking for anyone who recognises her to phone the hotline. Once we know her true identity, we'll be able to identify her husband. I take it you ran her DNA through the national database?'

'Of course, but she's not on the system. All that matters to me right now is getting this baby back alive. If you hear anything at all—'

'You'll be the first to know,' Grace said.

Suddenly, an idea popped into Grace's head. She still had a key to Maria's flat. If she took Croft there, he might be able to forge a stronger link to her? Grace was grasping at straws, and she knew it. Her heart desperately wanted him to be for real, but her head still whispered that he might be playing them all. She desperately wanted her heart to be right.

Chapter Fifty-One

Hannah was beside herself with worry about the baby. She had barely slept and felt heartsore at all that had happened. Why hadn't she realised that Maria was in trouble? Maybe if she'd been friendlier and not so caught up in her own stuff, she could have made a difference, maybe even saved her? She owed it to Maria to bring her killer to justice and find her baby, but Grace had warned her off the golf club. She was treating her like some stupid kid instead of an employee. Hannah was determined to show her worth and prove her boss wrong.

'Hannah, for goodness' sake, can you stop pacing? It's driving me crazy,' said Jean.

'Pardon me for breathing,' said Hannah under her breath, but loud enough to hear.

'I beg your pardon?' said Jean. They paused and glared at each other.

Hannah sighed and sat down behind her desk. 'Sorry,' she said. 'I know I'm being a pain.'

'I shouldn't have snapped. I'm as wound up as you are.'

'It's so frustrating sitting here doing nothing. We need to find the baby. Grace is off at some psychic thing and we're twiddling our thumbs. We need to do something. Anything!' she burst out.

Jean sat back in her chair and thought for a moment. 'How were things left at the golf club?' she asked.

'Brian said I was a good worker and they'd be happy to hire me from time to time on a casual basis, cash in hand. The trouble is that Matt now knows I work for Grace. He might have told other people there.'

'I doubt that,' said Jean. 'He's been banned from the club pending the outcome of criminal charges. I reckon if you show up there and say that Brian asked you to work for a few hours, no one would bat an eyelid. It'll take you out of yourself and you might dig up something useful.'

'Don't you need my help with anything?'

'No, that's me all caught up for now,' said Jean, looking worried rather than pleased. Hannah had come to realise that since the investigation had started Grace had stopped doing the legwork to get new clients. If they didn't solve this case, then the future was looking bleak for them all.

When Hannah had first met Grace, she had felt a bit intimidated by her. Lately, she worried that Grace might be crumbling beneath her capable exterior. She had been shocked to the core when she realised that Grace had recreated Connor's old bedroom in her new flat. That wasn't the action of someone who was moving on in their life, was it? Hannah was no stranger to the concept of adults not keeping their shit together. If only she could discover something that would enable Grace to wrap this case up pronto so that life could go back to normal. She would never complain about stuff being boring ever again.

Hannah grabbed her jacket and waved to Jean who was

now busy using the phone. Walking along Portobello High Street she wondered where best she should concentrate her efforts to try and achieve the elusive breakthrough. She could go to the golf club as Jean had suggested, but she was doubtful that would yield anything new. It would be too suspicious if she wandered round the college, as Xander Croft and Regan Bradley would recognize her from the golf club. Anyway, Grace had that covered. Hannah sighed, then brightened. She had it. Impulsively, she jumped onto a bus. Pulling out her small notebook from her bag, she flicked through the pages where she had made notes on some of the cases. She was sure she had Sylvia's address in here. Finding it and sticking it in a travel app, she was pleased to see this bus would take her fairly close. Grace had seemed increasingly worried that their client Sylvia might not be on the level. After all, financially, she stood to benefit more than anyone from Paul's death, and she was hardly acting the part of the grief-stricken widow. Megan had even seen her and Croft in a clinch, though it was probably a tit-for-tat thing when she'd learned of her husband's affair. But what if she'd bumped into Maria at the club and then confronted her? If Maria had told Sylvia that Paul was the father of the baby, then any woman would have completely lost her mind. Sylvia had no children. What if she'd wanted them? She probably figured Maria and Paul owed her that. If Sylvia had abducted the baby, then she would take good care of her, wouldn't she? But what if she hated the baby and wanted to snuff out her tiny flicker of life? Hannah shivered, pulling her coat tight around her.

Sylvia's detached house had a small front garden with a larger one behind and was set within a cul-de-sac. Fortunately, the light was on in the living room. As Hannah approached, she stopped to ostensibly fiddle with her phone and turned her head slightly so she could see inside. Sylvia clearly had a visitor and was laughing and animated. Hannah ducked down behind the hedge as Sylvia came over to the window and drew the curtains. The material was thin so with the benefit of the lamp inside Hannah was able to see a tall figure detach from the shadows and their silhouettes became entwined. *If only I could see who it is*, she fretted.

Hannah slipped into the garden unobserved and crept round the building, but the rest of the house was in darkness. Perhaps Sylvia's visitor was staying the night? Part of Hannah was so desperate to know that she felt like ringing the doorbell on a made-up pretext, but she couldn't risk doing that without knowing the man's identity. Suddenly, she froze to the side of the house as she heard the front door open. Light spilled out onto the path where she had been only moments earlier. She heard the sound of low, husky voices and a couple of quiet groans which made her scrunch up her nose and roll her eyes. The door closed once more, and she heard the sound of footsteps hurrying away. Hannah didn't dare race down the path in case Sylvia was watching from the window so forced herself to wait. She was messing this up big time. Somehow, she had to get this information and redeem herself.

Hearing water flow down the drain, she guessed that Sylvia was taking a shower. It was too late to try and follow the man. Hannah glanced at her watch to check the time. It had gone four. She then looked at it again, considering. The watch was the only nice thing that she owned – her ex-boyfriend had saved up for months to get it from a pawn shop for her birthday. She couldn't bear to lose it. A picture of the baby, tiny and vulnerable, came into her mind unbidden. It would be worth it if she uncovered anything that helped the tiny thing.

The sound of running water stopped and Hannah waited a few minutes before ringing the doorbell.

After what seemed an age, the door was flung open, and Sylvia Gordon stood there. Her hair was still wet from the shower, but she was immaculately dressed in a wrap-over dress.

Hannah smiled at her. 'Mrs Gordon? I work over at the golf club.'

'Oh yes, I remember you now,' Sylvia said, the confusion clearing from her face. 'But what are you doing here?'

'The manager knew I lived near you, so he asked me to pop by on my way home. A watch has been handed in and someone thought it might belong to you?'

'I doubt it.'

'Well... the light out here isn't all that great,' said Hannah. 'May I come in to show it to you properly?'

Hannah was shown into the living room and invited to take a seat. Removing the watch from her pocket, she held it out to Sylvia on the flat of her palm. She'd hoped Sylvia would disown it straight away, but seeing the woman's face light up as she picked it off Hannah's palm made her heart sink.

'Yes, it's mine,' Sylvia said with a wide smile as she undid the catch and slid it onto her wrist. 'Thank you for bringing it over to me. I hadn't even noticed it was missing.'

Hannah strove to master her temper, but really felt like smacking Sylvia in the face. Looking around Sylvia's detached home filled with beautiful things, she couldn't help but contrast it with her own family's mean and scratched-out existence on the fringes of society. *At least I'm bloody well honest*, she thought, though it was small consolation for losing the one treasure that she held dear.

'Hannah? Are you alright, dear?' Hannah slumped back in the chair.

'I'm so sorry,' she whispered. 'I feel a bit faint. Could I possibly have a cup of sweet tea before I go? It was so busy today I didn't have time to grab any lunch.'

Sylvia tutted in annoyance. She glanced at the new watch on her wrist and then suddenly brightened up.

'You rest there and I'll make us some tea,' she said before disappearing into the kitchen.

Hannah immediately sat up again and started investigating the space around her for clues. Her heart nearly stopped as she spotted a drinks tray on the sideboard. One glass had lipstick round the rim and the other had a small amount of drink in the bottom so had clearly been used by Sylvia's mystery guest. She also noticed an ashtray with two cigarette butts in it.

Jumping to her feet, she ran lightly across the room and placed each butt in one of the evidence bags Grace made them carry, then carefully pushed it into the bottom of her large bag. Flying back to her armchair she hurriedly slumped back down.

At that point the door to the kitchen opened and Sylvia walked through with a tray of tea.

'You're very flushed. I hope you're not coming down with something.'

Hannah sipped at her tea: she was so tense it was hard to swallow. 'I'm a bit rundown,' she said. 'It's been so stressful at work recently, what with the thefts and Maria's murder.'

'Yes, of course. Such a terrible thing to happen! That poor woman.' She looked away, but not before Hannah had caught sight of a gleam of triumph in her eyes.

'Maria was such a lovely person,' said Hannah, deliberately winding Sylvia up. 'She was so pretty, and everybody loved her. She'd have been an amazing mother. It's so cruel what happened to her and now her poor baby is missing.' Hannah surprised herself by breaking down in tears.

'Yes, very sad,' said Sylvia, her face closed off now.

'Did you know her from the club?' asked Hannah.

'No, I'm afraid not. Our paths never crossed.' She started to fidget with an earring and Hannah took this as her cue to leave. She'd pushed her luck far enough for one night.

'I'm so glad you got your watch back,' Hannah said, smiling sweetly. 'Thank you for the tea.'

'So am I,' Sylvia said, admiring it in the light thrown down from the glass chandelier in the hall as she closed the front door.

As Hannah turned the corner, her face tightened into a mask of fury. Sylvia Gordon was completely without conscience and Hannah was going to expose her for being a thief and a cheat if it was the last thing she did. Even if it meant losing her job.

Chapter Fifty-Two

Grace left with Croft through an inconspicuous side door. Fortunately, the bulk of the reporters had grouped around the front entrance. She could see the waving placards of Beverley's protest group to one side. Installing Xander Croft in the back seat of her car, she instructed him to lie down and cover himself with a travel rug. The last thing she wanted was the media to tail her to Maria's flat. Grace pulled the car out undetected, and within a few minutes arrived in the quiet residential street where Maria Rossi had managed to blend in, to the point of invisibility.

Parking in the communal car park to the rear, Grace opened the car door and took the blanket off Croft. She noticed it was smeared with a white oily residue. Had he been wearing makeup onstage? Had this simply been a theatrical performance to him? The two of them approached the property on foot. She handed Croft plastic gloves and coveralls for his feet and warned him not to touch anything without her say so. He hadn't wanted to come with her, and she felt a bit guilty for pressuring him. Anyway, he was here now. It wouldn't take long.

The air inside the flat felt stale and somehow oppressive as though it hadn't moved since her last visit. They walked through the eerily empty rooms in silence.

'He's not who he seems,' murmured Croft.

'What do you mean?' Grace asked but he held up his hand to silence her.

'She's with a young girl, aged about ten. She's showing me the wedding picture again. It's clearer here. Wait... no, that can't be right.'

'What? Tell me!' Grace snapped, frustrated that she wasn't privy to this one-way conversation.

Croft rounded on her, his eyes opening wide in fury. 'Look, Grace, I'm not a performing pony and your negative energy really isn't helping. I've had enough. The connection has broken. I need to go home and rest.'

Grace felt contrite. He was only here because she had asked him to come. 'I'm sorry. I'm terrified that if we don't find the baby quickly it's going to be too late.'

Croft sat down on an upright chair. 'I'm willing to try again, but I need you to stay completely quiet and let me do it my way,' he said.

Grace nodded in agreement. She left the room and came back with the photo and the candle from Maria's bedroom.

'These might help,' she said, lighting the candle and leaving him to it as she withdrew into the bedroom again. Sitting on the edge of the bed she explored the room with her eyes hungrily. Surely, Maria must have unintentionally left them some breadcrumbs for her to find?

Her eyes were drawn to the wardrobe. All those dry-cleaned clothes. What if she'd slid something into one of them? She'd checked the pockets, of course, but she hadn't examined them beyond that. Feeling a bubble of hope, Grace sent up a silent prayer as she opened the wardrobe door.

Her first thought was for the navy cashmere coat. Carefully she ran her gloved hands over the lining but drew a blank. She carried the other items one by one over to the bed and probed every inch of them. The last garment she removed was the flimsiest and she nearly didn't bother examining it – a sequin-covered dress seemed an unlikely hiding place. However, there was nothing else for her to do until Croft was finished so she set to with a sigh.

To her surprise she heard the faintest crackle of paper. She held it up to the light, expecting to see the paper shining through but it was uniformly dark. There was no hidden pocket, so she had no alternative but to unpick a seam with the small pen knife she carried in her bag.

Grace inserted her long, slender fingers and pulled out two folded pieces of paper. Opening them with trembling hands she realised that she had found Maria's birth and marriage certificates. Photographing them quickly, she put them back where she had found them. She would have to confess to Brodie that she'd been back snooping around.

A loud crash from next door startled her. Rushing through she found Croft sitting beside a smashed vase. His head was bleeding. He was shaking uncontrollably, and his eyes were wide with terror.

'What happened?' she demanded.

'The vase was on that table over there,' he stuttered. 'Then it flew through the air and hit me.'

Grace felt icy fingers dance up her spine. It was getting dark now and the gloom added to the eerie atmosphere.

Grace helped Croft to his feet and dabbed at his bleeding head with some tissues. Fortunately, he hadn't bled onto the floor. She gathered up the pieces of the vase and hoped the police wouldn't notice it was missing before she managed to get it fixed and return it. Hurriedly, they left the house before someone came to investigate the noise.

Grace felt spooked. Had something supernatural occurred back there? To even entertain such a notion flew against everything she believed, but how else could she account for what had happened? Could Croft have made the whole thing up? She supposed that theoretically he could have smashed the vase into his head then flung it down. Was he playing her for a fool?

Grace pulled up outside Croft's cottage on the outskirts of the coastal village of Aberlady in East Lothian. He'd declined to go to the hospital to have his head wound checked out.

'Will you come in?' he asked, not looking at her.

She hesitated.

'Please, I don't want to be alone right now.' The intense look Croft turned upon her made her shiver for all sorts of reasons. She supposed she couldn't blame him in the circumstances, and he'd only been hurt because she had dragged him there.

'Sure,' she said with a small smile. The cottage was whitewashed and set back from the road. She could smell the sea as the incoming tide sucked against the mud. The lonely cry of an oystercatcher pierced the air. Feeling the tension ebbing from her, she followed him up the path through the pretty garden.

Once inside, Grace looked round appreciatively at the cream walls, overflowing bookcases and comfortable leather sofas.

'Right, let's get a proper look at that head wound and get

it dressed.' They moved into the kitchen where she positioned him on an upright chair under a spotlight. 'First aid kit?' she asked.

'Kitchen drawer,' Croft said, pointing across the pine table. 'Anything else will be in the bathroom cabinet.'

Moments later, she had gathered all she needed. As she had thought, it was only a flesh wound which she hoped would knit sufficiently without the need for stitches. Grace was moved to see that he was still trembling. Surely no one was that good an actor? As she dabbed gently at his head, she admitted to herself that her interest in him far exceeded the professional. Croft stood for things she had never believed in, things she had never been able to accept. Yet, during this investigation she had felt her feet slide over the lines she had drawn in the sand as though tugged over them by tension from an unseen rope.

Once she'd installed him in an armchair in front of a lit fire with a generous measure of brandy, Grace slipped out to call Brodie.

'Hey, don't be mad but I went back to Maria's flat.'

'Grace, are you out of your bloody mind?'

She flinched. Brodie almost never swore so she knew he was raging.

'Do you want to know what I found or not?'

There was a pause during which she heard a deep sigh. 'Go on,' he said.

'I found Maria Rossi's birth and wedding certificates sewn into the lining of a dress – a cock-up by those searching the house. I'm sending the photos to you right now. They reveal her original name and also the name of her husband who I'm guessing you'll want to trace as a person of interest.'

'Thanks, Grace, I can't believe my team missed that. This

information could make all the difference,' he said, sounding rejuvenated.

'Can you do me a favour?' she asked, heart beating a bit faster.

'Sure, name it,' Brodie said.

'Can you swing by my flat and pick up Harvey? He's not had his supper yet.'

There was a brittle silence. 'Wait... where are you? You're not still with *Xander Croft*, by any chance?'

Grace desperately wanted to lie, but she knew he would see right through her.

'Yes, but—' she began.

'Tell me you're not sleeping with him. I've seen the way he looks at you, but I thought you had more sense. Tobias Sloan was bad enough!'

'Who are you to tell me who I can or can't sleep with?' Grace snapped, outraged and not a little insulted.

'Grace, this guy could be involved in some serious shit in relation to one of these deaths.'

'Or he could be completely innocent,' she shot back. 'You should see him, Brodie, he's really shaken up after... this afternoon.' She closed her eyes. She'd nearly given them away. Brodie would have a fit if he knew she'd taken Croft to the flat for another reading. 'There's nothing going on between us.'

'But you'd like there to be,' said Brodie, his voice hollow.

'Look, can you take Harvey or not?'

'Fine, I'll go get him now.'

He ended the call.

Chapter Fifty-Three

Jean sat nursing her drink, feeling sick with worry. Looking around her as the light from the log fire danced over the fanatical faces gathered there, she wondered how she was going to extricate herself from this situation. Somehow the group had accelerated from placard-waving eccentrics to contemplating real-life bodily harm. They'd been waiting for her as she turned the corner into her street after work, the implications of which made her feel ill. How had they known where she lived? Did they also know where she worked? If so, that didn't exactly bode well. They'd said they needed her help with an urgent situation. Her priority had been to get them away from her home, so she had allowed herself to be taken to Beverley's place again. What she hadn't expected, though, was that her phone would be taken from her the moment she walked inside. Leo had locked the door behind her and put the key in his pocket with a smirk. Beverley had greeted her warmly enough, though her eyes were glittering and she seemed a bit manic. Had she taken something? There was tinny rock music playing in the background. So far it was only the three of them.

'Can I use your bathroom?' Jean asked, getting unsteadily to her feet.

'Sorry,' replied Beverley. 'I'm afraid it's out of order. Why don't you relax and enjoy your drink?'

Jean took a few nervous gulps. It wasn't the type of gin she usually drank, and she had to resist the urge to screw up her face. Best not to antagonise them.

'Are you expecting more people?' Jean asked, hoping against hope that this was simply another party. She could make a run for it the next time they opened the door. The knowing looks she intercepted between Leo and Beverley told her that she had been rumbled. They must have found out that she had been trying to spy on them. That's why they hadn't left her alone for a minute, even to go to the toilet, so she'd have no chance to contact Grace.

Drinking deeply from her glass, Jean tried to work out how she was going to extract herself from this mess. Who was she kidding? There was no way she was getting out of here unless they decided to let her go. Never again would she moan about her boring life. That's if she made it out of here alive, she thought, gulping once more at her drink. The gin was relaxing her. And something else... it was making her... sleepy, she realised with horror. All of a sudden, her tongue felt too big for her mouth and her head felt too heavy for her shoulders.

'Have you drugged me?' Struggling to get to her feet, Jean collapsed back into the chair to mocking glances from the two of them.

Beverley came and loomed over her. '*You're* the serpent in our midst,' she hissed.

'No, I'm not!' Jean protested, struggling to sit up. If only the room would stop spinning. 'I'm just like you. Why are you doing this? I'm on your side,' she said, aware of how unconvincing she sounded.

'You've been sent to infiltrate our ranks. Another devil's whore.'

'Now, hold on a minute,' said Jean, bristling despite her predicament. 'I am no such thing. I demand that you let me go.'

'You're not in a position to demand anything,' sneered Leo.

'But you are going to play your part,' said Beverley, her eyes glittering with malice.

'What do you mean?' asked Jean.

'You'll see. It's all part of the plan.' Beverley turned away from her.

'I'll take her phone out and dump it somewhere,' said Leo. 'Don't want someone tracking her here.'

Jean stifled a groan. Her last hope had been that Grace would miss her and track her down via the app she'd made them all install.

What on earth were they planning? She guessed it was something to do with the college, but if they were prepared to abduct and drug her to get it, they were obviously aiming for something big.

Jean had a feeling that her life was trickling away from her when it had never felt so sweet.

Chapter Fifty-Four

Grace woke up and felt momentarily confused by her surroundings, before remembering she'd stayed over at Xander Croft's house. She'd slipped through to check on him a few times in the night, but he'd seemed to suffer no lasting repercussions from whatever the hell had happened to him yesterday. Her mind was still reluctant to grapple with it. Looking round the pretty spare room she turned her face towards the warmth of the sun streaming through the delicate white curtains. Glancing at her phone she groaned. It was already past nine. As if he'd read her mind there was a light tap at the door. Grace checked she was decent and pulled the duvet up under her chin.

'Come in,' she called.

Croft was fully dressed and had clearly been out to the local shop for fresh croissants and orange juice. There was also a steaming cafetière on the tray.

'You're spoiling me.' She smiled, feeling a bit awkward but pleased to see him nonetheless.

'Somebody should,' he said, patting her hand.

'Have you had any more thoughts about... the baby?' she asked.

'Nothing. Her poor mother is frantic in the spirit world. I'll try again later, when I'm alone.'

'Why did you do it the way you did? You know, in front of a large crowd?'

'Not because I wanted the publicity, if that's what you're inferring. I hoped that the energy of the crowd might strengthen the link.'

'Wasn't that a bit risky? I mean, presumably the reading could have been hijacked by any number of spirits desperate to reach out, if you...'

'Believe in that sort of thing?'

Grace looked away. Was this always going to come between them?

'I figured that no spirit would have the power of Maria's desperation. I only wish that she could have given us more about the baby's location. It's not a lot to go on.'

'The police have got a bit more now,' she said.

'Oh?'

'Yes,' she replied, not giving anything away. Grace might be drawn to him, but she wasn't a fool.

'Right, well... I'm off to the college. Pull the door closed behind you when you leave.'

He left and let her get on with her breakfast, which she devoured hungrily.

As soon as she was finished, she picked up her phone and called Jean to let her know she was going to be in later than normal. It went straight to voicemail. That was strange. Jean was always first in.

She tried Hannah.

'Hi Hannah, are you at the office? I've been trying to reach Jean.'

A baby started yelling in the background. Hannah sounded harassed.

'Sorry, Grace, I'm not in yet. My mum needed me to watch the kids for a bit. I'll be there in an hour, I promise.'

Grace told her to take her time through gritted teeth. She was annoyed that no one was in the office, but she had to be fair and Hannah had been working far too much of late.

Finally, she phoned Brodie.

'Where are you?' he asked. 'I tried to get you at the office, but no one is answering.' There was an awkward pause. Grace bit her lip. 'You're still there?' he said.

'Have you confirmed Maria's real identity?' Grace asked, sidestepping the question.

'Yes, her name is Gina Pagani. She's from London. Her husband's name is Felix Brannah. The certificates were authentic.'

'Have you managed to locate him?'

'No, he's not been seen in London since they broke up three years ago. Apparently, they're known to police and social services for suspected domestic abuse, but they could never pin anything on him because she wouldn't give a statement or cooperate with an investigation. She was hospitalised a few times over the course of the marriage.'

'Have you traced her next of kin?'

'She grew up in care. We haven't managed to find any relatives.'

'Okay, I'm heading into the office now. Keep me in the loop.' Grace terminated the connection.

She tried Jean again. Still no reply. Grace squashed down a small niggle of worry. She was probably out on an errand. It was time she devised a better procedure for her staff to keep in touch. It hadn't been necessary before now because Jean was always there, keeping things running like clockwork. In fact, maybe Grace had been taking her for granted. Perhaps that was what this was all about? Maybe Jean was fed up and looking for another job? She hoped not.

Her head started to throb, and she went in search of painkillers. She was aware of the trust that Xander Croft had placed in her by allowing her the freedom of his house when he wasn't there, but the investigator in her won over when she came across the open door to his study. Grace moved to enter, then worried that he would have a similar set up to Paul Gordon. Video footage would lead to a conversation she wouldn't relish. No matter how she sugar-coated it, she knew that what she was doing was a massive breach of trust.

Standing on the threshold, her eyes probed minutely for a camera but didn't find one. She drifted by the handsome walnut desk first. There was nothing of interest on top and she winced at the thought of having to open its drawers. All of them slid open bar one, which was locked. Grace quickly rifled through them, trying to disturb the contents as little as possible. It was mainly admin relating to the college. She knew she had to get into that locked drawer. Why would he lock a drawer inside his own home unless he had something to hide? She would never have another opportunity like this – to uncover the truth about him once and for all.

After a few frantic minutes she finally found the key in his cigar box. With shaking hands, she inserted it. The lock turned.

Pulling out the drawer, Grace realised that she had crossed a line there was no stepping back from. The first folder that she opened contained correspondence from a number of Edinburgh law firms acting on behalf of casinos which had taken steps to legally demand repayment, ban him from entering their premises and cut off his line of credit. Grace whistled when she saw the eye-watering sums involved. It looked like Xander had been robbing Peter to pay Paul to buy himself some time, but the whole house of cards was clearly on the verge of collapsing. It would also appear that since Paul Gordon had died Xander Croft had re-mortgaged the college building to the hilt. His finances were a complete car crash. Grace sat back on her heels as she thought about how this made him a desperate man. How far might Croft have gone to protect his secret and save himself from the circling wolves? She took photos of the most important items with her phone and then tried to close the drawer, but it was sticking on something. She pulled on it, but it was stuck fast. She couldn't leave it like that for Xander to find. Running through to the kitchen, she found a small vegetable knife and also retrieved her flashlight from her bag. Down on the floor she shone the light at the back of the drawer and found a sheaf of papers held together by a clip all scrunched up into the slider. Carefully, she inserted the knife and, wiggling it around, she managed to pry them free.

Her heart sank as she realised the papers were all about her. There were photocopies of news articles about her son's death and also her unfair dismissal case against the police. There was even a photograph of her agency. The thing Grace found most disturbing of all was the information pertaining to Connor. Croft had clippings from school shows, a swimming gala, even a copy of his death notice and headstone. She felt a rush of anger. She wished she'd thrown that vase herself. It was as Sloan had said – the man was a con artist and boy, had he done a good job of reeling her in. She took the items with her and vowed that Xander Croft had pulled the wool over her eyes for the very last time.

Chapter Fifty-Five

Grace burst through the agency door in a flurry of wind and sand then stopped dead when she saw only Hannah in reception. It was now gone eleven. Harvey had already been returned by Brodie and gave her a rapturous greeting.

'Where's Jean?'

'I don't know,' said Hannah. 'I've been in since before ten. I assumed she'd been in touch with you.'

'No, she hasn't and it's not like her,' said Grace, properly worried now.

She took out her phone and located Jean on the tracker. Frowning, she turned to Hannah and showed her the apparent location. It was static but appeared to be in a street rather than inside a building.

'Jean's the most organised, sensible person I know,' Hannah said. 'She's not going to take off somewhere without telling us on a workday. Something must be seriously up.'

Grace made a decision. 'Right, I'm going to look for her. Hannah, I need you to stay here in case she calls in.'

'Shouldn't you call Brodie?'

'I'm perfectly capable of conducting a search on my own!' Hannah looked crestfallen. 'Sorry, I shouldn't have snapped. He's got nothing to do with missing persons and she hasn't been missing long enough anyway.'

'Before you go, there's something else...' said Hannah, looking guilty. She caught Grace up on her antics from the previous night.

Grace was furious.

'Hannah, that was incredibly irresponsible of you. This isn't a game! People can and do get hurt during investigations. What if Sylvia's visitor had come back and recognised you from the office? What if Sylvia herself had remembered you from her one visit to the agency? As it is, you put yourself in harm's way for nothing.'

Hannah's face reddened and she was clearly trying not to cry. 'I proved that our client is dishonest and a liar,' she said. 'She's also got another man on the go that she's being all secretive about. What if it was her who killed Paul Gordon and now she's stolen his baby?'

Grace softened. It was partly her fault for not having updated her colleagues on her earlier visit to Sylvia's. She needed to keep her team better informed on the twists and turns of the investigation. Hannah's resolve and determination was admirable, and it wasn't as if the very same thought hadn't occurred to Grace. Still, it was one thing being an opportunist and nabbing a free watch, but it was quite another matter to murder someone under the guise of suicide then try to claim the insurance money by having it declared a murder.

'I think that highly unlikely, but we can't rule it out,' Grace said. 'This is the second time you've gone *off piste*, Hannah. This isn't an episode of *Nancy Drew*. I need to be able to trust you and you need to keep me in the loop at all times. If anything had happened to you...'

Hannah looked wretched. 'I'm really sorry, Grace. I won't do it again. I got to thinking about the baby... and I had to *do* something.'

'I know this must be difficult for you with your mum having a baby at home,' said Grace.

'Oh, I did manage to get hold of these.' Hannah pulled the cigarette butts out from a drawer in her desk. 'I thought maybe Brodie could use them to find out who the mystery man is?'

Grace looked at her aghast. 'Hannah, that is theft,' she said. 'And from our own client, no less.'

'Well, she stole my watch,' Hannah grumbled.

Two wrongs don't make a right, Grace was about to say but stopped abruptly. God, she was morphing into her mother.

'Brodie is in the police, so he has to abide by the rules or he'll lose his job. Also, any evidence gained unlawfully would be inadmissible in court.'

Hannah dropped her eyes.

'We'll talk more about this later but for now finding Jean is my priority.' Grace reached for Jean's diary, which showed no scheduled appointments for the day. A quick search of her desk threw up no clues to her whereabouts in terms of random jottings. She looked at her phone again. The location was still static. Her gut was telling her something was badly wrong.

Grace headed towards the college and dumped the car in the car park; the phone's location was only a few streets away.

Grace noticed as she got out that the usual protestors weren't there. She dug out her phone and jogged until she was as close as she could get to the signal. She stopped, breathing heavily, and looked around her. She was in an alley running behind a small strip of shops and restaurants. The signal blinked opaquely. She dialled the number, thankful that she'd had the foresight to make them all choose a very individual ring tone so that she would know immediately who was calling or texting. She could hear a sound from behind her. It sounded like a refrain from the hymn 'Morning has Broken' which was a very Jean sort of song. Grace hoped that the phone would have enough charge to continue to guide her as she inched closer, calling it repeatedly and examining everything between her and the sound. Finally, she stood in front of a skip.

'Of course you're in there,' she sighed. She couldn't immediately see it. Grace heaved herself over the edge and landed on something squishy that made her feel sick to the stomach. Strange fetid smells wafted up her nose and stuffed her throat as she pulled on some gloves and started turning over the rotting contents, home now to some rather unlovely life forms. Finally, the phone appeared. She took out an evidence bag and carefully placed it in there, turning it off to conserve the battery.

Pulling herself back out of the skip and jumping down to the ground, Grace now knew beyond a shadow of a doubt that something bad had befallen Jean. Whipping out her phone she called the office and got Hannah to check the file for Beverley's address. It wasn't far from here. It probably wasn't a coincidence that nobody had showed up for the demo today.

Grace then phoned Brodie. It went straight to voicemail. She swore in frustration. He could be ducking her call but most likely he was slammed chasing down leads in the missing baby case.

Hannah was still a kid. There's no way Grace could risk something happening to her as well.

Suddenly, she had it. Tobias Sloan could provide some muscle as back-up. She looked up his contact details on her phone. He didn't live that far from here. She'd go round in person. That way he couldn't fob her off. Grace suspected he was getting ready to pack up and head back down south. Of course, Tobias still had to spring his trap for Xander Croft and judging by what she had found in Croft's desk drawer that morning he probably wholly deserved to be publicly humiliated. Her stomach still lurched with misery every time he came into her mind.

Grace saw on the entry phone panel that Tobias lived in a flat on the first floor. She rang the buzzer but there was no response. About to turn away, she noticed a young woman with a baby in a pram approaching.

'Here, let me help you with that,' she said as the woman began to struggle up the steps with the squalling infant.

'Thanks, sorry about the noise, he's hungry,' she said with a smile.

'I'm here visiting my brother, Tobias Sloan,' Grace said. 'Tweedy chap, lives on the first floor?'

'Yes.' She nodded. 'I don't really know him, keeps himself to himself.'

Grace slipped through the door with her, trying to keep the conversation going but almost drowned out by the indignant baby.

Swiftly she ran up the stairs. She paused outside the door to Tobias's flat and listened. Not a sound. She rang the bell.

It echoed loudly but she could hear nothing else. She lifted the letterbox and peered into the gloomy interior. Turning away, she was about to leave when she heard the loud chime of a grandfather clock coming from inside the flat. She froze. Hadn't Croft said that there was a clock where the baby was being held? She thought back to what she had uncovered in his desk. But Croft was a complete fraud, wasn't he? However, something about seeing the baby on the stairs and then hearing the clock made her pause. It was a crazy idea, but still, Grace couldn't ignore this strange hunch – she knew that no matter how unlikely it was that Sloan had abducted the baby and stashed her in his flat, she couldn't risk not checking it out. Grace was also conscious that Jean was most likely in real trouble. She had to find her, too – *this better be quick*. Groaning, she dropped to her knees to search for a spare key in the plant pot and under the rug. Nothing. Stretching, she felt along the top of the door, again drawing a blank. Where would such a wily operator hide a key? She looked across at the other flat on the landing. The letterbox was raised with some junk mail poking out. Lifting the flap, she saw that the carpet beyond was covered in it. The flat was unoccupied. Turning over the mat she found a key and ran to try it in Tobias's door. Grace hesitated as it turned in the lock – she wasn't a serving police officer anymore. Grace thought of the baby and turned the handle.

The rented flat had seen better days. Mildew scented the air and it had a fusty, unloved feeling. She walked past the grandfather clock and did a quick search. Opening the bathroom cabinet, she saw something which froze her blood. A bottle of baby Calpol. She sped into the bedrooms. The first was a spare and the bed looked unslept in. She pulled out all the drawers, but they were empty. Next, she headed into the main bedroom. Tobias's trademark tweed jacket was hanging up on a hook behind the door. The bottom drawer of the large mahogany chest of drawers was protruding slightly further than the rest. Heart thumping, she slid it open. It was empty but the sight that almost stopped her heart was a tiny white baby sock in one corner. She left it there. There was no way of knowing if it had been left behind by the previous occupant or had come from the missing baby. She closed the drawer to exactly where it had been and after checking the rest of the flat, she let herself back out, locking the door and returning the key exactly where she had found it.

Grace ran down the stairs and almost collided with Tobias coming in the front door. Schooling her expression into one of relief she greeted him with a smile.

'Thank goodness you're here, I thought I'd missed you!' she exclaimed.

'What are you doing here?' he asked, his face grey and strained.

'Jean has gone missing. I tracked her phone to near here then realised I needed help. I couldn't raise Brodie, so my next thought was to come and find you.'

His face relaxed slightly and he nodded.

'Let's go then, you can fill me in on the way,' Tobias said.

Grace told him what she knew about Jean's disappearance, which wasn't much. Her mind was spinning as they walked back to Beverley's house. Was she right about Tobias, or had this case finally driven her insane? And what on earth would Tobias want with a baby anyway? There was no way of knowing and all she could do was keep him distracted and prevent him escaping until such time as she'd managed to track down Brodie. First Xander, now Tobias... how could she have been so wrong?

Chapter Fifty-Six

Grace stood outside Beverley's mid-terraced house with Tobias. So far, she didn't think he suspected anything. How in hell's name was she going to get Brodie mobilised? Without police powers behind her she felt impotent. She couldn't just call the regular police line because she knew that without any compelling evidence, they wouldn't treat this as an urgent matter. Brodie still hadn't even read her last text.

'I still haven't been able to get hold of Brodie,' she said to Tobias. 'We'll have to manage without him. Time could be critical. For all we know these nut jobs might already have killed Jean.'

Grace ground her teeth. She felt unsettled by Tobias's presence, but regardless of what he may or may not have done she still had to ensure Jean's safety and it wouldn't hurt to have a bit more muscle in her corner if things went awry. She was fairly sure that he liked Jean and wouldn't want any harm to come to her.

'I'm going to text Brodie again,' she said. 'Even if he's up to his eyes in it he should be able to spare a couple of officers to help us.'

Hurriedly, she typed it right in front of him. She kept it brief and to the point, saying that they thought there was a possibility Jean had been abducted and needed urgent assistance. She included her location.

They skirted the perimeter of the property, but there were no signs of life and all the curtains remained shut. Grace tried desperately to focus on the task at hand, but her mind was still reeling from the glimpse of the little baby sock in his dresser drawer.

'What do you want to do if no one answers?' he asked.

'I'm going to force my way in by any means possible,' Grace replied. *Like I did to get into your flat earlier*, she thought, and felt an insane desire to laugh as the absurdity of her situation sank in.

'I don't know that I signed up for breaking and entering,' he said, shaking his head.

His attitude enraged her, but she contented herself with a tight smile. 'I'll get in the front one way or another and you wait and tackle anyone trying to escape out the back,' she said. 'We can say that you happened to be passing and I shouted for help.'

'Fine.' He disappeared round the side of the house. Grace hoped that he wouldn't use the opportunity to scarper.

She walked up the steps and along the path to the front door. An upstairs curtain twitched. She rang the doorbell.

There was no sound of approaching footsteps, so she rang it again. This time she heard slow steps coming to the door.

Beverley opened the door a crack. Her hair was tidy, and she was immaculately made up. Grace had seen photos of her before, but the protestor's well-groomed exterior nonetheless surprised her.

Behind her Grace could see a strong powerful man with a shaved head. Both of them looked shifty.

'I'm looking for a friend of mine,' said Grace, her voice like chips of ice. 'If you bring her to the door now no one needs to get into any trouble. This can all be explained away as a misunderstanding.'

'You've got the wrong house,' snapped the other woman, moving to shut the door in her face but Grace was too quick for her, shoving hard with her shoulder and knocking the woman off balance. The man came at her, but she easily used his strength against him and put him down. 'Tobias!' she yelled. He came charging in from the rear and Grace was momentarily relieved to see him until she remembered what he might have done. She secured both of them with zip-ties to their hands and ankles, which she always carried with her as part of her basic kit.

'Stand guard while I search the house,' Grace said, as she took off, shouting Jean's name.

A few minutes later, Grace was forced to conclude that her employee wasn't there. Intercepting a smug grin between her two captives, she rounded on them.

'What have you done with her?'

Suddenly, she noticed the door to the under-stair cupboard they were both sitting up against. There was a bolt on the outside of the door.

'Move!' she shouted, toppling them to each side like skittles. This time, she read their look of alarm. Switching on the light, Grace stooped and examined every surface minutely. Someone had clearly been kept in here but there was nothing to prove that it had been Jean. A rumpled sleeping bag lay on the floor along with two empty water bottles and crisp packets. Right at the back to one side there was some writing on the wall in what looked to be red lipstick. She made out the words HELP ME but then the next word trailed off as though the writer had been interrupted.

Someone hammered on the door. Grace ducked back out of the cupboard to answer it and was relieved to see the cavalry had arrived: Brodie and a bulky-looking police constable.

'Grace, what's going on? I got your text.' He caught a glimpse of Beverley and Leo tied up in the hall and his jaw dropped.

She stepped out and pulled him to one side. 'They've taken Jean. I've no idea what they've done with her. I need your help, Brodie.'

'Officer!' shouted Beverley from inside. 'This man and woman have burst into our house uninvited and tied us up. I demand that you cut us loose.'

'What makes you think they've anything to do with Jean's disappearance?' Brodie asked.

Grace hurriedly explained about Jean infiltrating the group, her smashed phone being found in the skip and her failure to appear for work. She also told him about the words in the cupboard. Her heart sank as she saw the shadow pass across his face.

'I'm sorry, Grace, it's too thin. I don't have enough to hold them. I'm going to cut them loose and hope that they don't insist that I arrest you and Sloan for assault and false imprisonment.'

'Brodie...' she moaned, although she knew that if the positions were reversed, she would have done exactly the same. She could feel the pressure mount within her like a wave of molten lava. She turned and kicked the wall, causing the slab-faced constable to take a step towards her. Brodie waved him back.

'Grace!' he hissed. 'Keep it together!'

Even though she knew he was right, it was a struggle in the circumstances. Also, what was she going to do about Tobias Sloan? If Brodie thought that her evidence in relation to Jean was slim, there was no way he was going to act on her hunch about Tobias. After all, what did it really amount to? A psychic, who had almost certainly played her for a fool, telling them that the baby was somewhere with a grandfather clock and a chest of drawers? That didn't exactly narrow the field much. And anyway, that sock she'd found was in a rented property – it wasn't that unlikely that it had been left behind and missed by a cleaner in a hurry. Probably the last tenant had children.

Grace's head was spinning, and she sat down abruptly on the garden wall.

Tobias came out of the house with Brodie. They were talking in low voices and Grace felt her neck prickle with the realisation that they were probably discussing her. She could feel her face flush with colour as they came over.

'It's your lucky day: they're not going to press charges,' Brodie said, sounding weary.

'Go figure,' snapped Grace, seeing a flash of anger light up Brodie's face.

'We're going to go now. I suggest you head to the station and file a missing person report on Jean. I'm sure she'll turn up in due course.'

'What did they have to stay about the under-stair cupboard?' she persisted.

'She said her grandson had visited and was playing a game in there.'

'And you believe her?'

'What choice do I have? Stay out of trouble, Grace. I may not be able to bail you out the next time.'

She deflated like a burst balloon as she watched them walk away and get into the squad car.

'What now?' said Tobias, his expression giving nothing away.

'I have absolutely no idea,' said Grace.

Chapter Fifty-Seven

Grace was still smarting from her encounter with Brodie as she walked back along the street to her car, Tobias alongside her.

'Don't worry, we'll find her,' he said as they got into the car.

Back in Portobello, they hurried along the Esplanade to the agency. Hannah looked up hopefully as they entered but her face fell on seeing them. The three of them went straight through to Grace's room and sat down at her desk.

Grace quickly brought Hannah up to speed.

'I can't believe that Brodie blew you off like that,' she said. 'What do we do now?'

'Jean told me that Beverley said she was Xander Croft's mother. I'm going to go to the college and see what I can get from him. He might know about somewhere she could be hiding Jean. I also need to get inside Beverley's head and he's my best bet.'

'I can do a deep dig on this Beverley Thomson and her associates. What did you say their names were?' said Tobias.

'Jean said they were called Leo and Helen. I don't have a second name for Helen. Beverley appears to be living with Leo, so I assume they're married, given her religious leanings.'

'Is she affiliated to any particular church?' he asked.

Grace bit down on her lip. She should know all this stuff. She hadn't taken this strand of the investigation seriously enough and now Jean was paying the price.

'I don't know,' she admitted. 'What I do know is that like any fanatic she's extremely dangerous. Jean's life could be in serious jeopardy.'

'What can I do?' asked Hannah. 'Do you want me to follow her? She already knows what you both look like, but she's never seen me.'

'Absolutely not!' said Grace.

Hannah's face fell.

'Look, I appreciate your desire to do something to help but the last thing I need is for you to end up in Jean's predicament. Also, it's not as easy as you think to blend into the background. You've not had the appropriate training.'

'This is discrimination!' burst out Hannah.

'I beg your pardon?' said Grace, taken aback.

'You treat me differently because I'm young. You're not my mother!'

That one hit home. After all, she was nobody's mother. She could see the realisation flood Hannah's face.

'Grace, I'm so sorry! I didn't mean—'

She forced herself to smile. 'It's fine. We're all under a bit of strain at the moment. For now, locating Jean must be our main priority. But we can't lose sight of our main investigation into the murder of Paul Gordon. We know that he was having an affair with Maria. What we don't know is how that affair started. The photos we found in his office suggest to me that it may have started out as a honey trap. Perhaps Maria was offered money to seduce him for blackmail purposes but then developed genuine feelings?'

'The only two people that could have set that up would be our client or the man Maria was running from,' said Hannah.

Or Xander Croft, thought Grace. It would have been an easy way to discredit or influence Paul Gordon, not to mention getting additional funds to shore up his gambling debts.

'I think it more likely that the motive in setting Paul up was purely financial,' said Tobias. 'Hannah, you mentioned before that Matt Turner said he had a side hustle going on but later denied she had been involved in stealing the jewellery. What if Maria was involved after all? What if the pair of them had been hiring themselves out as honeytraps?'

'I'll see if I can find anything online,' said Hannah.

'I wouldn't bother,' said Grace. 'They're going to have false names and not show any photographs. There'll be no way to link anything to Maria or Matt.'

'True,' sighed Hannah. 'I can start a conversation with some of the staff at the golf club about honey traps in general and see what comes out?'

'That's a better plan.' Grace smiled.

Grace knew that she should pipe up now with what she had discovered about Croft's desperate financial position, but for reasons she couldn't quite fathom she kept quiet. Tobias was so determined to bring him down she didn't want to give him any more ammunition until she'd sorted it all out in her own head.

'Are you going to work from the office?' Grace asked him.

'No, I'm going to head into town to the National Library. I find the quiet there conducive to concentration. I have to post on all my fake social media accounts every day for them to seem authentic. It's grown more and more difficult to keep track of it all as so many other people are now interacting with my various sock puppet accounts. However, text me if you need me and I'll come running.'

'Thanks, Tobias, I appreciate this,' she said, scarce able to meet his eyes after the thoughts she had harboured about him this morning. Was Brodie right? Was she losing the plot?

'I still think Matt from the club could have killed Maria,' said Hannah. 'He might have thought she was going to try and pin the baby's paternity on him and bleed him dry.'

'In that case, he's not likely to then snatch the baby, is he?' said Grace. 'Both her parents are dead so it's not as though he could extort money for the baby's safe return. Though I agree with you that he would be capable of murder. The way he sought to frame her for the thefts was, frankly, chilling.'

'Are we going to keep looking for the baby?' asked Hannah.

'There's nothing we can do about the missing baby at the moment,' she admitted. 'Brodie and his team are all over that and their resources and manpower are infinitely superior to ours. Obviously, if we stumble across anything at all then we must contact him immediately.'

'I'd best get off now,' said Tobias. 'Keep me posted.' He unfolded himself from the chair and left, letting in a sudden gust of cold air.

Grace looked at the crestfallen face of her youngest team member. What else could she give her to do? Suddenly, she had it.

'I need you to do something for me, Hannah. You know

that feed from Paul Gordon's study? I need you to watch it in its entirety. So far, I've just seen the highlights that Tobias captured for me. Someone could dart in or out and their movements need to be accounted for. If you could do that while answering the phones and watching Harvey for me, I would be incredibly grateful.' She opened the file on her laptop and passed it over to Hannah.

Grace bent down to give Harvey a cuddle. He leaned into her, turning on the soppy eyes.

'Sorry, boy, I can't take you with me. I need you to stay and look after Hannah for me. I promise I'll walk you later and then we can chill out on the couch.'

He sighed as if he understood.

Grace rang the number for Jean's husband on her way to the car.

It was answered by a woman with a voice like a cheese grater.

'Derek! It's for you,' she yelled, nearly busting Grace's ear drum. This did not bode well.

'Yes? Who is this? said the man on the other end of the line.

'It's Grace McKenna. I'm Jean's employer,' she said.

'What are you calling *me* for?' he asked, sounding bored already.

'I'm afraid she's gone missing.'

'Not my responsibility,' he said. 'We're divorced. I'm sure she'll turn up. Probably having a bit of a strop. You know what women can be like.'

'Can you at least tell her children and give them my contact details, please?' she said, trying not to show her anger at his complete indifference to the plight of his ex-wife.

Grudgingly he noted her number down and then hung up without saying goodbye.

What a charmer, she thought. Jean must have had a terrible life with that man. It was down to her now to find her before she was robbed of the chance to find a better one.

Chapter Fifty-Eight

Jean awoke in darkness. She'd lost all concept of time and had no idea if it was night or day. Her tongue was stuck to the roof of her mouth and she had a raging headache. Her hands were tied behind her back and she was lying on a mattress whose provenance was dubious.

'Don't panic, Jean,' she whispered. It was freezing cold and draughty. There was some light penetrating the gloom from a window high in the brick wall. She seemed to be in some form of basement.

Feeling panic bubbling up, she took some deep breaths which came out more like sobs.

She had to get a grip. Getting hysterical would help no one. Her shoulders were aching. She had to get her arms free at the very least. She rolled over on to her knees and with a bit of huffing and puffing managed to stand up. Thank heavens for her Pilates classes. She wouldn't have been able to do that a year ago.

The space she was in was large but afforded no clue as to what was outside its walls. Jean was bursting for the loo and eyed the bucket and toilet roll combo with horror. This could *not* be happening to her. How long did they intend to keep her here?

She hobbled across to what looked like a housekeeping trolley and discovered a glass bottle of water. Picking it up by gripping it round the lid with her teeth she whipped her head round and threw it down on the floor where it shattered. She then got down on her knees and selected a suitable piece of glass and gently picked it up with her teeth. As it pierced her lip, she felt a sharp sting and blood started gushing from the fleshy part of her bottom lip. She had an insane urge to laugh. This vanished when she tried to get up and toppled back on to her face amidst the glass, closing her eyes in the nick of time. More cautiously this time, she raised herself to her knees, then her haunches and thrust herself upright, her thigh muscles burning with the unaccustomed effort.

Moving away from the glass she hobbled over to the far wall from where she could watch the door and carefully bent over to drop the piece of glass that she'd been carrying in her mouth onto the floor. Turning round she went on to her knees then sat down pushing her legs out in front of her. Carefully she felt behind her for the glass and grasped it firmly. She started sawing at the rope binding her, but it was like cutting through steel. Tears sprang from her eyes, stinging the cuts on her face. She'd been so sure this would work. Her shoulder muscles were on fire, but she persevered, knowing there was no other way to get her hands free. She lost all sense of time as she sawed but she could feel the fibres fraying now.

It was working.

Chapter Fifty-Nine

Grace walked into the college with a heavy heart. Even though her original view of Croft's psychic skills had been vindicated, she took no pleasure in being right. If Xander Croft had murdered Paul Gordon she would do everything in her power to ensure that he paid for his crime. But for now, her biggest priority must be finding Jean and she was hoping he might be able to help her.

The receptionist told her to take a seat in the light-filled atrium. As she looked around her, there was no hint of the impending financial collapse of the college. People were filing into seminars looking happy and engaged. It was a community of sorts and she might be the one to send in the wrecking ball.

'Grace! To what do I owe this pleasure?'

She looked up to see Xander Croft striding towards her, arms outstretched. Conjuring up a smile, she allowed him to embrace her briefly. Already she could feel herself mourning the loss of who she thought he was. Grace closed her eyes briefly, inhaling the scent of him for perhaps the last time.

When she reopened them, she was shocked to see Regan Bradley staring across the room at her with hate-filled eyes. What was her problem? Turning away, Grace spoke urgently to Croft.

'Jean, one of my team, has been abducted. It's not looking good.'

'How can I help?' he asked at once, his blue eyes crinkling in concern.

'This is difficult...' she said, still feeling Regan's eyes burning into her like lasers. 'Is there somewhere more private we can go?' As usual, Croft seemed blissfully unaware of his colleague's apparent obsession with him.

'Come to my office,' he said, leading the way. Grace smiled at Regan to wind her up on the way past. The woman was ridiculous.

Croft showed Grace to a comfortable leather sofa and sat down beside her.

She pulled out a photo of Jean that Hannah had taken in the office and showed it to him. 'I'm working on the theory that she has been abducted by your mother, Beverley Thomson, and her husband, Leo.'

Croft sat back, looking shocked.

'My father died years ago. I don't know a Leo. Are you sure she's involved?'

Quickly Grace filled him in on what she knew about the situation so far.

'We haven't spoken since I was a teenager,' Croft said. 'I hadn't realised she'd become so unstable. I was, of course, aware of the protestors outside, but I never dreamed that she would be one of them. Then, when I saw her in the college the other day, I was stunned. I couldn't even think what to say to her. You really think that she might have taken Jean against her will?'

Grace had hoped for some more recent contact between them. 'You've really not spoken to her at all?'

'Not entirely by my choice,' he said, looking sad. 'She's getting on now. I would have happily reconciled – I tried to reach out – but she simply can't accept this side of me.' He waved a hand to encompass the college and all its activities.

'Does she have access to any lock-up garages, buildings or the like?'

He shook his head. 'I wouldn't know if she did, sorry.'

'What about other family members?'

'She drove them all away years ago.'

'The only motive that I can come up with for Jean's abduction is that she stumbled upon something that Beverley was planning.'

'Like what?'

'I don't know.' Grace shrugged. 'Could she be changing her strategy to more direct action? Maybe planning an attack against you personally or the college?'

'She's never done anything like that before. Are the police involved?'

'Jean's not been missing long enough for them to be actively concerned. They spoke to your mother, but she had an answer for everything.'

'She can be very convincing.'

'What could have triggered her recently? I mean, up to now she's been happy with simply demonstrating.'

Croft pondered, his brow creased in worry. 'Maybe the new TV show sent her over the edge? The thought that I'd be disseminating the "work of the Devil" on a large scale. She really believes this stuff.'

'I see.'

'It's not entirely her fault. Her own father was a fanatic. Zealotry can sometimes be a mask for those with cruel appetites to hide behind. She didn't stand a chance. They were dirt poor, and she fell between the cracks.'

Grace looked at him, her heart heavy. He might be a flawed man – had done unforgivable things – but she did not consider him to be, at heart, a malicious one.

Croft reached out for her hand, and she let it rest there for a moment before gently pulling away and sitting up straighter.

'I found these in your desk drawer,' she said, pulling out the sheaf of papers, knowing that this would change everything.

The colour drained from his face. 'You broke into my desk? But I trusted you—'

'And I trusted you. It is what it is,' she said, her cool expression belying the turbulence she was feeling inside.

'I'm sorry you found all that, but believe it or not, it changes nothing. I've always used research to enhance my readings and clarify them – I told you that. The spirits don't give speeches in BBC English. Everything is opaque and can be open to interpretation at times. The research is just a tool to help me divine meaning.'

'Dress it up how you like,' Grace snapped. 'You manipulated me, and I almost fell for it.'

'I don't see how you think you occupy the moral high ground after abusing my hospitality and breaking into my desk. If anyone has been manipulated here it's me, Grace.'

'Whatever. Right now, I need to concentrate on finding Jean.'

'Of course,' he said, his face now closed off from her. 'I want to help you. I really do, despite everything.'

'I know you do. If anything occurs to you then please call. I have a bad feeling about all of this.'

Chapter Sixty

Hannah blew back in the door with Harvey. Her hair was standing on end with the wind, much like his fur. She grabbed a towel from Grace's office and dried him off. Then, after she'd given him a titbit, she stuck the heater on and took her seat behind the large desk where Jean normally sat. Hannah really missed her older colleague. What if she was never found? What if she was already...? She wrenched her mind away from where it was headed. A sudden lash of rain against the windows startled her. It was likely going to be a quiet day. Not many people would be daft enough to venture out in this weather. The office was starting to warm up now and smelled of wet dog. She didn't mind. It was somehow comforting. She wiggled her toes under Harvey's heavy head, which he had rested on her feet. His eyes were shut and he sighed contentedly.

Hannah began to watch the camera feed from the very beginning, determined not to miss a single frame. Clearly, it was activated by motion sensors as it didn't record when the room was empty. It was mind-numbingly dull, but such was her dislike of Sylvia Gordon that it kept her focus sharp. Even though he was in his forties, Hannah had to admit Paul Gordon had been a good-looking man. She paused the footage and scrutinised him. He looked kind, unlike his klepto wife. Hannah was still scorching mad over the watch. She pressed play again: Paul's mobile rang and his face lit up as he answered it. His voice was deep and pleasant. Hannah guessed he might be talking to Maria as he looked so happy and animated. It was impossible to hear what he was saying as he had lowered his voice.

Sylvia burst in with some mail and he hurriedly terminated the call.

'Don't mind me,' she snapped, banging it down on his desk and turning to leave. She slammed the door so hard a picture fell off the wall. Gordon's expression became bleak as he jumped up to restore the picture. *Wait a minute! What was he doing?* He had turned to face the camera and shrugged, pointing to the door.

'See what I have to put up with?' He shook his head then left the room. Could he have installed the camera to gather evidence against his wife? Their marriage looked grim. Perhaps she really had wanted him dead, thought Hannah. Perhaps the only reason Sylvia had instructed them at all was to get her hands on the insurance money.

The next time Hannah looked up from the screen, it was nearly lunchtime. Her eyes were sore and her stomach was rumbling. She'd been desperately hoping for something to impress Grace with from the footage, but it was like looking for a needle in a haystack. With a pang, she wondered how Jean was managing. It was like she'd vanished off the face of the earth. Grace had texted to fill her in and Jean's ex-husband sounded like a right pig. Even her kids hadn't bothered to get in touch. Although Hannah and her mum had their ups and downs, if anything happened to her, she wouldn't rest until she was safe.

There must be something she could do to help Jean. Paul Gordon could wait. After all, he was already dead, so it wasn't exactly time critical. Not compared to Jean.

The rain had stopped and the sun was trying to come out.

'What about it, boy? Fancy an adventure?' she asked. Harvey's head came up and his tail thumped. She copied down Beverley's address from Grace's desk. Then, clipping on Harvey's lead, she stuck some poo bags in her jacket and flipped the sign on the door to 'Closed'. She also grabbed Jean's cosy scarf off the hook. It was freezing cold and she wouldn't mind.

They walked up to the bus stop on High Street and a suitable bus arrived almost immediately. She knew that Grace would be furious about her taking matters into her own hands again, but it would be worth it if she found something that would help to locate Jean. She figured that if Beverley and Leo had stashed Jean somewhere they would most likely have to visit that place at some point to take in supplies. Hannah could watch them and follow where they went. *Unless they've already killed her*, a dark voice murmured inside her head. She shoved it away.

Stopping opposite Beverley's house, she pretended to fiddle with poo bags. There were two vehicles parked in the driveway. One was an old Mini with racing stripes but the other was a white van which would be ideal to transport someone unseen from the house. She managed to surreptitiously take photos of the licence plates. Grace hadn't mentioned a van, so it probably hadn't been there earlier. Harvey tugged on the lead, giving her a puzzled look. She really hadn't thought this through in bringing him. He sat down and gave her a paw, his warm brown eyes locked on hers. Hannah crouched down and buried her head in his fur. Why was she such a screw up?

She stiffened as she heard the front door open and a stocky, powerfully built man came out. He was dressed in a dark green boiler suit with a peaked cap and had a lanyard with what looked like an employee ID round his neck. If she could only get a peek at it, she would know where he was going with his van. Hannah crossed over the street and walked towards him with a smile on her face just as he opened the van door.

He wheeled round with a glare, causing her heart to skip a beat but on seeing Harvey he cracked a smile and bent down to stroke him. Harvey promptly went on a charm offensive as if he was deliberately playing along.

'Cute dog,' he said, turning to Hannah. 'Did you want something?'

'Thanks, my phone has run out of charge and I'm a bit lost. Can you point me in the direction of the park?'

'Sure,' he said. 'Walk down to the end of the road, turn left and it's the first street on your right.'

'Thanks, I appreciate it.' She smiled and set off in the direction indicated. The van overtook her going in the same direction. Hannah quickened her pace. She'd seen what was around his neck and it changed everything.

Chapter Sixty-One

Grace smacked her hand down on the front desk at Leonard Street Police Station in frustration.

'Look, I'm telling you, Jean is not like that! There's no way she would pick up some man and disappear with him without letting on. I'm telling you, something bad has happened to her, something criminal!'

The dough-faced constable sighed as though she was putting a big wrinkle in his day by making him do his job. Grace itched to slap him.

He laboriously completed the report. Grace asked for his name and serial number in as intimidating a manner as she knew how to persuade him to bloody well get on with it. She rubbed her temples, feeling a headache coming on.

'Right, now that you've done that, can you tell DS Brodie McKenna that I'm here to see him?'

The constable looked alarmed. 'Oh. I'm afraid that won't be possible without an appointment. The DS is very busy at the moment.'

'Tell him I'm here, please,' she snapped, holding on to her temper by a slender thread.

He sighed, but did as she asked. A few seconds later he turned back to her.

'He said I've to buzz you through and that you know the way.'

She grunted a thank you she didn't feel and took the stairs two at a time. Arriving at Brodie's open office door she tapped lightly and he waved to acknowledge her. The paperwork on his desk had multiplied since her last visit.

'Grace? Any word from Jean?'

She shook her head and sat facing him across the desk. 'Not a thing. I've filed a missing person report with the jobsworth on the front desk. Can you please make sure it finds its way to someone halfway decent?'

'Consider it done,' Brodie said.

'Any luck tracing the husband? He's got to be a key suspect in Maria's murder and also snatching the baby.'

'His present whereabouts remain unknown.'

'Do you have a photo?'

'We received one, just before you came in, from DVLA. I haven't seen it myself yet. I'll dig it out and get it across to you.'

'What about the baby?'

'My only hope is that she's found her way to someone who is at least able to take care of her. Of course, she could be dead,' he said, his voice bleak. 'There's another appeal going out tonight on the news.'

'I shouldn't really be telling you this, but a missing baby trumps all other considerations. Can I rely on your discretion?'

'If it leads to information that might help the case, I'm

willing to turn a blind eye as long as no one was actually hurt,' Brodie sighed, running his hands through his hair.

'I've become increasingly concerned that my client Sylvia Gordon might not be on the level. She had no children with Paul Gordon, but she told me she desperately wanted them. Think about it, Brodie. She would feel cheated. She might even have convinced herself that the child is legitimately hers.'

Brodie sat forward in his seat. 'Do you think she has the child?'

'No. I visited her house and there was no sign of her. However, a junior member of my team then took leave of her senses and visited her on a false pretext.'

'Go on.'

'She said she was clearly seeing a man but trying to conceal the relationship. I had also noticed signs on my own visit that she had a man staying over regularly.'

'Did she get a look at him?'

'No, she was round the side of the house... er... hiding.'

'Great,' said Brodie.

Grace persevered, feeling the ice thinning beneath her feet.

'Anyway, Sylvia invited her in and while she was making tea my colleague got a bit carried away and took these.' Somewhat embarrassed, she pulled out the cigarette stubs. 'It occurred to me that if Sylvia was involved, she might well have an accomplice and who better than a besotted new man? The only reason I'm doing this is because the welfare of a baby is at stake,' Grace said, hoping she could trust him. She didn't want this backfiring on Hannah.

'Fine. I'll have them tested in the hope they inform the investigation. They certainly wouldn't be admissible as evidence.'

'This is all so complicated. The one thing I keep going back to is that Paul Gordon must have felt completely paranoid to have installed a camera in his study the way he did. But paranoid about what?' Grace continued.

'It could be so many things.'

'Usually, in a domestic setting you would expect it to be about suspected infidelity, but the only camera seems to have been in Paul Gordon's study,' mused Grace.

'To me, that suggests that it was more to do with the financial side of his life – his business and business partners.'

Grace froze in her seat. *What if the man that Hannah saw leaving Sylvia's was Xander Croft?*

'Grace, are you all right?' asked Brodie after a few moments.

Startled, she gave him a weak smile. 'Sorry, been mulling things over in my head. What did you make of Croft's psychic display?'

'It didn't convince me, put it that way. A grandfather clock and a chest of drawers? Not a lot to go on. You know I don't believe in all that stuff anyway. I had to be seen to leave no stone unturned.'

Grace was silent. She debated whether to mention what she had found in Tobias Sloan's apartment but decided against it. She was already starting to feel faintly ridiculous for reacting the way she had.

Grace got up to go. 'Thanks, Brodie. I'll keep in touch.'

Grace was almost back at the office when the passport photo of Maria's ex-husband pinged on her phone. Pulling over to look at it, her blood ran cold.

Even though he had a thick beard she would recognise those eyes anywhere.

Hurriedly, she phoned Brodie only to be told that he'd left the office and they didn't know when he'd be back. No chance of back-up then.

She fired off a text to Brodie.

> The man in the photo is Tobias Sloan. I'm heading to his address now. Please send back-up as soon as you can. Attaching the address.

She pressed send.

Grace pulled out into the traffic and, when it was clear, she did a U-turn, her heart racing.

Chapter Sixty-Two

Hannah entered the college grounds with Harvey. Walking round the side of the building she joined a path that cut through a lawn. *I couldn't have planned it better*, she thought, with rising excitement. If anyone stopped her all she had to do was say she'd been in the café meeting someone but needed to let her dog stretch his legs before heading back home. She'd redone her hair in pigtails and looked younger than her age. No one would suspect she was up to anything. Once Hannah had made it round the back of the building, she was more circumspect. She spied Leo's white van parked against a brick wall. The rear of the building had fewer windows and they were smaller than the ones at the front. On the far side, she spied steps leading down to some kind of basement complex. She would hazard a guess that if Jean was being held anywhere in the building by Leo, it would be somewhere in there. She walked over to the back door of the van. Crouching down beside Harvey, who was clearly revelling in the unexpected turn of events, she pulled the scarf from around her neck.

Frowning, she suddenly realised that the fact that it had her scent on it, too, now might confuse him. As far as she knew, Harvey hadn't received special training to track someone, but like all retrievers he was very food oriented and Jean often sent titbits his way. Maybe it would work?

His snout poked into the soft rainbow coloured material, snuffling.

'Find Jean, boy. Seek her out.'

He looked up at her expectantly. Hannah pulled a titbit out of her pocket.

'There's plenty more where that came from. Now, seek, seek!' She unclipped his lead then rolled her eyes when he immediately rushed off to the grass for a wee. This wasn't going to work. Feeling scared but determined, she walked down the stairs. The door was locked fast and there was a security pad to key in a four-digit number. Now what? Breaking out in a sweat, she figured it was worth a try and keyed in 0000. Nothing. Then she tried 1234 and – hey presto! – there was a loud buzzing sound and she was in. As she pulled the door towards her, she felt a wet nose against her leg and Harvey followed her inside.

'Good boy,' she whispered, pulling out another treat and presenting the scarf once more. He took off down the corridor, his tail high and wagging from side to side. She rushed off after him hoping that he was looking for the same thing she was and not following the trail of someone's meat sandwich. It was a maze inside and Hannah started to worry about finding her way back to the door again. They came to another flight of stairs leading further down into the bowels of the building. Harvey headed down them, his nose close to the ground and Hannah gritted her teeth and followed him, feeling more and more scared by the minute. The corridors were narrower on the lower level, and it smelled musty as though not much air circulated. The lights were spaced out and on a timer, which meant she was tormented by what lay ahead of her in the darkness and what lay behind. She could feel panic creeping in. Harvey abruptly stopped and started scratching at a door. He whined deep in his throat and turned beseeching eyes on Grace.

'Jean!' she shouted. 'Are you in there?'

There was no reply. Harvey continued to paw at the door and whine.

She heard a door bang further along the corridor, followed by approaching footsteps. Dragging Harvey back around the corner, she cuddled him to her to keep him quiet. Peering round the edge of the wall, she saw Leo take a pile of keys from his pocket and unlock the door. He went inside. Hannah strained her ears and heard him talking to someone, but she didn't hear another voice reply. He came back out, locking the door behind him. Then, to her horror, she realised that he was coming her way. Feeling along the wall in the darkness she found a handle and turned it. To her relief it opened noiselessly, and she managed to get herself and Harvey in there in the nick of time. Shaking, she heard the footsteps pass and recede. Sitting in the darkness, Hannah realised that she couldn't rescue Jean on her own. Taking out her phone she was frustrated to see that there was no reception. She ran back along the hall to the door she had stood at before.

'Jean, it's Hannah. If you're in there, I want you to know that help is coming.'

Still no reply, but if her friend was in there she would most likely have been gagged. The thought made Hannah want to cry but there was no time for tears.

She was about to turn away when there were three thuds against the other side of the door.

She answered them with three knocks of her own.

'I'll be back. Stay strong!'

Hurriedly she made her way back to the door she had entered by. To her relief the white van was gone. Once she had made her way past the college gates and emptied her pockets of treats to a grateful Harvey, she quickly phoned Grace, biting her lip as she thought about how angry her boss was going to be. There was no reply and she decided not to leave a message. There was no time to lose, and she had a plan.

Chapter Sixty-Three

Grace crept back into Tobias's flat with the spare key. She'd placed her phone on silent and had checked that he was still researching at the library by phoning him before entering the building. The loud tick from the grandfather clock was the only sound punctuating the silence as she crept from room to room. She entered the main bedroom and pulled out the chest of drawers. Everything was as per her last visit. No sign of a baby or any wipes or nappies. It could, of course, mean that the baby was no longer alive. It was ridiculous to cling on to the hope that she was on the say-so of Xander Croft's reading... and yet he'd been right about the grandfather clock and the chest of drawers.

Grace walked over to the wardrobe. There were only two changes of clothes hanging there. She pulled on gloves and then removed a pile of crumpled clothing from the back of the wardrobe and examined it. There was nothing in the pockets. She was about to put the garments back when she noticed a ragged tear in one of the trouser legs. Now that she thought about it, she was positive she hadn't seen Tobias wear them before.

Turning round, she now examined the bed. It was unmade and there were two indentations on the pillows. She felt along the underside of the mattress and looked under the bed frame. Nothing. Heading for the toilet, she noted the presence of an additional toothbrush which squared with her suspicions. This was bad. Really bad. He'd played her for an absolute fool from the beginning. Grace needed to find some proof of his true identity. He surely must have stashed his passport somewhere close to hand in case he needed to go on the run. This place would be a rental, so a built-in safe was unlikely. Glancing at her watch, Grace groaned. She couldn't stay here indefinitely. The library would be closing in a few minutes.

She lifted the lid on the cistern and smiled. Got him. Fishing out the sealed waterproof bag, she dried it with a hanging towel and shoved it in her own evidence bag. Time to get out of here. Walking along the hall the grandfather clock started to chime, startling her. Grace was reaching for the door handle when she sensed a disturbance of the air behind her. Her skin prickled a warning. She tried to whirl round but it was too late as she found herself caught in a choke hold from behind. The sharp tang of aftershave overwhelmed her and made her shudder with fear: her mind threw her back to the attack in her office.

'It was you!' she gasped, struggling to free herself.

A large hand covered her mouth, and she bit down firmly on the fleshy underside of the palm causing him to exclaim in pain and briefly release her. Grace kicked back at Tobias's legs as she swung round to face him, driving up with her knee into his groin, causing him to stumble backwards. She advanced with her fists raised, ready to do battle, but was silenced by the sight of a gun pointing at her. Breaking out into a cold sweat she nonetheless lifted her chin and stared directly at him.

'You were after the pictures of your wife that night,' Grace said.

His face became suffused with anger, his mouth cruel. 'She was nothing but a filthy whore,' Tobias spat.

'Where's the baby?' she demanded.

He looked momentarily puzzled, then laughed outright. 'How should I know?'

'I know all about you and Sylvia! It's pointless denying it. How long have the pair of you been together? Which one of you pushed Paul Gordon off that roof?'

'There you go again,' he said, looking irritated. 'Jumping to conclusions.'

'Says the man pointing a gun in my face.'

'It appears to be the only way I can prevent you from leaving until I've persuaded you to see things my way. Let's talk about this in a civilised manner.'

He gestured for her to enter the lounge, which she did reluctantly; she was moving farther from the door and her escape. Grace positioned herself on an upright chair, ready to spring to her feet in an instant when she could.

'It's over. I know who you really are and so do the police. In fact, I'm expecting Brodie any minute. I have to say, though, your cover was well constructed. Even I couldn't poke any holes in it. You had a fake website with fake articles, the whole nine yards.'

'You get what you pay for.' He shrugged. 'The person who made it is very accomplished. The death certificates were real. A nice touch blending truth with fiction.'

'Tell me where the baby is,' she pleaded. 'She's the innocent in all this. It'll knock years off your sentence if you hand her back unharmed. This is your opportunity to do the right thing.'

'That man stole my wife from me. Why on earth would I wish to bring up their brat? You're barking up the wrong tree. And not for the first time, I might add.'

Grace flinched as the grandfather clock started chiming the hour.

Tobias looked at her and groaned. 'Tell me you didn't believe that guff about the grandfather clock? Do you still not get it? Xander Croft is a mentalist and a conman, nothing more.' Grace strove to keep her face expressionless though his words were stabbing her through the heart. 'All he had to do was throw out some bullshit about your dead son and you were putty in his hands.'

His mention of Connor stiffened Grace's resolve. Tobias – or Felix Brannah, as he was really called – was going down. She wouldn't rest until he was behind bars. Perhaps he hadn't abducted the baby, but he was far from innocent.

'So how long have you been romantically involved with my client?'

He laughed unpleasantly. 'Seriously? You really expect me to spill my guts to you? Not happening. I want that bag you stole out of my cistern. Easy does it now,' he said, training the gun on her as she tossed it across to him.

She had to keep him talking until she could figure out a way to get the gun out of his hands, without getting her head blown off in the process.

'Time's running out for you, Tobias. The best thing you can do to help yourself is admit to killing Maria. If you say it was an accident it would plead down to culpable homicide. You'd be out in no time. As for the break-in to my office? You were after the photos of Maria and Paul, weren't you? You didn't want me sharing those with the police. You can still do the right thing.'

'The right thing?' he scoffed. 'What a simplistic world you inhabit. Ever heard of survival of the fittest?'

As she saw him stripped clean of his veneer of charm, Grace wondered how she had ever trusted him. Seeing the cruel set of his mouth as he sneered at her, she recognised him fully for the cruel predator that he was.

'You must have enjoyed helping Paul Gordon off that roof,' she said. 'The ultimate payback.'

'I certainly would have done, but unfortunately the bastard killed himself before I had the chance. I'd been looking forward to stamping him out of existence,' he said, his expression so wistful that Grace realised he might actually be telling the truth.

'What makes you think someone else didn't kill him?' she asked. 'It sounds like quite a queue was forming.'

'I have my reasons.'

'He left a note, didn't he?'

'You really are a thorn in my side!' Tobias burst out, waving the gun in her face.

'So, what's the plan then? Running off into the sunset with Sylvia? Cue violins?'

Sloan looked shifty.

'I get it, you're only romancing her until you get your hands on your share of the life insurance policy,' said Grace. 'What a charmer.'

'We had a deal,' he growled.

'You can't get away with shooting me. There's no silencer on that gun. The neighbours will have the police here in no time. I was in the police. I was married to a serving officer. Every copper in the country will be looking for you. Why not tie me up and get a head start? You can be on a flight out of here before they even decide to look for you. They've got nothing concrete on you in relation to Maria. Not yet, anyway.'

He stood staring at her as he analysed his options.

She held out her hands together in front of him and crossed her ankles.

'Look, I'm cooperating here. Tie me up and scarper. You know it makes sense. I have plastic ties in my bag. It's the easiest solution and will buy you some time to plan your exit strategy.'

Grace's heart was beating nineteen to the dozen and she could feel the sweat trickling down her back. Was he going to go for it?

He switched the gun into his left hand and reached with his right inside her bag, open beside her on the floor. As his attention wavered, Grace made her move. Grabbing his left wrist with both hands she squeezed a pressure point, causing his hand to jerk open and release the gun. Kicking it across the room, she stabbed him in the stomach with her elbow as she twisted and kicked out at his knee, causing him to crumple to the ground with a muffled curse. She then grabbed for the gun and pointed it firmly at him while he was stumbling to his feet.

'I should have put a bullet in you while I had the chance,' he snarled.

'Hands in the air!' she ordered.

Reluctantly, he complied.

Determined not to get drawn into any further debate, she jammed the gun into the base of his spine then made him apply the ties to his ankles and wrists and pull them tight until she could see them cutting into his flesh. Once he was immobilised, she removed his phone from his pocket. There was no land line in the flat. Finally, she removed the bullets from the gun and put both items in her bag.

'I'll arrange for the police to pick you up,' she said, as she scooped up her bag. 'I'd tell you to have a good day but, let's face it, that ship has sailed.'

With that parting shot she left him sitting there and locked the flat behind her, slipping the key into her pocket. As much as she wanted to see him taken into custody, she couldn't afford to be delayed with red tape when Jean was still missing.

Chapter Sixty-Four

Grace jumped into her car and with a shaking hand inserted the key in the ignition. Before putting the car in gear, she looked at her phone and was concerned to see a number of missed calls from Hannah. Hurriedly she called her back.

'Hannah? Everything okay? Any word on Jean?'

'Yes, Harvey and I rescued her and she's back here with me in the office.'

'What? Is she alright?' asked Grace, scarcely able to compute this bewildering turn of events.

'Yes, she was being kept in the basement of the college by Beverley's husband. She was drugged, tied up and gagged but apart from that she's fine,' said a cheerful Hannah, sounding as though she was discussing nothing more important than the weather.

'How did you...?' began Grace. 'Oh, never mind, it'll keep. I'll be there as quick as I can. Close the office and *do not move* until I get there. Got it?'

'Got it,' replied Hannah, sounding slightly huffy. That

girl was going to be the death of her.

She fired off a quick text to Brodie.

> Tobias Sloan is secured and awaiting collection at 3 Huntingdon Terrace. I have his gun and ammunition.

Her phone rang. She ignored it, too frazzled to deal with Brodie right now. If he wanted to speak to her, he could come to the office. She was exhausted and needed to check on her staff. She turned on the ignition and drove off.

Bursting in the office door Grace was so relieved to see Jean sitting at her desk cupping a hot chocolate that she felt tears spring to her eyes.

'It's cold outside,' she managed, fooling no one.

Harvey rushed to her side, welcoming her with a loud woof. She sank down, burying her face in his neck until he wriggled to be free.

Grace ushered her employees through to her own cosy room, turning up the living flame fire and installing Jean on the sofa. Hannah came through carrying a steaming mug of coffee for Grace and they sat down to debrief.

Grace didn't know whether to laugh or cry when she heard about Hannah and Harvey's antics in finding Jean. Looking down at Harvey, snoozing in front of the fire with his head on her shoe, she marvelled that he'd been able to track Jean from the scent on her scarf. More likely he simply remembered her scent from seeing her most days – but either way it was impressive.

'But how did you actually get her out?' Grace asked.

Hannah looked a little embarrassed. 'Well, first of all I tried to call you a few times. Then I tried to call Brodie, but he was out and I didn't know who else to ask for. I was really panicking in case that horrible man Leo came back and hurt Jean, so I decided to go into the college and ask for help.'

'Who did you ask?' said Grace.

'Regan Bradley. She was at reception when I ran in with Harvey. Of course, that got her attention as dogs aren't allowed so she was starting to tell me off when I burst into tears and blurted out that one of their employees had kidnapped Jean and locked her in a room in the basement.'

'Bet that got her attention,' piped up Jean.

'She grabbed a couple of big security types, and we rushed down to the basement from the inside. Harvey came, too, because I refused to let him out of my sight. They had a set of master keys and when they opened the door, I saw Jean lying there all trussed up and with duct tape over her mouth. She was facing away from us. I even thought she might be dead.' Hannah teared up as she remembered.

'I'd passed out: dehydration, apparently. I'm right as rain now,' Jean said with a bright smile which Grace suspected was more for Hannah's benefit than anything else. 'The paramedics gave me some rehydration sachets and I've been taking them with copious amounts of water. They were happy I was improving after treating me, so I didn't need to go to hospital.'

'Regan was great,' said Hannah. 'I'd never have believed she could be so nice from the way she behaves at the club. I reckon that's all a big show and she likes people to think she's tough when she's not like that underneath.'

'Right... What about the police?' said Grace. 'I assume the college have dismissed Leo and he's been arrested?'

'Regan said she'd take care of it. She really was ever so kind,' said Jean.

'Who'd have thought?' said Grace.

'Did you call my ex-husband?' asked Jean. 'He must have been worried sick. What about the kids? Have they been in touch?'

Grace felt sad for her.

'I did speak to him,' she said. 'He may not have been able to get hold of your children yet. You know how busy they are.'

Jean's face fell. 'I see,' she said.

The door to the office opened and Grace knew immediately it was Brodie as Harvey bounced happily to his feet, his tail wagging furiously.

'In here!' she yelled, and he came striding in, his face lightening as he took in the sight of the three of them and bent to greet Harvey.

'Grace, one of these days your texts are going to give me a heart attack,' he admonished her. 'Jean, I'm relieved you're safe and sound. You've had quite a time of it. As for you, Hannah, I suspect you're going to give me as much trouble in future as this one does currently.' He pointed to Grace.

Hannah decided that must be a compliment and beamed at him. Grace wasn't so sure.

'We've arrested Leo and Beverley and they'll appear at the Sheriff Court tomorrow. The Procurator Fiscal is going to oppose bail, but much depends on who hears the case.'

'You mean they could get out?' said Jean in alarm.

'It's possible but try not to worry. Do you know what they were planning?'

'They planned to burn the place to the ground that night with me in it,' Jean said with a shudder. 'They saw me with Grace one day and then saw Grace chatting to Xander Croft and thought he'd sent me to infiltrate the group and thwart their plans.' Jean now looked tired and strained as her relief at getting away from them ebbed into exhaustion.

Grace shook her head at Brodie and he changed the subject.

'We took Sloan – aka Felix Brannah – into custody and he's being questioned in relation to Maria's murder. As you would imagine, he's denying everything. I'm going to need that gun from you, Grace. I need to log it as evidence.'

'He had a gun?' said Jean and Hannah in unison.

She waved away their concern. 'I suspect he'll cave and admit to culpable homicide,' she said. 'And it was no big deal. It's in the car. I'll get it for you now.'

As they walked out into the crisp night air the smell of the sea soothed Grace and she inhaled deeply, the adrenaline finally draining from her system. Walking along the Esplanade together to where their cars were parked, Brodie put his arm around her and she leaned into him. It felt good.

'Can you also come into the station now and give me a statement?' he asked. 'I can drive you and get someone to bring you back.'

'Yes, of course,' she replied.

She fired off a text to Hannah telling her where she was going and to make sure she and Jean got taxis home from the office that evening.

'Any leads on the baby?'

'Nothing concrete.'

It would be a big feather in his cap – arresting Felix Brannah for Maria Rossi's murder – but she knew that, like her, he wouldn't rest until the baby was recovered alive and well.

She also knew that happy endings were few and far between.

Chapter Sixty-Five

Grace woke up the following morning feeling stiff and sore after her tussle with Tobias Sloan. She felt sick at the thought of how he had wormed his way into the heart of her investigation. Clearly, with the benefit of hindsight, he had done it to ensure that Croft went down for a murder he didn't commit, thus enabling her client to obtain the substantial payment from the insurance company and split it with him. All those times he'd disappeared off to the library he'd either been with Sylvia or doing something completely unrelated to the case. He'd used Grace to gain access to the golf club and bided his time until he revealed himself to his poor ex-wife, Maria. She suspected he'd intended to murder her all along.

Staggering to the bathroom, she gloomily surveyed her haggard appearance in the mirror. Her hair hung limply round her pale face and she had dark shadows under her eyes. Last night she'd harboured the illusion that she and Brodie might get back together again in the future. In the cold light of day that notion seemed ridiculous. As he had hugged her goodbye, it had taken all her willpower to let him go and not cling on to him.

She heard Harvey getting revved up next door. The need to care for him was sometimes the only anchor she had to this world.

Despite the beauty of the early morning, Grace couldn't shake the weariness from her bones, though her mood lightened on seeing Harvey bouncing around on the sand trying to kill a long strand of seaweed. After he'd had his run, she called him to the water's edge and he settled down to wait for her, his warm brown eyes never leaving her as she dove under the icy waves. Gasping with the shock of it as she surfaced and swam out in a straight line, she emptied her mind of everything but the rhythm of her stroke and the creeping numbness up her body.

As Grace returned to shore, she felt calmer and the cold water had soothed her aching muscles. Her first proper case was winding its way to a conclusion. She now felt quite sure that Paul Gordon had committed suicide and that Sylvia had decided to cover it up for her own financial gain, forging an unholy alliance with Tobias Sloan in the process. Grace wouldn't be a party to fraud and was going to have to persuade her client to come clean. She also wanted to know whether Sylvia was aware that Tobias had murdered Maria. Even if she didn't know, surely she must have had her suspicions? At the very least, Sylvia had withheld valuable information when being questioned by the police. As to what had happened to poor Maria's baby... that still remained unclear. The trail was getting colder by the minute. There had been so much publicity about the tragic situation on the TV that anybody could have seen it and made off with her. Grace fervently hoped that she was still alive and being well cared for at least. The alternative was too horrible to contemplate.

Once she'd fed Harvey and got dressed, she called in at The Espy with him for a cooked breakfast. She had barely eaten yesterday and was ravenous. She was pleased to see that Brodie's arrest of Tobias had made the front page of the Scottish papers. This should take the pressure off him for now. If he could only find the baby safe and well, he would be a national hero. Draining the dregs of her coffee, she contemplated her empty plate. Well, it was empty apart from the obligatory sausage that had all of Harvey's focused attention. She passed it to him and it was gone in a flash.

'You really need to learn mindful eating, boy,' she murmured whilst patting his big head. He loved sausages so much they were down his throat before he had a chance to even taste them.

Walking along the Esplanade to the office, she was surprised to see that Jean was already at her desk, even though Grace had told her to take as much time as she needed off work. Hannah was in bright and early, too.

Harvey made a beeline straight for Hannah and Grace walked over to Jean.

'Why aren't you on the sofa watching daytime TV?' she asked.

'The walls were closing in on me a bit. I felt I'd be better off working,' Jean said with a bright smile, but Grace wasn't fooled for a minute. She'd been through a terrible ordeal, but if it helped her to be here then she wasn't going to argue.

'We've been quite lost without you to keep us all in order,' she said.

Hannah nodded vigorously. 'Don't worry, Grace, I'm going to stick to her like glue today.'

Jean's eyes misted up. 'If it wasn't for you, Hannah, I might not have made it out of there alive.'

'Harvey was the real hero,' Hannah grinned, patting him fondly and sneaking him a titbit.

Grace put some notes on the table. 'Lunch is on me, you two. Have it at The Espy so you can take a proper break from the office. I'm heading off to see our client and see if I can't wrap things up.'

Chapter Sixty-Six

Sylvia flung open the door as Grace raised her hand to ring the bell. She had dressed to impress and was wearing a full face of makeup. Her expression was hostile and belligerent.

'I suppose you'd better come in,' she said.

Grace followed her through to the sitting room and took the seat offered.

As Sylvia sat down opposite her, she noticed her fingernails were bitten down to the quick again and there was a muscle twitching at the corner of her eye.

'I take it you've heard about Tobias Sloan,' Grace said. 'I'll keep using that name for now as I never knew him under his former one. The two of you were in cahoots this whole time.'

'I suppose there's no point denying it,' Sylvia sighed.

'Did you know he'd murdered Maria?'

'I suspected him at first, but he denied it. He was very convincing. By that time we were involved and I believed him. He told me he'd decided not to ask her to come back to him as he wanted to be with me. I thought he loved me.'

'Loved your potential insurance cheque more like,' said Grace. 'You couldn't tell the police what you knew because you didn't want your role in this whole sordid affair coming out.'

'I've no idea what you're talking about.'

'You were the one who set in motion this whole chain of events. Maria Rossi was barely scratching out a living. Paul's star was rising, and you became obsessed with the amount of female attention he was getting. You wondered if his head might be turned and decided to set a trap for him. A honeytrap.'

Sylvia tightened her lips but said nothing, so Grace pressed on.

'Seeing the way men responded to Maria in the club, you decided to pay her to tempt your husband to stray. That way you'd be in control the entire time. Of course, she was only meant to report back as to whether or not he passed the test and that would have been the end of the matter.'

'She told me he passed,' said Sylvia. 'I blamed myself for doubting him and then made a renewed effort in my marriage.'

'But they started a passionate affair behind your back. The fact that you were the one who had thrown them together must have been a bitter pill to swallow.'

'I loved him more than life itself, but I could see him slipping away from me.'

'Someone got wind of the affair and started to blackmail him. You found the photos and that's when you knew,' said Grace.

'I confronted him. I begged him to stop, but he refused.

He said he couldn't live without her. I managed to track down her husband from some information in her student application form for the college. She'd had to disclose her real identity in that as she couldn't vouch her new one with proper identification. When she applied, she'd made an appointment to come and see me. She said she was estranged from her family and didn't want them to find out her whereabouts. I saw no reason not to enrol her and agreed to keep her real identity a secret.'

'So, she owed you,' said Grace. 'A robust new identity didn't come cheap.'

'Yes, well, when things went so badly wrong with Paul, I remembered this and used it to track her husband down. At that stage he was known as Felix Brannah. I told him where she was and what she was up to. He said that he still loved her. I thought they would reconcile and that he'd take her back down south. I thought that Paul would come back to me then. My only intention was to save my marriage, I swear!'

'Had you not done what you did Maria would be alive today and her baby wouldn't be missing. You may not be legally responsible for the woman's death, but you are morally culpable.'

'I was distraught. I wasn't thinking straight,' Sylvia said.

'I think that you knew exactly what you were doing. You executed a cold-blooded plan that resulted in two deaths and a missing child who will be an orphan if she's found. I don't know how you can sleep at night.' Grace sighed. 'You're my client and you paid me to find out what happened to your husband. Well, I have.'

Sylvia looked alarmed rather than pleased.

'Paul Gordon committed suicide but, of course, you knew that already, didn't you?'

'How can you say that?' she said, pulling out a lace hankie and hiding her face in it.

Grace sat back in her seat and laughed.

'Really? That's how you're going to play this?'

Two dry eyes glared belligerently at her over the top of the hankie.

'As things stand at the moment, you've done nothing that the police need to know about. If you had actually murdered Maria in person rather than been just a catalyst, I would have handed you in to them without compunction.'

'Thank you,' Sylvia sniffed.

'However, you needn't think that I'm going to stand idly by while you frame Xander Croft for a murder that he didn't commit as petty payback for rejecting your advances. He didn't attempt to force himself on you, it was the other way round, wasn't it? You were looking for a revenge affair, a way to hurt Paul as much as he'd hurt you.'

'He pushed me away as if I disgusted him. He didn't need to be so cruel.'

'I'm not going to be party to a fraudulent insurance claim either.'

'What do you mean?' Sylvia gasped. 'I'm due that money. You can't... you'll ruin everything. Please, Grace, I'll give you a third of it on top of your fee—'

'Save it!' snapped Grace, her eyes like flint. 'Here's what's going to happen. You're going to get me that *suicide* letter *right now*.'

Sylvia reluctantly got up and unlocked the writing bureau in the corner. She extracted an envelope and handed it to Grace before sitting back on her perch.

Grace unfolded it and read the letter which was heart-breaking and utterly clear in its intent. It would seem that Paul hadn't known about the baby. Maybe if he had that would have given him a reason to live? She photographed it and handed it back to Sylvia.

'There's no advantage to anyone now in having all this come out.' Grace sighed again.

Sylvia sagged in relief.

Grace produced a typewritten letter to Paul Gordon's insurance company that withdrew the claim and handed it to Sylvia for signature. She scrawled on it with bad grace.

'That simply leaves the matter of my fee.' Grace produced a detailed breakdown and passed it across. 'I will take payment directly into my bank account,' Grace said.

Sylvia sighed and transferred the outstanding balance via her phone. 'You strike a hard bargain. Maybe you're more like me than you think?'

'I'm *nothing* like you,' Grace almost shouted. She couldn't help but feel she'd made a deal with the devil, but she knew that in the circumstances the courts would have no power to punish her client for what she had done.

They both stood up.

'One more thing,' said Grace. 'I want the watch back that you took from Hannah. It doesn't belong to you.'

Sylvia took it off and flung it at her.

Grace caught it in one hand. 'I'll show myself out,' she said.

Chapter Sixty-Seven

Grace felt as though a great load had been lifted from her shoulders as she turned her face up to meet the spring sunshine. Regan Bradley had been incredibly helpful and kind to Hannah and Jean yesterday. She felt a little guilty that she'd misjudged her and decided to drop off a thank-you note and some flowers. Grace didn't want to have to go into the college if she could help it so, scrolling through her phone, she located Regan's address from the witness statements she had copied. She lived at The Jewel, which wasn't far away, and there was a florist's shop on the way. She could always leave the flowers and card with a neighbour if Regan was out. She left Harvey snoozing in the flat as he was tired out from all the excitement yesterday.

Grace found the modest detached house without difficulty. Ringing the bell, she stood back to admire the spring display of daffodils in the garden.

Regan looked flustered when she came to the door. Her eyes widened in shock as she saw Grace standing there. A baby started screaming from within the house as the grandfather clock in the hall started to chime. Grace could hear a train going by in the distance.

'I'm sorry, it's not a good time,' gasped Regan, already trying to slam the door shut.

Grace threw down the flowers and shoved the door back open with her shoulder as she charged into the house. Rushing past Regan, she followed the screams into a bedroom where she discovered the baby girl lying on a changing mat.

She scooped the baby up and held her close, the screams gradually subsiding. She turned to face Regan who stood staring at her in shocked silence.

'Please, give her to me,' pleaded Regan. 'I'm begging you! It's not what you think.' She broke down in tears, utterly distraught. 'Paul would want me to have her. I loved him. He was all I ever wanted.'

'It was you!' said Grace. 'You were the blackmailer.'

'I wanted him to break it off, to stop seeing that woman. He'd already gone off his bitch of a wife. Paul and I were such good friends. I thought he would turn to me if I could only open his eyes, make him realise,' she wept. 'He would hug me and hold me. We had grown closer and closer. It would only have taken a tiny spark to ignite the flame.'

'Instead, you helped to drive him off that roof to his death,' said Grace.

'No... he really jumped?' Regan whispered. 'All this time I thought that Xander Croft pushed him off, but I had no proof.'

No wonder she had seemed so hostile around him. Grace was struggling to wrap her head around this latest revelation.

'Why would you think that?' asked Grace.

'That night, I followed Paul up onto the roof. I thought he might be seeing Maria again. I thought she was already up there waiting for him. As soon as I got there, I heard him and Xander arguing. Going at it hammer and tongs they were. I couldn't make out what they were saying.'

'Did they see you?'

'No, I hid. I saw Xander storm off then I waited a bit but there was no sign of Paul. He'd have had to go past where I was hiding to get off the roof. I went looking for him, but he was nowhere to be seen. I looked over the edge and that's when I saw him lying there...'

'You didn't call an ambulance?'

'No, I could tell he was already dead. And I was in shock, I suppose.'

'Regan, Paul left a note. Xander didn't kill him.'

'But that's so much worse,' she cried. 'I blackmailed him. I drove him to it!'

'He was obviously in a bad place anyway,' Grace said, taking pity on her. 'It wouldn't be the only factor. There was a lot going on in his life at the time.'

'It was so hard watching Maria and seeing her swell with his child. I tried to distract myself with Matt Turner but as her pregnancy grew so did my remorse for the blackmail. When Maria was murdered but her baby survived, I felt it was a sign. I thought that the universe was giving me Paul's baby to take care of so I could atone for what I'd done.'

'Nobody gave you this baby, Regan. You took her for your own selfish ends.'

'Please, give her back to me. All you're doing is condemning her to a life in foster care and children's homes. Don't you see? She'd be better off with me! I love her. She'd want for nothing. I'm her mother now. She needs me.'

Her shaking hands stretched out to Grace in supplication. She looked wired, like she was running on adrenaline.

'I've got money. Lots of money. I'm begging you. Give

her back to me. You were a mother. You know what it is to love and lose a child.'

'You're right, Regan,' Grace replied, her words spiked with anger. 'I do know. And this isn't it. You've no claim on this child.' Her voice softened as she looked into the wild eyes of the frantic woman before her. 'You need help.'

Regan broke down in tears and collapsed onto the bed. She had no fight left in her.

Grace took out her phone and called Brodie. Wrapping the baby up in a warm blanket she left the house to wait for him. She felt empty, completely hollowed out.

A few minutes later, Brodie and a uniformed officer arrived, followed by another police car with a social worker and the police surgeon. He took the baby from her to check she was in no immediate danger. After a tense few minutes the police surgeon pronounced that the baby was stable and seemed to have been well cared for.

Meanwhile Brodie and the officer led Regan Bradley from the house in handcuffs and put her in the police car.

'Grace, you're white as a sheet,' Brodie said, rubbing her two lifeless hands within his to get some warmth into them. 'Did you bring your car?'

She didn't look at him, just nodded her head. It was as if her body had shut down. But there was one more thing that she needed to do.

Chapter Sixty-Eight

As she drove through Edinburgh, Grace managed to rouse herself sufficiently to phone Jean and Hannah to let them know that the baby had been found safe and well and she planned to take the rest of the day off. She was bone tired.

Grace pulled into Merchiston College car park and switched off the ignition. Slowly, she walked indoors. The foyer was crowded with students changing classes, so she was able to slip over to the door leading to Xander Croft's private quarters unobserved. She keyed in the number she had memorised and slipped inside to the muted passageway where the mediums had their consulting rooms. At the end she came to his office. She listened at the door. The phone rang inside the room and she heard Xander's voice as he answered it. It was a brief call. After it had ended Grace opened the door and walked in without knocking.

'Grace! I've heard about Regan. It's all over the news. I can't believe it. Why would she do such a thing?'

'Love makes fools of us all,' said Grace. 'She was on the

roof that night. You and Paul Gordon were arguing. Why didn't you say anything?'

'Why do you think? I swear to you, Grace, he was still alive when I left him. Sylvia would have done her level best to have me put away for a crime I didn't commit. She became obsessed with having a revenge affair after she found out about Paul and Maria. I rejected her and she didn't take it well.'

'He left a note. Sylvia hid it.'

'You mean that he'd already made up his mind before our argument?'

'Yes, it would seem that way.'

'Ever since it happened, I've tormented myself with what could have been. He'd discovered that I'd borrowed some money from the college funds to dig myself out of a hole. I repaid it but he was furious at the time.'

'Perhaps he planned things that way to punish you?' said Grace. 'If life has taught me anything at all, it's that we can never truly know what is in the mind of another, no matter how close we may be to them.'

'Thank you for telling me. It has brought me some peace. I'm trying to put things right. I'm getting help for my gambling.'

Grace hesitated before speaking what was on her mind. 'When I found the baby... it happened as you said. One of the things you mentioned in my reading... about my dad... that was true, too. I'm finding it hard to reconcile these things with what I found in your drawer. Also, that woman in the audience the first time I saw you, the one in the purple coat, she was a plant, wasn't she? I saw someone pay her off in the car park.'

He smiled at her, though his eyes were sad. 'Yes, she was. The research I do and the tricks I employ give me the reassurance I need to stand there in front of an audience and do what I do. Sometimes things come through strongly. Other times there is nothing, a deafening silence. People need more than that. They need hope and reconciliation. It can't always be conjured up out of the ether on demand.'

Grace thought about it for a moment. It made sense on one level. 'The only thing I know for sure is that I can't deal with this stuff. It makes me second-guess myself and doubt everything. I'm not comfortable around it—'

'Or comfortable around me...?'

'I'm sorry,' she said softly. 'Have you been in touch with your mother?'

He shook his head. 'Some wounds can't be healed.'

'Take care of yourself,' she said, as she turned to leave.

'I'm not going to see you again, am I?'

Grace gently closed the door behind her.

Once back in Portobello, Grace went straight upstairs and let herself into the flat. Harvey sensed her mood right away and after she'd petted him, he followed her into the bedroom. She lay down, but all the recent events whirled around her head like some macabre kaleidoscope. Harvey jumped up and lay down beside her with his head on the pillow and for once she didn't shoo him down. Nothing seemed to matter much anymore.

After a while, Grace realised that she wasn't going to be able to sleep. Maybe another swim would shake this strange, disconnected feeling and help ground her again.

She pulled on her swimming costume and robe. Harvey perked up and watched her with his head cocked to one side.

'Sorry, boy, you can come next time,' she said.

It was after six as she walked on to Portobello Beach and

the sun was dropping in the sky. Families were making the most of the last rays in the sky. Reaching the edge of the sea, Grace removed her robe and laid it out of the tide's reach. There was no one else in for a swim. The cold deterred most from even a paddle.

Still feeling strangely detached, she dived underneath a wave feeling the welcome slice of the cold into her bones and pulling away strongly from the shoreline. The voices receded and she felt her energy return as her body tried to defend itself from the cold temperature. Her thoughts drifted from the shock of the last few days to her son. Her soul called out to him as she swam ever further from the beach. Grace fancied him swimming a phantom crawl alongside her. He'd always loved the water. She had thought he'd loved life, too, but she'd been wrong. She felt a peculiar warmth and realised that she was crying. Crying for what might have been. She'd lost everything because of that night: her son, her husband and her career. All that was left was a shadow existence and it wasn't enough to sustain her.

Treading water, she looked back at the shore. The wind and tide were pulling her out to sea. There was no fight left in her.

Suddenly, she heard her son's voice, clear as a bell, coming from the direction of the beach.

'MUM! THIS WAY!'

Her heart caught fire and she plunged back into the waves, swimming with all her might, clawing her way to shore with every muscle and sinew, until she emerged gasping from the sea, looking frantically around her.

'MUM! THIS WAY,' she heard once more, closer this time. She gasped as she saw a gangly teenager swoop on a football and hold it up laughing as he lobbed it back to a dark-haired woman.

Suddenly, Grace understood. It was not her time.

She grabbed up her robe and headed for the flat. As she stepped up on to the Esplanade she saw Hannah standing there with a buggy. Smiling, she went over to meet her. As she glanced into the buggy, she was transfixed by the cherubic little boy sitting there, his brown eyes sparkling with mischief. Her heart melted. She knew without having to be told.

'Grace, I didn't know how to tell you... I'd like you to meet your grandson,' said Hannah.

A Letter from the Author

Dear reader,

Huge thanks for reading *Murder by the Seaside*, I hope you were hooked on Detective Grace McKenna's first case. If you want to join other readers in hearing all about my new releases and bonus content, you can sign up for my newsletter.

www.stormpublishing.co/jackie-baldwin

If you enjoyed this book and could spare a few moments to leave a review that would be hugely appreciated. Even a short review can make all the difference in encouraging a reader to discover my books for the first time. Thank you so much!

This story sparked into life for me with the image of a solitary woman swimming out to sea at Portobello Beach where her son had drowned and fighting the urge to keep going. A dog was awaiting her return at the water's edge. This was my lockdown book and Grace McKenna was a woman on the edge struggling to come to terms with a heartrending loss as so many people were at that time. It was a battle I wanted her to win.

Thanks again for being part of this amazing journey with me and I hope you'll stay in touch – I love hearing from readers and I have so many more stories and ideas to entertain you with!

Jackie Baldwin

www.jackiebaldwin.co.uk

Acknowledgments

I'd like to thank my wonderful editor, Kathryn Taussig, for her words of insight and encouragement as well as a forensic attention to detail which helped to turn this book into the best version of itself. Thanks also to the copy editor, Liz Hurst. A special thank you to the cover designer, Eileen Carey. It was love at first sight! The whole team at Storm have been outstanding. Thanks to writing friends Linda Wright and Irene Paterson for their feedback on my first draft.

I'd also like to thank my lovely daughter-in-law, Rhanna, who helped me with some of my medical questions. Any mistakes are mine alone. A big shoutout to Kelly Lacey and Love Books Group for organising a terrific blog tour.

However, the biggest thanks must go to my husband, Guy, who reads everything I write and supplies me with endless cups of tea to keep me going. He stops me setting fire to each book when I am about 60,000 words in and have a crisis of confidence. I also owe a big debt to my lovely dog, Poppy, who sadly is no longer with us. She had a large head, a square jaw and everyone thought she was a boy. She also had more heart than any dog I've ever known, and she is the inspiration behind Harvey in the book. It is my way of making her live on.

Finally, to any reader who has made it this far, I hope that you enjoyed it! A book without a reader would be a very lonely thing so thanks for sharing this story with me.

Printed in Great Britain
by Amazon